GAMES OF DECEIT

by
Pan Pantziarka
A Fairfax and Vallance mystery

CRIME & PASSION

First published in Great Britain in 1997 by
Crime & Passion
an imprint of Virgin Publishing Ltd
332 Ladbroke Grove
London W10 5AH

Crime & Passion series editor: Pan Pantziarka

Copyright © Pan Pantziarka 1997

The right of Pan Pantziarka to be identified as the Author
of this Work has been asserted by him in
accordance with the Copyright, Designs and Patents
Act 1988.

ISBN 0 7535 0119 8

Typeset by Avon Dataset Ltd, Bidford on Avon, B50 4JH
Printed and bound in Great Britain by
Mackays of Chatham PLC, Chatham, Kent

ONE

Sarah Fairfax glanced in the rear-view mirror again. He was still there. Up ahead the road was clear, the dark strip of tarmac banking gently into a long curve that skirted the grey town below them. The sky was mottled grey with dark clouds low on the horizon, obscuring the brightness of the sun that had warmed the start of her journey. The light was starting to fade and already some of the other cars on the motorway had their lights on. Not the dark car behind her. Not her, either.

She was already above the speed limit but the gap with the cars ahead seemed to be getting wider. The gap with the car behind shorter. He was practically on her tail already. What the hell was he doing? If she slowed suddenly he'd plough into her, his heavy dark Mercedes would cleave her car in two and take her with it. There were cars behind them, but they were too far behind. For a moment she considered slowing down in the hope that he'd pull into the lane beside her and accelerate away for ever. But then why should she give him that pleasure?

Faster. She stepped hard on the accelerator and her car responded smoothly. 'Don't look back,' she whispered to herself under her breath as she watched the speedo clock higher and higher. What if he was a cop? No, the police didn't drive big black Mercedes that cruised along way above the speed limit. Her car was buffeted by the sharp gusts that cut across the motorway but she was still in control, still able to handle the speed and the acceleration.

The cars up ahead were not so far, the red tail lights another measure of how quickly the daylight was dying. The town below them had given way to a countryside of neat fields, ploughed earth and thick woods. The low cloud seemed to make the fields dark and heavy, an oozing mass rather than a green carpet swaying in the breeze. A plume of smoke was rising in the distance, a white trail drifting into the sky. She looked suddenly. He was still there. On her tail.

She was doing over a hundred and he was still following only inches behind. Who was he? What the hell did he want? White, male, middle-aged. His face was obscured by the reflection of cloud on his windscreen; she couldn't quite see his face. Dark glasses, she saw that.

She flicked her headlights on, hoping that the sudden flash of red in her tail lights would force him to slow down but there seemed to be no response. Had she cut him up earlier? Perhaps that was it. A stupid man with a big car who couldn't handle being over taken by a woman. Damn him! Why didn't he back off?

'Go away!' she muttered angrily, aware that her hands were gripped tight on the wheel. It was pointless trying to out race him; the only way to do that would be to take her car to the limit and that was both stupid and dangerous. She started to ease off the throttle, slowing down gently so that he didn't smash into her. Was his car blue or black? It was so dark that she couldn't really tell. He was there in her wing mirror, slowing down at the same rate.

The way was clear for him to overtake, the outside lane was completely empty; there was nothing stopping him. They were down below the speed limit and the bastard was still there. What did he want? Her hands were clammy and she was starting to get worried. The road ahead looked busier and she felt relieved. If they got caught up with the flow of traffic there'd be more chance to shake him off.

How much further? The drive down to the New Forest from London hadn't seemed such a big deal; now it felt as if it was taking for ever. The lights came on behind her, fierce headlights catching suddenly in her wing mirrors so that everything turned black for a moment. A motorway sign flashed passed and she realised that she'd picked up speed again. She indicated left, started to slow down again as she approached the slip road. The car behind her started to indicate too, slowing down proportionately as she turned off from the motorway.

Her foot went down hard and her car shot forward, crossing from the slip road and out back onto the motorway. Her heart was pounding and the fear was making her sweat. She looked back. There was no sign of him in the rear-view mirror. Thank God! She turned and looked quickly over her shoulder, not quite willing to believe that the bastard, whoever he was, had finally gone.

She breathed a long, slow sigh of relief. God, she was jumpy. The road ahead was busy and that was comforting too. There wasn't long to go. Carol had assured her that the Hunting Lodge Hotel, in the heart of the New Forest, was a relaxing, comfortable place to meet. It even had a pool and the food was supposed to be excellent, though knowing Carol it was hard to say whether her recommendation was good or bad.

Sarah would have preferred to take the more scenic route to Lyndhurst, driving down towards Hythe and then in through the heart of the New Forest. The heathland was always so beautiful, the dark purple of the heather stretching for miles before giving way to the greens and browns of the trees in the distance. Instead she took the direct route, heading down the more thickly wooded main road that cut through the forest.

The Hunting Lodge was a big square building lit up by pale orange light and set well back from the road. The neon sign at the entrance of the gravel drive boasted recommendations and three stars but the sturdy Victorian façade did nothing to inspire confidence. A maiden aunt of a building: staid, conservative and unwelcoming.

She parked her car at the side of the hotel, alongside half a dozen others, switched off the headlights and sat back, relieved that the long drive was finally over. The forest lay across the road, a dark brooding presence that was both peaceful and yet strangely unsettling. The sky was heavy with dark cloud that looked fit to burst and a stiff breeze swept down through the trees. Terrible weather. Walking shoes were stowed in the boot of the car but there was no way she was going to take a walk in the rain.

She grabbed her case and trudged across the car park towards reception. The breeze hissed through the trees, making her shiver with cold. Just as she got to the door she looked back suddenly. Nothing. She was still spooked by the black Mercedes. It was stupid. A bored driver playing silly buggers on the motorway, it happened all the time.

Registration was a quick formality. The receptionist, a young man in his early twenties and too camp for his own good, went through his routine with a fixed smile on his face but nothing behind the eyes. He was bored rigid and it showed. She grabbed her key and headed up to her room before she realised that she hadn't asked after Carol. What was there to ask?

The room was a double, with a big bed and lots of space. And an en-suite bathroom with a real bath, that at least was something. A cubicle shower would have been the end; there was nothing like a long hot soak to ease the back after a long drive. There was a small TV in one corner, and beside it a dressing table-cum-desk with a selection of brochures spread across the top. She dumped the glossies without a second glance, clearing the space for her own things. Laptop, notepads, pens, tape recorder; she carefully positioned them on the desk, marking out her work space clearly.

The heating was on, she realised, switching on her computer. There was a heavy cast iron radiator under the big square window opposite the desk. She crossed the room to turn it down; the room could easily get stifling no matter what its size. The window was draped with big heavy curtains which had once been lilac, now they looked grey and seemed to serve no other purpose than to hide the filth caught in the net curtains. Looking to one side of the window she saw that the wallpaper had started to peel just under the picture rail.

The first impression of comfort and space started to give

way. Dirty net curtains, peeling wallpaper and clanky old radiators which gave out too much heat, what next? She struggled with the radiator and finally it gave way and she switched the valve down. For a second she contemplated opening the window but a quick look at the darkness outside made her change her mind. It still looked like it could rain and the darkness was so heavy that she was half afraid it would leak into the room.

She went back to the computer and checked that everything was running: her files were still there, complete with preliminary notes on the story she was supposed to be getting from Carol. Next she checked the tape recorder, rewinding the tape to make sure the batteries were still working.

With that out of the way she relaxed a little. She unpacked her clothes and started to stow them neatly in the wardrobe when she was startled by the phone. The antique ring sounded strange to her ears, but given the surroundings there was nothing incongruous about its percussive call.

'Sarah! You made it then.' There was no mistaking Carol's voice on the other end of the line.

'Yes, I made it,' Sarah agreed, deciding to save the story about the black car till later.

'What do you think of this place? It's a find, isn't it?'

Sarah glanced around the room. If she ignored the peeling wallpaper, the dusty net curtains and the ancient heating she could see that the room had a faded elegance that some people might find appealing. 'It probably looks better in the sunlight,' she said.

There were no such reservations from Carol. 'I love this place,' she gushed excitedly. 'Have you tried the pool yet?'

'I've only just –'

'You've got to go for a swim. It's not the biggest pool in the world but a swim makes such a difference.'

'Do you want to meet in a few minutes?' Sarah suggested. 'We can talk and swim at the same time.'

Carol laughed. 'I've already had my swim. Why don't you have a swim and then we can meet for a drink before dinner?'

Sarah had planned for a long hot soak before dinner; a swim sounded less appealing. 'I can swim tomorrow,' she said.

'Come on! After that drive from London I'm sure you need to relax a bit. A swim will do you good. What time shall we meet for dinner?'

'What time do they stop serving?'

'Nine, I think. Let's meet in the bar at eight thirty. That leaves you plenty of time for a swim. It'll do you good, Sarah, you know it will.'

'OK, I'll see you downstairs at half eight,' Sarah agreed.

'Good. And Sarah?'

'Yes?'

Carol laughed again. 'You're not going to wimp out of a swim because it's cold, are you?'

'Of course not,' Sarah responded instantly.

'Good. See you later.'

The pool was at the far end of the hotel and Sarah had to wind her way up and down stairs and along two corridors lined with rooms before she got there. There were two changing rooms just outside the pool building, both of them converted toilets with cold tiled floors and faintly disturbing smells. They were also bloody cold and she shuddered at the thought of stepping across the icy tiles.

The pool itself lay on the other side of a heavy fire door and at first glance it was hard to see what Carol had been so excited about. The bright blue water was steaming in the ice cold air, tendrils of mist rising lazily from the surface that was so still it might have been glass. It *was* freezing. In the summer it would have been an outdoor pool surrounded by greenery and glistening in the sunlight. Now it was covered over by a plexi-glass dome mounted on castors. The cover kept the rain out but did nothing to keep the place warm. Rivulets of water cascaded from the glass sides, making the darkness outside seem hazy and indistinct.

Sarah shivered as she looked at the cool water. The glassy surface was broken suddenly as a trickle of water dripped from the roof, eddies and ripples spreading across the square pool. She hoped it was warmer than it looked; underwater lighting and the deep hum of a pump suggested that it was heated. It was no surprise that the pool was empty.

She turned back with the intention of returning to her room when she saw footprints near the shower in the corner. Looking back she traced the prints back to the water and from the shower out to one of the changing rooms. Carol hadn't been lying; she had probably only just finished her swim when Sarah had arrived at the hotel. Damn it! Carol hadn't wimped out, which meant that neither could she.

The changing room seemed cramped and claustrophobic, the smell of chlorine over-powering. Sarah changed quickly, shivering tightly as she slipped into her black one-piece. The floor was colder than she had imagined and she had to grit her teeth to walk the short distance to the edge of the pool.

The water did not look inviting. It stared at her: cold, blue, icy. The best thing, she knew, was to dive straight in. That would get the shock over and done with, then she'd be able to enjoy the swim. And she would enjoy it, no matter what. The longer she dithered the worse it would seem. Still she stared at it and it stared back implacably.

Was it heated? She tested the water's edge with her toes. Freezing. There seemed to be no difference between the water and the surrounding cold air or the floor seemingly tiled with slabs of frost. There was nothing for it. She took a step into the water, gritting her teeth as it lapped uninvitingly against her legs. Her teeth were chattering and she tensed hard to keep quiet. Two steps in and the water was above her knees. She felt cold all over, from the tips of her toes to the tips of her fingers.

She inhaled deeply and then launched herself into the water. The shock hit her as she immersed her body in the icy blue. She swam a few strokes into the centre of the pool and then stopped, breathing fast in the hope that she'd warm up. How long before hypothermia set in? The only way to get warm was to swim. The pool was long enough to get in a few good strokes before having to turn.

She swam for a while, back and forth slowly, until the icy feeling started to subside. It wasn't exactly warming up, but it was becoming bearable and she had stopped shivering. When she switched to swimming on her back she could appreciate the eddies of water cascading down the sides of the glass dome and the fingers of steam rising from the rippling blue surface of the water.

Perhaps Carol had been right after all. A nice slow swim was a good way to relax after the long drive. Trying to hold a proper conversation would have been a waste of time. There was a lot to talk about though, and she hoped that Carol wasn't going to be so difficult to pin down later on. Carol had always been like that, even at university. She was good at giving the impression that she was being direct and forthcoming when in fact she was being vague and uninformative. It was probably why she had gone into public relations. In any case her talent, if that was what it was, had enabled her to convince most of the *Insight* team that she was sitting on a good story. Sarah had yet to be convinced. It was hard to imagine that Carol – hedonistic, flirtatious and irresponsible – could have stumbled on to a story important enough to warrant a TV exposé.

There was no clock. Sarah sighed inwardly. How could anyone have a swim without a clock on hand to keep track of the time? She was at the far end of the pool, at the deep end, and she pushed off, pushing powerfully against the side to propel herself forward quickly. As she moved into her stroke something caught her eye, a dark shadow moving on the periphery of her vision. She turned over quickly, splashing noisily in the water as she did so. It was hard to see through the misted glass . . .

She turned back again, her heart pounding powerfully in her chest as she pulled herself through the water. She was up and out in seconds, the cold water cascading from her body as she ran towards the door. The air was colder than ever and the steam rose from her body. She stopped at the door and looked back, shivering from cold and fear. Somebody had been there. Staring through the misted glass. Spying on her. Peeping at her.

She shuddered at the thought but felt compelled to stand her ground. Whoever he was he had gone. She had glimpsed him from the corner of her eye, his face pressed against the misted glass, his face distorted by the droplets and rivulets of water. He had gone even as she turned towards him,

8

disappearing into the bushes that surrounded the pool-side building.

The changing room seemed even more forbidding and claustrophobic than before. Not risking it, she covered herself in a big white towel, grabbed her clothes and then headed back to her room. The whole place seemed deserted, the long corridors eerily silent as she padded back, splashing water with every step.

Part of her wanted to scream, to shout out her anger and her rage but another part stood back calmly. The same impulse which made her stand in the doorway to stare back where he had been also made her want to deny him the pleasure of her anger. A bloody peeper, getting his kicks from spying on women. Had he been waiting for her to strip off and get into the shower after her swim? The cover of darkness and the misted glass gave the impression of privacy and solitude; having a shower after the swim would have been exactly what she would have done.

By the time she was in her room she felt calmer. Had it really happened? For a moment she doubted that it had. Perhaps it was a left-over from the incident on the way to the hotel? But then she didn't doubt what she had seen. Damn him, whoever he was. She couldn't describe him; a fleeting glimpse was all she had but it had been real and not imagined.

Carol hadn't aged a bit. She was just as Sarah remembered her from university: long blonde hair, a round face with prominent lips, clear blue eyes and a smile that showed perfect white teeth. She hadn't put on weight either: she was still slim around the waist and it seemed to push her boobs higher and make her legs appear longer. God, she been popular with men and hated by their girlfriends.

'Sarah, you haven't changed a bit,' Carol said, crossing the bar to meet her.

Sarah smiled in return. Carol was lying, of course, but it was still the right thing to say. 'And neither have you,' she said. 'I ought to hate you for it.'

'Come on, Sarah, you know as well as I do that men have always lusted after you. Anyway, I hear you're hitched.'

Sarah's smile wavered. 'Who told you that?'

Carol shrugged. 'Can't remember. So, it's true then?'

The last thing that she wanted to do was to talk about Duncan. 'Sort of,' she admitted. 'What about you?'

'I've given up on looking for Mr Right,' Carol sighed. 'These days I'm willing to settle for second best.'

Sarah glanced at her watch. The room was empty apart from the two of them and a bored-looking girl behind the bar. 'Shall we skip drinks and go straight in to dinner?' she suggested.

'If you like,' Carol agreed. 'I just hope the food's up to the usual standard.'

The dining room was huge, ornate, lit with pale orange light and almost completely empty. An elderly couple occupied a table by the door; their table had been cleared and they were sitting in silence staring glumly at their coffee cups. A waitress in black and white uniform was hovering nearby, obviously waiting to usher them out. She looked up at Carol and Sarah and the irritation was there in her dark brown eyes.

'Are we late?' Sarah whispered to Carol as she led them to the far end of the room.

'Ignore her,' Carol replied, 'she's always in a mood. She was the same last night and I was down at eight.'

The table that Carol had chosen was in the very corner of the room. Behind it a large potted plant reached up towards the ceiling, its large olive green leaves vivid in the light from a nearby chandelier. To one side there were French doors leading out into the garden and beyond that the door leading into the kitchen.

'It's great, isn't it?' Carol said, taking her place at the table.

There was something wonderfully elegant about the surroundings, as though the entire history of the building were invested in the grand room. Sarah nodded, admitting that there was something deeply attractive about the Victorian atmosphere.

The waitress arrived a second later. She was young, possibly still in her teens, but she could barely muster a smile as she handed out the menus. Dressed in a simple uniform of white blouse and long black skirt, she too seemed to be in tune with her surroundings.

'Is it the same chef as last night?' Carol asked, not even bothering to look at the menu.

'I think so.'

Carol smiled to the young woman. 'Good, he was excellent last night.'

The waitress tried a smile and almost made it. 'I'm sure he'll be just as good tonight.'

Sarah waited until the girl was gone before looking at the menu. A three course meal was included with the cost of the room, which usually meant something dire in the way of food. 'What did you have last night?' she asked.

'A brilliant wild mushroom ragù with rice, roast aubergine stuffed with onions, apple and herbs followed by crème caramel with kumquats. Lovely.'

'You're vegetarian?' Sarah said, her heart sinking. The first thing she'd seen on the table d'hôte menu that had taken her fancy was venison in blueberry and red wine sauce.

'Yes, I stopped eating meat a couple of years ago. What about you?'

Sarah had tried giving up meat in the past but had failed dismally every time. 'I don't eat much meat,' she said, trying not to sound so apologetic.

'Really? When we were are at uni you were always so political, I thought that you'd definitely be a veggie.'

'No, I'm not.'

Carol smiled sympathetically. 'Well, it's good that you don't eat too much dead animal,' she said. 'It's just not healthy.'

The condescending tone would have been bad enough had Sarah not felt as though she'd just failed some important test. She had been outdone by Carol, whose interest in politics and the environment had been non-existent. If her appearance hadn't changed with the passing of time, it seemed that her views and behaviour had. The menu seemed suddenly to be a minefield to be navigated carefully.

'The venison's meant to be good,' Carol remarked from behind her menu. 'I've heard it's one of the chef's specialities.'

'Really?' Sarah remarked stiffly. She knew she ought to

order it just to show that she didn't care what Carol thought, but then there was part of her that rebelled at the idea of being so outrageously carnivorous.

'What about the fish?'

'What about it?'

Carol put her menu down. 'Do you eat more fish if you've cut down on meat?'

'Yes,' Sarah stated defiantly. 'Do you eat it or are you *properly* vegetarian?'

'Well,' Carol said, lowering her voice slightly, 'I give in sometimes. It depends on what's available. This fresh fish terrine sounds good.'

'And the baked sea bass as a main course.'

Carol picked up her menu and flicked to the wine list. 'What's it to be? A Muscadet or do we go the whole hog and order a decent bottle of Chablis?'

The price of the Chablis was extortionate, and even the bottle of Muscadet was robbery. 'It's not exactly cheap, is it?'

'Expenses?'

Carol was paying for her own stay at the hotel as the research budget wouldn't extend to paying for more than Sarah's stay but Carol had been insistent that she would not meet anywhere in London. 'Our accounts people will hit the roof,' Sarah said. 'They'd rather we went to a burger bar . . .'

'It's all right,' Carol said, 'I'll cover it.'

Sarah was adamant. 'No way, Carol. We'll have the Chablis and I'll argue the toss later.'

'Are you sure?'

'I'm sure. OK, are we ready to order?'

'Yes, I'm starving. And we've got a lot of catching up to do.'

'And some work to get out of the way,' Sarah reminded her.

'No, not until we've had a good old natter about us,' Carol insisted, waving over the waitress.

Sarah waited until they had finished ordering before picking up again. 'I know we've got a lot to talk about,' she said, 'but there's more to this than socialising. I've got to decide whether you've got a story or not, Carol. It's an important decision, you know that.'

12

'Of course I know that, and what I've got to say is important, but that doesn't mean we can't spend a few minutes catching up on news. Come on, Sarah, we don't see each other for five or six years and then you want to get straight down to work. It's not exactly friendly, is it?'

Put like that it wasn't. 'We do one programme a week,' she explained. 'That's one half hour slot when we have a chance to make a difference. It's not much, is it? If you take out the commercial breaks, the credits and the lead-in we've probably got under twenty minutes to present a story. It's important, that's all I'm saying.'

Carol sighed. 'I know it's not much, Sarah, and I really admire the commitment you put into it. I always knew you'd get into something like that. It's good, I mean there's not many people who show that amount of dedication. And you know I wouldn't be here if I didn't think I've got something that's worth exposing. I know I was never into politics the way you were, but things change, I've changed. We're talking about hundreds of thousands of pounds being stolen from public money, from money that should go to better causes than to line people's pockets. I know it's not high government sleaze, but it's still wrong, and it's still news, isn't it?'

At last, it seemed as though Carol was ready to talk things through. So far she had spoken in riddles, dropping broad hints and insinuations but without the solid fact that would give everyone an idea of what it was she had actually uncovered. 'Do you mind if I record this?' Sarah asked, reaching into her bag to grab her cassette recorder.

Carol looked slightly alarmed. 'I'm sorry, Sarah, but I'd rather we didn't.'

'What?'

'I'd rather not do it, I'd rather not talk on tape.'

Sarah sighed inwardly; Carol's concerned speech had sounded too good to be true. 'Why not?' she asked wearily.

'Because it puts me in a difficult situation. I'm supposed to be working for these people . . . I know what they're doing is wrong and I think it has to be stopped, but what happens to me after that? No one in the world's going to want to employ a whistle-blower. Are they?'

It was a valid point, but it irritated Sarah nonetheless. 'This is just for me,' she said, tapping the machine absently, 'it's not for broadcasting. It certainly won't get used in the programme. We've already talked this through, we've guaranteed that you'll not be identified.'

'Come on, Sarah,' Carol said, 'can't we just carry on without it? I'm sorry but I get scared sometimes. You know how things are when the defence industry's involved? It gives me the creeps.' She obviously wasn't joking. The look of concern on her face was real.

'OK,' Sarah said, putting the recorder back in her bag, 'no tape.'

The waitress arrived with the chilled bottle of Chablis. She poured and Sarah tasted then she poured for Carol before departing.

'Carol,' Sarah said, leaning across the table, her voice almost a whisper, 'just who are you scared of?'

Carol half smiled, as though embarrassed. 'Spooks,' she said quietly. 'You know the kind of people involved in the defence industry.'

'What kind of people?' Sarah asked. The kind of people who harass drivers on the motorway? The kind of people who spy on lone females swimming?'

Carol shrugged. 'There's all kinds of people involved. You're the one with all the politics, Sarah, you should know who I mean.'

That wasn't good enough. Sarah needed more than veiled hints and a sense of paranoia. 'Are you talking about the security services?' she demanded.

'I don't know,' Carol admitted disarmingly. 'All I know is that there are guys out there who are creepy. They frighten me and that's what they're there for.'

Sarah debated telling her about the incident in the pool then decided against. Anything that fuelled Carol's fear was a bad idea; it just made it more likely that she'd not talk at all. 'Have you been threatened?'

Carol closed her eyes and nodded. 'Phone calls,' she whispered.

'Have you recorded them?'

For a second there was silence and then Carol laughed. 'I'm not you, Sarah. You might be used to that kind of pressure but I'm not.'

Only a few months previously someone had tried to run Sarah down. Before that, at the Ryder Forum, someone had tried to poison her. She smiled. 'OK,' she admitted, 'I'm probably more used to that. The food's going to be arriving soon,' she added, 'do you want to eat first and then talk?'

Carol looked relieved. 'Sure,' she agreed. 'Tell me about your other half. He's a bit of a hunk from what I hear.'

Duncan a hunk? He was conventionally good-looking in a bland, blond kind of way, but Sarah had trouble thinking of him as a hunk. 'Who've you been talking to?' she asked.

Carol smiled. 'Never you mind. Well, what's he like?'

'He's OK.'

'OK? OK? You don't exactly sound happy with him. What's wrong?'

Sarah's private life was off limits. She hated talking about it, hated talking about him. 'What about you?' she said. 'What are you up to these days?'

'Don't change the subject,' Carol said sternly. 'Come on, what's wrong with him? Let me guess, he's the type that can't stand commitment, right? He's getting jumpy?'

Sarah sighed deeply. 'I'm the one getting jumpy,' she admitted. 'It's just that he's so boring sometimes . . .'

Ditch him. That had been Carol's stark advice. Ditch him immediately; don't dither, don't beat about the bush. Sarah had wanted to talk about anything but Duncan, but in the end the conversation had been dominated by talk about men, relationships, careers and men again. And once conversation had started on relationships, and Sarah's relationship in particular, it had been impossible to shift Carol on to any other subject.

Sarah sat at the desk in her room and stared at her notes. There was nothing substantial to add to them; not one new fact had emerged from the evening's discussion. No, that wasn't true, she realised. What had emerged most strongly was Carol's real fear. In the telephone conversations leading up to their meeting Sarah had put it down to unjustified paranoia or else silly posturing. Now, having been harassed on the motorway and then spied on in the pool she wasn't so sure.

The room was still too hot, even with the radiator turned down. The wine hadn't helped. They'd finished the bottle of Chablis and started on another bottle before Sarah had a chance to protest. Not that she would have objected too much; once she'd started talking about Duncan the wine seemed to help.

Ditch him. It was harsh advice really but Carol was right. Sarah knew that her relationship with Duncan was going nowhere. That's what happened when you met someone on the rebound. After things with Chris had collapsed so painfully Duncan had been there to help her pick up the pieces. He'd helped her through the worst and then, before she knew it, they were together. Together. And now, nearly two years later she was stuck with him, inexorably bound to him by ties of guilt and gratitude.

Sarah exhaled heavily. Her throat was dry and the room was growing closer. She stood up and a wave of dizziness assailed her suddenly. Too much wine? A bottle and a half between two of them? It hadn't seemed to affect Carol at all; her laughter had grown brighter perhaps, her smile warmer, but other than that there had been no visible sign that the alcohol had done anything to her.

There was a decanter of water by the bed and a travel kettle in an alcove by the door. There were sachets of tea and coffee by the kettle too, but things were not so bad that she felt inclined to risk them. At just before midnight it was too late for room service, and the bar downstairs had closed too. That left nothing but a glass of tepid water to slake her thirst.

She sat on the edge of the bed and reached for the decanter. The scream – a wrenching female cry of panic – startled her. A car alarm started up in sympathy, its electronic pulse piercing the momentary silence after the scream. She jumped up quickly and ran to the window. Thrusting aside the tangle of curtains she looked down into the car park. The lights were flashing on one of the cars, pulsing in time with the shrill cry of the alarm. Beside it, down on the gravel, was Carol, on her knees and in distress.

Lights were flicking on all over the hotel and the first people were running across to Carol before Sarah moved. Justifiable paranoia? She dashed out of her room and down the stairs. An old man in striped pyjamas and a tartan dressing gown was peering out of the door towards the commotion in the car park.

'Someone's been attacked,' he said as Sarah came running into the foyer.

'Is she hurt?'

'I don't know,' he admitted, making way for her.

The cold night air felt good as she stepped out of the lobby. The sky above them was dark but for the brilliant light of the half moon. Carol was on her feet and the car had been silenced. Two of the night staff from the hotel were tending her, talking softly as they tried to calm her down. She looked up and saw Sarah and came running towards her.

'It's all right now,' Sarah whispered softly, holding Carol tightly to reassure her. 'What happened?'

Carol was shivering, though whether it was from the cold or the shock it was impossible to tell. 'I came out for some air,' she managed to say, her arms still locked tightly around Sarah. 'I was just . . . just walking when I heard a noise. And then . . . And then he attacked me . . .'

'Who attacked you?'

She shook her head. 'I don't know . . . I don't know, Sarah. I'm scared . . . Please, I'm scared.'

'Have you called the police?' Sarah asked, turning towards the hotel staff.

'No, not yet,' the camp young receptionist replied. 'I'll do that now, they're not too far from us.'

Carol's reaction was instantaneous. 'No, don't call the police. OK? No police.'

Sarah stepped back to look at her. 'Why not? If someone's attacked you then they need to be called.'

'No. I mean it, Sarah, I don't want the police involved in this.'

She was adamant. Despite the fear and shock there was not an element of doubt in her voice.

'Are you sure?' the receptionist asked. 'He might've been trying to break into the cars.'

'Yes, that must be it,' Carol said, jumping at the excuse. 'I must've disturbed him . . . You see, Sarah? It wasn't me he was after, he must've just brushed past me as he ran off.'

Sarah looked towards the forest further on. Like a dark, brooding mass, it gave nothing away. Carol was lying and lying badly. 'Have any of the cars been damaged?' she asked, walking towards the car which had been screeching earlier.

'We'll look,' the other hotel worker, another young man, volunteered.

'Let's go back now,' Carol suggested softly.

They walked back quickly, Sarah convinced that none of the cars had been damaged. Carol had been the intended target, not the cars.

'Someone trying to break into the cars,' Carol told the man in pyjamas.

'Out here? My God,' he exclaimed, 'you would have thought we'd be safe from that kind of thing. Are you OK?'

'Just a bit frightened, that's all,' she replied, managing a smile.

'They ought to string the buggers up,' the man complained bitterly. 'Damn it, I'll have to go out and check on the car now.'

Sarah watched him storm off to his room. 'He wasn't so quick to complain when he thought that it was you who'd been attacked. Threaten his car though . . .'

'That's just the way people are,' Carol said. 'I'm sorry I went outside now. I'll be all right, it was just a shock, that's all.'

'Come on, Carol,' Sarah snapped angrily. 'Just who do you think you're kidding? That was no car thief and we both know it. Who was it?'

'I don't know,' Carol said quietly.

The two hotel workers came in. 'Everything looks fine,' one of them reported. 'Whoever it is has disappeared. Are you sure you don't want us to call the police?'

'It was probably just some kid,' Carol suggested. 'Let's just pretend it never happened.'

The receptionist looked doubtful. 'We've never had anything like this happen before. I apologise of course, and I'm sure that if there's anything we can do to improve security . . .'

'How about installing some lights out there?' Sarah suggested sharply.

The man smiled, trying to placate her. 'Of course, madam, we'll look into that.'

Carol tugged Sarah's hand. 'I'm bushed,' she said, 'I'll see you for breakfast in the morning.'

'I'll walk you to your room,' Sarah suggested.

'Sarah! Look, I'm OK now, OK?' Carol was smiling.

'We need to talk properly tomorrow,' Sarah told her.

'Over breakfast,' Carol promised. 'Now, we both need a good night's sleep.'

TWO

Lucy and Damian were already in the meeting room when Sarah arrived. As always they were sitting next to each other, huddled close and in quiet conversation. Lucy glanced up and smiled. Her hair had been cut close and it seemed to make her smile broader and more relaxed.

'We were just going through your report,' she said.

Damian nodded. 'There's not much to it,' he added, as though Sarah were not already aware of it.

'I know,' she agreed, taking a seat on the other side of the table. The sky outside was bright, blue and lightly dusted with thin wisps of cloud, and the sunlight streamed in through the big square window at the end of the room.

'We're just waiting for Alex,' Lucy said.

Sarah resisted saying 'I know'. Alex would complete the triumvirate of series editors; they were the ones who made the final decisions as to which stories would go ahead and which would be spiked.

'Have you spoken to Carol since coming back?' Damian asked. He leant back in his seat so that his face was bathed in bright yellow light. He looked relaxed, at ease in the bright sunshine, the light reaching across his face and down to touch the dark hairs visible where his shirt was undone.

'This morning,' Sarah said. 'She says she's fine, a bit nervous but fine.'

'No more attacks?'

'I'm not sure she'd tell me even if there were,' Sarah admitted. 'She's stubborn like that. On the morning after the attack in the car park she was still insisting that she'd disturbed a car thief.'

'Why?' Lucy asked, shaking her head in a gesture of disbelief. 'I mean from what you say it was obviously not a thief. Why pretend otherwise?'

It was a good question. 'Because she doesn't want to admit the truth to herself? Because she's frightened? I don't honestly know,' Sarah admitted. 'All I know is that the fear I saw on her face was real, and that I wasn't imagining things when I was followed along the motorway.'

Damian sat forward again, his face now a picture of concern. 'You've not had any more trouble, have you?'

'No. It's been a week since I came back from Lyndhurst and there's been nothing weird going on,' she reported.

Damian laughed. 'Except for all the flak you've been taking from accounts. What was it? Three bottles of champagne?'

Lucy was grinning too. So, the story was doing the rounds already. 'Two bottles of Chablis,' Sarah corrected them, allowing herself a smile too. 'You'd think I'd drunk the place dry the way Peter was going on.'

'Has he coughed up yet?'

Sarah nodded. 'Eventually,' she said.

'Yes,' Damian said, 'we could hear you putting him in his place all right. I've never heard a grown man cry like that before.'

The door opened and Alex breezed in. As always she managed to wear the brightest of colours and the coolest of fabrics and still look like the boss.

'We were just talking about Peter,' Damian explained.

Alex smiled as she sat down. 'Yes, what did you do to him, Sarah? I've never seen him look so defeated before.'

Sarah shrugged. 'I just had a little word with him, that's all,' she said. She turned and caught Lucy's eye, kept the contact for a moment and then Lucy looked away. She and Lucy had come to words in the past; neither of them had enjoyed it and there was still a certain tension between them. It couldn't be helped. Sometimes it was necessary to put aside friendships and fight for what you believed in.

'Right,' Alex said, taking control of the meeting, 'we might as well get on with it. There's not a lot here, is there, Sarah?'

'I know, but it's enough to suggest that there's something important going on. Carol's been blowing hot and cold over this, but the facts that I've managed to corroborate all bear her out. There's big corporate money behind the building of Epsley Science Park. The main players at the park seem to be a hub of software companies, most of them with big defence contracts. I've also checked out some of the names she's mentioned and they come across as squeaky clean.'

Alex looked down the list of names. 'Doesn't that suggest that there's nothing going on?'

Lucy, who had also been looking down the list of names, looked up suddenly. 'Maybe they come across as squeaky clean because they are,' she suggested. 'I mean what have we got that's concrete?'

'One of the companies, Software Solutions, has been awarded three big defence contracts worth over two million pounds. The first and smallest of the contracts went to tender, and the company came in as the lowest bid, but the following two were awarded directly to the company. Somewhere along the line the company's managed to side-step all normal procurement procedures. There's definitely something under-hand going on here. A few discreet questions to people I know have confirmed the fact that no one seems to know what's going on here.'

Alex looked up from the notes. 'Do we know what these contracts are for?'

'No, we don't,' Sarah admitted. 'That's classified information, but I'm sure we can work it out ourselves. The only thing we do know is that neither of the second two contracts is finished. No software's been delivered yet and from what Carol says things are way over deadline.'

Alex turned to Damian. 'Comments?'

He shrugged and pushed himself back in his seat again. 'Software contracts are notorious: late delivery, overspending and crap results are an industry standard. What's the big deal here?'

'The big deal here,' Sarah stated calmly, 'is the suggestion of deliberate fraud. These contracts are deliberately late because it guarantees a steady income to the company. The last three delivery dates have been missed and the testing schedule has been dumped – we've got documentation from Carol to back all that up – and yet the payments from the MoD are still coming through.'

Damian looked unconvinced. 'There'd be penalty clauses,' he pointed out. 'Not to mention loss of confidence and an end to future contracts.'

He was right; Sarah had pointed the same thing out to Carol. 'What if the contracts don't include penalty clauses? What if future contracts aren't an issue when the current ones can be made to drag on for ever?'

Lucy cut in quickly. 'Are you alleging corruption at the Ministry of Defence?'

'Yes, that's a part of what's been suggested by Carol,' Sarah confirmed. 'She's seen the payment schedules and she's overheard the head of the company chatting about it to one of his contacts at the ministry. She doesn't have any names for us yet, but she's prepared to get copies of all the information she can.'

'That's the problem,' Alex responded, 'it's all so vague at the moment. So far we've only got a *suggestion* of ministry corruption.'

'Is she alleging high level involvement? Are we talking political corruption as well?' Lucy added.

Political involvement would mean the threat of censorship – a D-Notice would effectively put a lid on anything developing – and a host of other problems. It would turn the story into something so hot that Sarah doubted whether anyone on the other side of the table would want to touch it. 'No, there's no mention of politicians being involved,' she said. 'She only talked about civil servants. Look, I know there's a paucity of hard fact. I pointed it out in my brief, remember? I'm not arguing that we don't have anything concrete to go on. What I'm saying is that we can dig deeper here, that's all.'

'This Carol, she's a friend of yours, isn't she?' Lucy pointed out unexpectedly.

Sarah clenched her fists tightly. 'I hope you're not saying that that's got anything to do with my conclusions?' she said coldly.

The temperature in the room seemed to have dropped a couple of degrees despite the bright light. Lucy looked a little bit flustered. There was a smile on her face but it had lost its earlier brightness. 'I'm not saying that at all,' she said hastily.

'Then why mention it?' Sarah demanded.

'Because it might have a bearing on this story,' Alex suggested. 'You know her more than we do, we've only ever spoken to her on the phone. We need to know if it's a factor, that's all. What are her motives in all this?'

'Firstly,' Sarah began, doing her best to control her anger, 'Carol and I are hardly best friends. We were at university together and until last week I hadn't seen her in years; that's a measure of how close we are. I do know that she's frightened about what's happening, and that she knows more than she's letting on at the moment. I think there's a story here, Alex, but if you want to put someone else on it then go ahead.'

Alex smiled. 'No one's suggesting that,' she said.

'I'm sorry, Sarah,' Lucy added. 'I really wasn't getting at you. It's just that we're more removed from this, that's all.'

'I'm as objective as you are,' Sarah insisted. She was doing her best to remain calm but it wasn't easy.

'We know you are,' Damian agreed. 'To be fair, I've spoken to Carol a few times on the phone now,' he added, 'and she comes across as remarkably together. I agree with Sarah on this one; we need to dig deeper.'

'How have you left things with her?' Alex asked.

'I told her that we'd probably need more information before going ahead with the story,' Sarah said.

'Good. I think that's a reasonable conclusion. I've looked at the schedules, we've got six weeks to decide whether this one goes into pre-production. Do you think we can come to a definitive decision in that time?'

With everything else Sarah was working on six weeks was

a pitifully short space of time to fully investigate a story's potential value. 'I'm still working flat out on the Chrysler story and we're coming up to head on the Irish drugs and guns programmes,' she said, 'but I think I can manage a few clear days to spend on this one, so long as the other stories don't go haywire.'

'What are your next moves?' Lucy asked.

Sarah already had the answer. 'I'm going down to Epsley Science Park for a good look around.'

Alex smiled. 'Good. And Sarah? This time go easy on the Chablis.'

They were expecting a placatory smile in return. Tension over, all friends again. 'Don't worry,' she said, 'I'll make sure that I drink nothing but tap water.'

Epsley University was the first stop, Sarah decided. It had provided the land, the concept and the academic gloss required to build the Science Park; the hard cash had come from a diverse group of venture capitalists and entrepreneurs. It was an arrangement that seemed to suit both sides, though who actually gained the most from the partnership it was hard to tell. From what she had learned the university's day to day involvement with running the Park appeared to be minimal. However, it was still the best place to start, as far as she was concerned.

The drive down through London to the suburbs was a headache-inducing nightmare of a journey. The roads were polluted, congested and unbearably hot. With the sunroof open and the windows down the car was awash with waves of carbon monoxide and diesel fumes. Closing the windows meant keeping in the blistering heat that burned Sarah's face and arms. There was nothing for it but to sit and cook, or else to suffocate, as the traffic crawled along dismal streets more suited to cold and rain than to the sharp heat that burned down from the sky.

Finally the cramped south London streets gave way to the dual carriageway that led out of the city and down towards the heart of Surrey and beyond. Sarah pressed her foot down and the car leapt forward, moving up in speed as the road ahead cleared at last. With the open road the blue sky was transformed from an instrument of oppression to something inspirational. From wishing for a refreshing burst of rain, Sarah now hoped that the sunshine would hold out for the rest of the day.

Epsley lay to the south-west of London, a suburban satellite which had once been a village but which had now been swallowed up completely. There was nothing left of a village atmosphere; to all intents and purposes it was functionally part of London, albeit on the very edge of the capital. The university had probably started life as a local technical college and in turn had been transformed into a polytechnic and, most recently, it had been promoted to full university status. If it had any kind of reputation, and Sarah wasn't sure that it had, it was for dull competence. Its students had no history of radicalism, its academics no flair for brilliance, its courses no sign of innovation.

It was not the kind of place that Sarah had considered for her own education, though in her day her choices had been driven more by snobbery than anything else. Brilliance was everything, nothing else would have been acceptable. In some ways, she reflected, things had changed and in others they hadn't. She was still determined to be the best, to prove herself first and foremost, yet how she defined that brilliance had changed. Reputation alone was no guarantee of anything; no longer could she accept things, or people, at face value.

The university was signposted from the main road. She turned off and headed along through open countryside before turning again towards a more built-up area. She rounded a final corner and the grim façade of the university came up ahead. The main building looked like a concrete and glass tower block rather than an institute of higher education. Smaller buildings, most of them also constructed from preformed blocks of grey concrete, were spread widely across the rest of the site.

Entry was through unmanned double gates and a road that wound through to a number of different car parks. She drove round, stopping at each in turn until she found a place that allowed visitors to park. Spotting the pay and display machine at the end of the car park she revised her opinion. The university building was more like a run-down shopping centre than a tower block.

What was she doing there? It had seemed a good place to start, but now that she had arrived she was at a loss as to why she had thought so. The Science Park was sited elsewhere, the buildings were newer and the environment was presumably better. She had phoned the university press office earlier in the day and they had given her all the background she needed.

She locked the car and decided to walk around for a while. If the university had been the inspiration for the Science Park then she wanted to get an idea of the atmosphere which had produced that inspiration. The concrete buildings were more widely spaced than she had first thought, with wide open lawns and tarmac paths between them. Scattered beds of flowers were wilting in the sun, the bright colours bleached by the light and the soil starved of water. Glancing at her watch she saw that it was still well before lunch time, which explained why there were so few people around.

The path nearest the car park wound its way into the heart of the campus: a main square which bordered the university bookshop on one side, a number of offices on the other and the entrance to the library building on another. There were more people around there: groups of students sitting on a low brick wall near to the path, people going in and out of the library and the bookshop. Ordinarily the library would have been her first port of call; she loved books and always saw libraries as massive stores of information waiting to be discovered. However, with the sun so bright and the stillness of the air she knew that the atmosphere in the library would be close and uncomfortable.

Now that she was closer to the university buildings it was possible to see that they were in a poor state of repair. The concrete was falling apart, cracks ran along the walls and the steel frames around the windows were in dire need of paint. The long paths around the site were littered with paper, discarded sweet wrappers and drink cans, all adding to the feeling of drift and decay. Was there no spark of life anywhere on campus?

A cluster of signs pointed to the different departments, many of them housed in the tower block that dominated the skyline. She walked round, aware of being in the dark shadow of the tower. Even in the shadow there was no cooling breeze, no escape from the heat that seemed to ooze from the ground and drift down from the sky. She hesitated before approaching the entrance to the main building, but the hope that it would provide some respite from the stifling atmosphere proved stronger than her desire to get back to her car.

Inside, the lobby looked shabby and uncared for, with worn carpets on the floor, an array of defaced posters on the wall and queues of people waiting for the lifts. She walked past a group of students — loitering in sullen silence near the entrance to the toilets — to a noticeboard on the wall beside the list of departments located in the building. There was nothing of interest in the student union notices: concerts, discos, clubs. There seemed to be no sign of political activity, and even the adverts for clubs and discos seemed curiously apathetic. Had things changed so radically with young people? Or was the apathy a reflection of the atmosphere endemic at Epsley?

Looking at the list of departments proved only slightly more interesting. Clearly the focus of the departments in the building, and perhaps of the entire university, was on applied science and technology. The humanities were poorly repre-sented, unless one counted business studies as a humanities subject, which Sarah could not bring herself to do.

The engineering department was located in the top two floors of the building; it was where the original impetus for the Science Park had come from. From what she had read, and from what Carol had said, the original idea for the Science Park had come from the head of the electrical engineering department, though it was actually his former assistant, Dr Gerald Graham, who had taken the idea to fruition. She debated going up to take a look around but in the end she decided against. She had seen everything she needed to see. The university was not the hive of industry that she had hoped to find; the decaying buildings, morose students and dead beat atmosphere told the whole story.

It took a while to find her way back to the car, the paths

through the different buildings all looked so similar. In the blistering heat her car had cooked well, its shiny surface too hot to touch and the air inside unbreathable. She opened the doors and windows and sat for a while, hoping that the worst of the heat would dissipate while she wrote up her notes.

Not that there was much to write. She listed her key words for the university: depressing, stagnant, dispirited. The bright sunshine should have added a summery gloss to the university, it should have yielded an atmosphere of quiet energy and excitement. Instead it had served to highlight the decaying buildings, the lethargic atmosphere and a strange, pervading sense of depression.

What kind of environment would have been spawned from such an atmosphere, she wondered, finally starting the car.

Epsley Science Park sat squat and red beside a small lake that glistened in the harsh light of the afternoon. Access to it was via a single slip road from the main dual carriageway. Sarah followed the road round slowly, waiting until she had a clear, unobstructed view before slowing the car to a halt. The Park lay below her, a collection of buildings at the bottom of a shallow incline, surrounded on three sides by landscaped grounds and facing a man-made lake in front of it, with only the dark grey road to break up the symmetry of land and water.

She took her camera from the glove compartment of the car and took several shots from the high vantage point. If only she'd done the same with the university; the differences were striking. Here there was no single building to dominate the view; instead the half dozen units shared a common architecture with each being slightly different to its neighbour. Each two-storey unit was built of dark red brick, with a sloping roof of red clay tiles and dark windows tinted black but reflecting the light in sharp white strips.

Once the photos had been taken Sarah drove down to the site, taking her time, tracking the view in terms of camera angles and lighting. Already she could see the opening scenes of the programme, fading from the apparent decay of the university to the modernist gloss of the Science Park. She was jumping the gun of course, assuming that the contrast was significant, but the idea was as appealing as the power of the images.

The road diverged near the entrance to the estate, turning off onto the Park itself on one side and then heading on towards a fenced-off section of land on the other side of the lake. A large billboard beside the lake announced PHASE TWO: A JOINT DEVELOPMENT OF EPSLEY UNIVERSITY AND VENTURE CAPITAL INTERNATIONAL. As well as listing the main contractors the billboard featured an impression of the new addition to the Park: another six units on the opposite side of the lake, though in the artist's picture they appeared less glossy and more in tune with the landscaped surroundings.

Sarah turned onto the estate, slowing to glance at the list of companies signposted near the first of the buildings. Carol was working freelance for a company called PR-Tech, its offices sharing a building with another small company, a typical arrangement for most of the units. Running through the list of companies confirmed the facts – Software Solutions, InfoSoft, Advanced Micro Technologies, Networks Inc, G-Man Software and more – computer and software companies predominated. Nearly every unit on the site was occupied. If the level of occupancy was a measure of success then the venture was clearly doing well.

There were car parks in front of and between the different units. Sarah smiled to herself as she parked near Carol's office – the place looked like the forecourt of a BMW dealership. The sleek bodies of the fast, expensive cars gleaming in the sunshine were another measure of prosperity and success. It made another good image to contrast with the decrepit state of the university. She made a mental note to list all the images that highlighted the change from university to Science Park, instinctively linking the pictures to the words and phrases she had been composing on the drive down.

'Sarah! You're here!'

She turned to find Carol crossing the car park towards her. The sunlight sparkled in her long blonde hair, making her flesh seem pale and contrasting with the vivid red of her lipstick. Her eyes were shielded by black sunglasses that matched the short-sleeved cardigan worn over an ankle-length checked dress which again seem to draw attention to the gold of her hair and the red of her lips. The dress did nothing to flatter her figure, Sarah noted absently. Was she putting on weight? Perhaps the intervening years hadn't been so kind after all.

'A good drive down?' Carol asked as Sarah stepped from the car.

'From London? You've got to be kidding,' Sarah responded. 'The traffic's even worse when the sun's out.'

'Isn't it gorgeous though? It's only April and already it feels like July. It's going to be a good one this year, I can tell.'

'How have things been?' Sarah asked, deciding that the weather talk could wait until later.

Carol smiled broadly, her red lips parting to reveal perfect white teeth. 'Fine, fine,' she insisted quickly. 'Listen, before you go in,' she whispered, 'there's a few things you need to know. Firstly I've told Liz that you're a TV director; you do documentaries. I've told her that you're here to talk about doing a programme on the Science Park. I've said it's just exploratory, nothing's confirmed –'

What the hell was she on about? 'Stop!' Sarah cried, unwilling to keep up with the fast stream of information. 'I thought I was here to talk to you. What's going on?'

'We did say you needed to find out more, didn't we? This is the best way, Sarah, the only way really. Don't you see? You can go undercover . . .'

'You're joking, right?' Sarah snapped. Perhaps all the talk about spooks and the security services had gone too far. There was no way that she was prepared to act out a charade, no way at all.

Carol smiled and shook her head. 'I'm not joking,' she stated quietly. 'I've taken too many risks already, Sarah. I've already told you that there's something major going on here, but if you want to dig it all up you'll have to get your hands dirty too.'

'I can't do this,' Sarah insisted. She wanted to look Carol in the eye but the dark glasses gave nothing away.

'I'm frightened enough as it is. Look at what happened to

me at Lyndhurst. Do you really think that that's the first time? Do you?'

'Have you been to the police?'

Carol laughed, her hair falling back over her shoulders as her head went back. 'Get real, Sarah,' she said, losing the laugh abruptly. 'I thought you were the hardened cynic, not some naïve kid. How did you think you were going to get this? Walk in and –'

'Stop it!'

Carol stopped instantly. 'I'm sorry,' she said quietly. 'I just assumed that you'd use some form of subterfuge to get to the truth. If I'm wrong I'm sorry, but I can't let you walk in and blithely announce who you are and what you're doing. This might be dangerous, Sarah.'

There was no time to talk things over. Sarah could see someone looking down on them from one of the windows of the upper storey of the office. An argument out in the blazing heat did not augur well. 'Can't we go for lunch somewhere? Just the two of us?' she asked.

Carol looked round. 'That's Liz,' she reported, 'she runs PR-Tech. She's expecting you. She thinks it's a real coup having you here. A TV programme on the Science Park is the sort of thing which she dreams about.'

There seemed to be no way out. Sarah had never gone for the cloak and dagger stuff. She preferred to keep a distance and to use other methods to get her stories. This time, with all the implications of security service involvement, there seemed to be no other way. 'OK,' she agreed, 'this is just an exploratory meeting. Nothing's been agreed. Who do I work for?'

Carol looked relieved. 'Thanks. You work for an independent production company.'

'Name?'

'You make it up, she didn't ask.'

Sarah looked around the Park. The serried ranks of garishly coloured German cars provided no inspiration. 'I work for . . . I don't know . . . Penis Substitute Productions . . .'

Carol laughed. 'OK, you work for a company called PSP. You're looking around at a number of possible stories and this is just one of them. We met at uni — that part's true at least.'

'Is there anything else?'

Carol turned and waved to Liz. 'No,' she said, turning back, 'just remember that she's keen to impress you. Tell her you need to know everything there is to know about this place.'

The whole thing sounded ludicrous. It was going to fall flat on its face, and when it did the whole story was going to go with it. 'Let's just get on with it,' Sarah said, turning to flash a smile in Liz's direction.

'Don't worry,' Carol assured her, 'I'm sure this is going to be a breeze.'

Within minutes of meeting her, Sarah could see that Liz was indeed keen to impress. In her late thirties or early forties, impeccably dressed, with dark brown hair and a rather plain face dominated by dark, intelligent eyes, she was in many ways the opposite of Carol. Several inches shorter than Carol and Sarah, Liz spoke with a quiet determination that was immediately apparent and which was in stark contrast to Carol's endless equivocating. And where Carol was an immediately engaging character, Sarah could see that Liz was more guarded, keeping something back behind her dark brown eyes.

Her office was large, open plan and dominated by glossy posters advertising both the Science Park and many of the individual companies on it. A large square meeting table sat in the middle of the room, the focus of the office. Computers and desks were arranged along one wall, clearly marking out the working area, and on the other side there were filing cabinets, bookshelves and the rest of the office furniture.

'I hope you don't mind,' Liz said, showing Sarah to the table, 'but I've put together a presentation pack for you. I wasn't sure how you wanted things to run.'

Carol answered before Sarah had a chance to. 'We thought that a run down on the history of the Park and then a list of the major companies here would be a good place to start,' she said.

Sarah sat down. 'That's a good a place as any to start,' she agreed, taking a copy of the presentation.

Liz smiled. 'It's nothing too grand,' she said, taking the seat on the other side of the table to Sarah. 'It's just something I put together on the computer this morning.'

'Do you fancy something cold or would coffee be OK?' Carol asked.

Sarah looked up from the thick pile of papers, realising that Liz was intending to go through things in fine detail. 'Coffee, please,' she said, guessing that they were in for a long day.

'We can break for lunch in a while,' Liz added. 'Then, if you like, we can look at some of the most interesting of our clients in the afternoon.'

Everything had been clearly organised in advance. It was a pity no one had informed her, Sarah thought, but then she doubted if she would have come if Carol had told her what was being planned. She turned back to the presentation pack, padded out with organisation charts, bullet points, colour graphics and pages and pages of text. Liz may have put it together earlier in the morning, she realised, but the individual items in the pack had been used before.

'How was the drive from London?' Liz asked while Carol made the coffee.

'Hot and hectic,' Sarah remarked. 'You're miles from the nearest station here, aren't you?'

'Yes, we're not exactly well served by public transport,' Liz said. 'But that doesn't seem to adversely affect us here.'

'They're all road demons here,' Carol called from the other side of the room. 'There's probably more BMWs and Mercedes per square metre here than anywhere else outside Germany.'

Mercedes? Sarah's heart skipped a beat. Was it possible that the big black car which had tailed her so intimidatingly on the way to Lyndhurst had come from the Park? If someone on the Park knew that Carol was onto something . . .

'Shall we start?' Liz said as the coffee arrived.

It broke Sarah's train of thought. There were questions that Carol had to answer, but the way things had been arranged

34

meant that there was probably little chance of asking them directly.

'Can I make notes?' Sarah asked, suddenly realising that Liz was about to start.

THREE

Sarah had hoped that the break for lunch might give her a chance to breathe a bit. Liz was clearly good at her job, though Sarah had never been one to appreciate the finer arts of public relations. Some of what Liz had to say was mildly interesting, but most of it was tediously dull. The history of the Science Park was boring except for the story of the government's policy with regard to the universities, but Liz had skated over that quickly. Even a few direct questions on the subject had yielded nothing worth quoting.

The official story was that the university had decided that closer links with industry were a 'good thing'. That these links revolved around the whole question of the state funding of education were of no apparent concern to Liz, nor to Carol come to that. These academic–industrial links had been, according to Liz, extremely useful for all sides, and the culmination of these was the setting-up of a consultancy business at the university. Lecturers with appropriate skills were being made available, at a fee, to private industry to solve problems, transfer skills, improve technology and provide specialist training.

At one point Sarah had asked, pointedly, what the students thought of such consultancy business. Didn't they mind missing out on lectures while the university cashed in? Liz had merely smiled, suggested that the question was off-topic and had swiftly moved on with her presentation.

Lunch, much to Sarah's disappointment, had been a working affair. Her heart had sunk at the news. She knew what a working lunch meant: sandwiches – except for Carol who refused to eat bread that wasn't organic – and more talk. Liz took her chance to ask questions, wanting to know about the proposed documentary in detail. Sarah had done her best to bluff it out, though she was certain that Liz would soon realise what a load of rubbish her questions were eliciting in the way of reply. When she didn't, much to Carol's obvious relief, Sarah guessed that if you were in PR and talked bullshit for a career your own critical faculties atrophied soon enough.

After lunch Sarah was given a quick tour of the Science Park, where Liz acted as guide as they walked across from one unit to the next. Each of the companies on the site was introduced in passing, with Liz giving a quick précis of the work the company did and who the key players were. It was second-hand information as far as Sarah was concerned: she'd done her own homework on the Park and Carol had also supplied her with the low-down on who was who. She listened attentively all the same, pretending interest when she felt nothing but a desire to get away.

Once they returned to the PR-Tech office things did get more interesting. Liz had wanted to know on which companies Sarah was going to concentrate. The truth was that the only company of real interest was Software Solutions and any of the other companies which might be involved in its schemes. Carol had previously mentioned two other companies; G-Man Software and Advanced Micro Technologies.

'Software Solutions is an obvious choice,' Sarah replied after a moment. 'They're the biggest company here. It makes sense to focus on them a good deal.'

Liz did not looked convinced. 'They write specialist software for the defence industry mainly. To be honest,' she said, 'I'm not sure they'd be that interesting . . .'

Sarah sat back, affecting surprise. 'Why? They're a client of yours, aren't they?'

'Don't get me wrong,' Liz replied defensively. 'Every company on this site is a client of ours – we handle the press, publicity and PR for every single company here – and we don't favour one more than another. It's just that, well, I'm not sure there's anything really dynamic going on there.'

'Why don't I talk to Brian Quigley at Software Solutions first?' Sarah suggested. 'Perhaps he can persuade me that his company's interesting enough for the documentary. Who else?'

It was Carol who spoke first, clearly pre-empting Liz's reply. 'It's got to be G-Man Software,' she said. 'They're the smallest company here; it's a two-man band. Two brothers actually, Grant and Gavin, hence the G-Man name. They're interesting, you'll like them.'

Again Liz did not look convinced. 'Come on, Carol, you know that the boys are struggling to make a go of things. They're hardly representative of the Park as a whole.' It seemed to Sarah that Liz was trying to keep a tight lid on her emotions. Her dark eyes had narrowed and she was leaning forward in her seat, her arms crossed tight around her chest.

'To be honest if they're struggling then it makes it more interesting to me,' Sarah said.

Liz shook her head. 'Can I be frank here, Sarah? Gavin's a good lad, he's tough, he's sharp, he's going places and he'll be keen to co-operate with you. His younger brother, Grant, is bad news and I doubt if you'll find him at all helpful.'

'Oh, come on, Liz!' Carol cried. 'That's unfair. Just because Gavin wears the suits that doesn't mean –'

Liz was about to respond when she caught Sarah's eye. She inhaled deeply and forced a smile. 'I'm sorry,' she said, 'we're not very together at the moment. To be blunt I'm worried that someone like Grant Newman's going to give everybody the wrong impression of what life is like here.' She turned to Carol. 'I'm not saying he's a bad person, just that he's not really representative of the people working on the Park.'

Clearly the two brothers were important in some way. 'Why don't we mark them down as candidates for the programme at this stage,' Sarah suggested, trying to placate Liz while keeping her options open. 'Even if Grant isn't typical, he might still be worth including in the film, even if it's only to highlight the differences between him and the profile of the other people on the Park.'

'I can't see him agreeing to that,' Liz said, 'but it's your call.'

'OK,' Sarah said, writing the names down on her pad. 'Who else?'

There was another difference of opinion, with Liz suggesting InfoSoft and Carol a company called Advanced Micro Technology. The argument drifted on for a while, with Sarah trying not to appear to be taking sides. In the end, after an interminable period of wrangling, it was agreed that Sarah would look at both companies. By then it was late and Sarah felt desperate to get away. The day had dragged on for longer than she had anticipated and had yielded little of the hard facts she had been after.

It looked as though Liz was about to start arguing about G-Man Software again as it obviously rankled that her objections had been so quickly overruled. Sarah cut her off quickly. 'It's getting late and I've got a long drive back,' she said.

Liz looked at her watch. 'Is that the time? Surely we've still got time to meet Dr Graham.'

'The Director of the Park,' Carol added, although Sarah already knew the name and what he did.

'It's getting late,' Sarah said, unable to muster any enthusiasm. It had been a long meeting and all she wanted to do was to take a break. She still needed to talk to Carol alone, but even that she was willing to put aside for another day.

'You've got to meet him,' Carol insisted. There was something about her tone that suggested an order rather than a request.

Sarah sat back, resigned to her fate. 'Sure, go ahead,' she agreed.

Dr Graham was tall and well-groomed, with a neatly trimmed beard, short black hair streaked with the first signs of grey and light brown eyes that shone with intelligence and good humour. He was wearing a dark blue suit and an off-white shirt to contrast with his silver and blue silk tie. Sarah wasn't sure what she had been expecting, a fusty old bureaucrat perhaps, but certainly not the lively and attractive individual who strode into the room wearing such a relaxed and welcoming smile.

Carol, smiling, decided to handle the introductions. 'Sarah, this is Gerry, Dr Graham to the rest of the world, and Gerry, this is Sarah Fairfax.'

'Hello, Sarah,' he said. 'I'm so glad you could make it.'

They gripped hands momentarily, his fingers warm and strong, and then he took a seat at the table, to Sarah's left. His voice was strong, masculine, with a hint of an accent that she couldn't quite place.

'We've had a good meeting,' Liz reported, 'and I think we've made a fair bit of progress.'

Were the arguments about the Newman brothers to be glossed over? Sarah smiled. 'We have,' she agreed, deciding to toe the line for the moment. 'I can safely say that there's more than enough here to work on.'

'Good, that's just what I want to hear,' Dr Graham said, fixing Sarah with his eyes. 'Now, what can we do to facilitate things for you?'

Sarah tried to look away from him but his eyes held her in place. He spoke with a certain amount of forcefulness; not that it made him sound pushy, it was more subtle than that. 'I'm not sure yet,' she said, realising that he was waiting for an answer.

His smile broadened. 'I had been thinking of providing some office space, computer equipment, comms, that kind of thing.'

He was thinking along the right lines, of course. But then he had had time to think things through. Damn Carol! Sarah nodded her agreement. 'That's the kind of thing we'll need,' she said, 'but that's a while down the line yet. Initially I'll need access to information. If you could make people available for interview, and arrange perhaps for me to visit each of the companies that we're interested in.'

'That goes without saying,' he assured her. 'Which of the companies have you selected?'

Sarah listed them quickly, searching Dr Graham's face for clues as to his feelings about each of them in turn. The only one in which she detected a flicker of reaction was G-Man Software, the hint of a frown appearing on his face. Liz keyed in to his disquiet too.

'It's a short-list,' Liz hurried to assure him. 'The plan is to home in on three of the four companies.'

'Good. In that case I'm sure that Sarah's going to make the best selection,' he said. 'What's your plan of action?'

'Obviously I need to get back to base to go through all of the information I've already collected,' she said. 'I need to sit down and talk with the rest of my team.'

'Will you be coming back with more of your people?' he asked. 'I'm thinking that perhaps we can arrange to get the university's media resources team involved at some point.'

Like all deceptions, once started it was going to get harder and harder to keep up with. 'I think that might be jumping the gun a bit,' she said. 'This is still at its earliest stages. We might not even get beyond the next commissioning meeting.'

Carol was the first to respond. 'But from what you've seen today?'

'I'm keen to continue with this,' Sarah said, 'but I need to dig deeper. I need to identify the story, the hooks which will grab the viewers and draw them in.'

'Of course,' Liz said blithely, 'and we'll do everything we can to make that happen.'

Dr Graham broke in before Sarah had time to respond. 'What is your angle?' he asked. 'What's the story you're looking for?'

Liz and Carol had avoided asking anything fundamental, but Dr Graham seemed not to be the type to let anything slip. 'My angle?' Sarah echoed. 'Well, er, we want to focus on the trials and tribulations of small companies in the high technology area. What are their needs? How best are these needs met? How do they compare to traditional small companies? That kind of thing.'

'So the Park itself, as a separate entity, isn't the focus of your programme?' he asked, sounding slightly disappointed.

'It is in so far as it meets, or fails to meet, the specific needs of these companies,' Sarah lied. 'Obviously we can contrast the kind of environment you provide with the more traditional industrial base.'

His next question was even more direct. 'Why us?'

It took Sarah by surprise. 'Pardon?' she said, aware that the other two women were letting him do all the talking.

'Why us? Why Epsley Science Park? Why not South Bank in London? Or the Surrey Research Park in Guildford?'

Sarah had not heard of either of them. She tried hard to think of an answer that sounded truthful. Her mind went back to Liz's presentation, though already it had started to fade from memory. 'Because you're newer,' she said. 'I mean, you're still at an early stage of development; things are more flexible here.'

'We're also fully networked for the future,' Liz reminded everybody. 'Every unit on the site has its own local area network, and these in turn are linked up to a site wide intra-net.'

'Have you approached anyone else?' Dr Graham asked next.

Sarah felt as though the tables had been turned. Earlier in the day everyone had been keen to impress her; now she was the one who was on the line. She felt as though she were being interviewed, and, she guessed, she was doing poorly. 'No,' she admitted. 'We had a list of potential places, but as Carol and I are old friends I thought I'd short-circuit things. I know it's not the most methodical way to work, but then it seemed to me the most immediately useful.'

The explanation brought a smile to Dr Graham's lips. 'I'm sure that we've all worked that way before. OK, I'd still like to involve our media resources unit. We publish a newsletter and I'd like to mention it there. It's not much, but it keeps our investors happy, and if it raises our media profile even slightly then that's a bonus.'

Sarah was too tired to argue. 'If that's what you wish,' she agreed. 'I'll need to come back in a few days to start interviewing people. When I come back I'll talk to your media people.'

'Good,' he concluded. 'I'm sure that this is going to work to the benefit of all of us.'

He looked relaxed again, the good humour still in his eyes and in his smile. He was definitely an attractive-looking man, Sarah admitted to herself. There was a hint of cologne which suited him well.

'That, I think,' said Liz, 'wraps it up for the day. Unless of course you've got any more questions, Sarah?'

Sarah declined with a slight shake of the head. It was late. The tinted windows made it difficult to judge the true colour of the sky but it was getting darker by the minute. The clock on the wall was nudging towards six; it was later than she had realised.

'No,' she said, 'I've got a long drive back to look forward to.'

Dr Graham laughed. 'Don't worry too much,' he said, 'you're driving against the flow of traffic. The rush hour's in the opposite direction, the roads out of London are a nightmare.'

'I hope you're right,' Sarah said, sorting through her notes. She gathered everything together and then stood up. 'It's been a useful day, long and tiring, but useful all the same.'

'It's been nice meeting you,' Dr Graham said, shaking her hand once more. His eyes seemed to linger for a moment too long. She turned to Liz and said her goodbye, aware that he was still looking at her.

'I'll walk you to your car,' Carol offered.

At last, a chance to talk alone. 'Thanks,' Sarah said. 'Well, 'bye, everybody and I'll be in touch.'

Together she and Carol walked out of the office onto the landing at the top of the stairs. The office opposite was unoccupied, the plain wooden door without the brass plaque which each of the occupied units boasted. The single flight of stairs leading down to the entrance lobby was also quiet.

'Well?' Carol whispered, stopping at the top of the stairs. 'What do you think?'

'I'm tired,' Sarah said, exhaling heavily. The long day was beginning to take its toll.

'Come on! What do you think?' Carol persisted.

'It's too early to tell yet. From what you've said before this Quigley's the prime mover in whatever's going on. I think I'll –'

Carol cut in quickly. 'Not that! What do you think of Gerry?'

The question took Sarah by surprise. 'What about him?'

'He's gorgeous, isn't he?'

Gorgeous was not a word that Sarah used. Neither was cute, dishy or hunk. 'He's good-looking,' she said.

'What?' Carol sounded outraged by the half-hearted comment. 'I saw the way you were looking at him. You fancy him, don't you?'

'I do not,' Sarah snapped. 'Look, that's not the reason I'm here.'

'He fancies you too,' Carol continued, completely ignoring Sarah's objections.

Did he? 'He doesn't,' Sarah stated coldly.

'You know he does.'

Sarah suppressed the smile that gave her away. 'There's no time for that. Come on,' she said, 'I need to get going.'

'Yes, you've got Duncan to get back to,' Carol said, her smile at odds with the derogatory tone of her voice.

'Stop that now!' Sarah muttered angrily. What the hell did Carol think she was playing at? Talking about Duncan was off-limits. It had been a mistake to talk about him at Lyndhurst; now Carol imagined that he was a reasonable topic of conversation.

'Don't be so touchy,' Carol replied, patting Sarah's hand comfortingly. 'I was only kidding. Sorry, it's a sore point, I know.'

'I'm going,' Sarah snapped.

'I said I'm sorry. Come on, Sarah, don't be upset with me. Please?'

Sarah looked at her, trying to fathom what was going on behind Carol's innocent blue eyes. She sounded genuinely contrite. 'OK, it's just that the subject is closed. Understand?'

Carol nodded. 'I know. What about Gerry? Is talking about him off-limits too?' she said, smiling.

'Oh, for goodness' sake,' Sarah sighed. 'Come on, you were going to walk me to my car, remember?'

They walked down the single flight of stairs in silence, Sarah looking through the glass doors at the sky which was dark blue and cluttered with thick grey cloud. The heat and light which had made the day so oppressive and uncomfortable had been replaced suddenly by a night sky thick and dense with the threat of rain. It looked cold outside, and Sarah, like everybody else, was dressed for the heat.

'It doesn't look good,' Carol remarked, stopping at the door.

It was an understatement, entirely untypical of Carol. 'I boiled on the way up here and I'll freeze on my way back,' Sarah complained softly.

'Listen, I just need to go to the loo,' Carol said suddenly. 'I won't be long. You'll wait, won't you?'

'Be quick,' Sarah urged. 'We need to talk.'

'OK, wait here.'

Carol turned and headed back up the stairs to the office. Sarah watched her go then turned back to peer impassively at the darkening skyline. The edge of the car park was lined with dense shrubbery, bathed in the soft orange glow of the street lamps, and beyond that a sloping lawn led down to the thick black pool that was the lake.

'Hello? Can I help you?'

Sarah swirled round, startled by the male voice which had appeared from nowhere. The look of surprise on her face was echoed by the young man behind her, equally startled by the way she had jumped. Clean-shaven, with thick black hair slicked back, a stud in one ear and a suit that looked sharp enough to cut with, the man stared at her for a moment before remembering to smile.

'I'm sorry I made you jump,' he apologised.

'You didn't make me jump,' Sarah responded instantly.

He grinned. 'OK, sorry I didn't make you jump,' he said. 'Are you waiting for somebody?'

Sarah looked beyond him to the door through which he had presumably emerged. The brass plaque signalled that the office belonged to G-Man Software. As he was dressed in a sharp suit and a tie that contravened every law of good taste she guessed that he was the acceptable one of the Newman brothers.

'You must be Gavin,' she guessed.

He raised his eyebrows questioningly. 'You're one up on me then,' he said. 'I've got no idea who you are.'

She smiled at last. 'Sarah Fairfax,' she said, offering her hand. 'I might be working on a documentary on the Science Park. You're on my list of people to meet.'

'Really?' he said, his eyes lighting up. 'What's it for, this documentary?'

'Television.'

'Wow! What channel?'

She smiled, his enthusiasm was touching. 'I work for an independent production company. This programme's at an early stage of development, we might not even –'

Gavin turned suddenly as Carol came down the stairs. He looked at her coldly and she looked back equally disdainfully. 'Listen,' he said, turning back to Sarah, 'here's my card. Give me a ring and we can talk properly.'

Sarah just had time to take the card before he pushed the door open and walked out.

'What's all that about?' Sarah asked, tucking the card into her bag.

Carol shrugged. 'Gavin and I aren't getting on,' she said, as though Sarah hadn't noticed it for herself.

'Come on,' Sarah said, 'we need to talk.'

Gavin shot past in his car as Sarah walked out into the cold night air. His car – bright red and sporty – zoomed by in a squeal of rubber and acceleration. It figured, of course: the sharp suit, slicked-back hair and boyish grin were all part of the same boy-racer image. She watched his car travel fast to the entrance to the Park, turn right and then head towards the main road.

Carol joined her outside, wrapping her arms tight around her chest as the cold hit her. 'He's such a flash little bastard,' she muttered, watching the car finally disappear into the distance.

'Why aren't you getting on?' Sarah asked. There was probably something personal going on, something sexual, knowing Carol.

'He just doesn't like the fact that I get on with his brother,' Carol reported glumly.

'You mean that Gavin fancies you but you fancy his brother?'

Carol grinned. 'You're beginning to sound like me,' she cautioned. 'What makes you think that I fancy either of them?'

Sarah was about to respond when she stopped herself. It

was a stupid way to talk, like a silly schoolgirl talking about her crushes on older boys. 'Let me guess,' she said, 'Dr Graham's more your type.'

Carol shook her head. 'Not my type at all,' she said. 'Come on, it's freezing out here.'

They started to walk across the road towards the car, keeping in step. The lake and the rolling lawn meant that the breeze was cold and strong, whipping up viciously across the open space of the car park. Sarah clutched at her bag and the presentation folder, holding them tight as they were buffeted by the breeze. The street lights on the edge of the car park rattled noisily, the lamps shaking slightly, casting strange shadows around the cars. She looked up at the thick cloud, low and menacing and moving steadily across the sky.

'It's not summer yet,' Carol remarked, also looking up at the sky.

'It's all over the place,' Sarah said, sucking in the air through gritted teeth. Next time she'd bring a jacket, no matter what the weather forecasters promised.

Lights flashed suddenly ahead of them blinding Sarah completely. She stopped and shielded her eyes, caught in the harsh white glare. Carol was beside her, also covering her eyes and trying to make out the car in front of them. The engine was gunned loudly and roared with an angry, suppressed power. The tyres screamed against the tarmac and at the same time Carol cried out.

Sarah could feel the car racing towards her, the raw power of the engine pushing the vehicle to its limits. The lights were so powerful . . . She stood still, unable to move, trapped by the twin beams as the car accelerated towards her. Time stopped. It felt as if her heart were bursting inside her; her hands were shaking so much that the papers fluttered from her fingers.

It was almost upon her.

Suddenly she was swept aside and her scream was one with the scream of the car as its slipstream touched her. She fell to the ground heavily, her arm crashing under her, the thud of her body lost in the roar of engine and voices. The pain was sudden and intense, a jolt of sensation that knocked the wind from her.

'Are you all right? Sarah?'

Carol's urgent cries brought Sarah round. She sat up on the cold tarmac and watched the car disappearing into the distance. Carol had saved her. It had been so close, so bloody close that she had felt the air gliding over the car as it stormed past.

'I'm all right,' she managed to say, her voice giving the lie to her words. She wasn't OK. She was scared to death.

'Jesus, that was close,' Carol whispered, holding Sarah's hand tightly.

Sarah looked up and saw that Liz and Dr Graham were running towards them. Even though her legs felt shaky she forced herself to stand. No matter what the cost she couldn't let them see her so obviously afraid. She hobbled over to the nearest car and leant back against it.

'Are you all right?' Dr Graham demanded. 'Carol?'

'We're OK,' Carol said, her teeth chattering.

He took Sarah by the arms and looked her in the eye. 'Are you hurt?'

She looked at him, surprised by the confident way that he touched her and by the real concern that she could see in him. For a second she held his gaze and then, suddenly, she looked away, slightly embarrassed. 'I'm fine,' she insisted, moving away so that he let go of her.

'You're bleeding,' Liz pointed out.

Sarah looked at her elbow, which was stinging sharply. 'It's nothing, just a graze.'

'Let's get it looked at,' Dr Graham suggested quietly.

'It's all right,' Sarah snapped. Why were they all fussing? And then she remembered the most important point. 'Did anyone get his number?' she demanded.

'No, he had his lights on full beam,' Carol said. 'The bastard almost blinded us, we couldn't see a thing.'

'We didn't see anything either,' Liz added quickly. 'We just heard the car and then your screams.'

'Damn! Carol, do you have any idea who it was?' Sarah said.

48

Carol shook her head. 'Of course not,' she said. 'I've no idea.'

'I doubt if it's anyone who works here,' Liz said.

'We'll have to make enquiries,' Dr Graham added. 'It might have been a visitor. Someone who's had too much to drink by the sound of it.'

They were all talking nonsense. 'Call the police,' Sarah instructed. The pain in her arm was still there but it was nothing compared to the anger flaring suddenly inside her. It hadn't been an accident, she was certain.

'The police?' Dr Graham repeated. 'But the driver's gone now. If he's drunk he'll get pulled up on the motorway.'

'He wasn't drunk,' Sarah said coldly.

Carol looked alarmed. 'You don't know that,' she said.

'Come on, Carol!' Sarah spat angrily. 'How many times has this happened before?'

'It hasn't,' Carol maintained. 'I don't know who it was, but I'm sure it was an accident.'

'Are there security cameras on site?' Sarah demanded, her mind racing to find ways to prove what she knew was the truth.

'On the perimeter,' Dr Graham said. 'Near the phase II site. There's nothing here.'

'Carol? Did you get the colour of the car? The make?'

The answer was no to both questions. Dr Graham was looking at Sarah as though she was being hysterical.

'Have you told them about Lyndhurst?' she demanded of Carol.

Carol's eyes widened. 'There's nothing to say, Sarah. Come on now, relax, please.'

Sarah noted the pleading look in her eyes. Was Carol saying that Dr Graham and Liz couldn't be trusted? She closed her eyes, letting the burst of angry energy drain away. It had been a long day and now she felt exhausted.

'I'm sorry,' she said finally. 'You're right, I'm getting this out of proportion.'

'I'm not surprised,' Liz agreed sympathetically. 'It must have been a real fright for you.'

Sarah nodded meekly. 'Yes, that's right,' she said. 'I'll be fine once I've sat down for a few minutes.'

'Would you like to come back for some coffee?' Dr Graham suggested quietly. His eyes looked hopeful and there was a hint of a smile on his face.

It was tempting to go back to the warmth and to a cup of good strong coffee but Sarah resisted. 'No, I'm OK. Please,' she said, 'you get back and I'll be off home. The sooner the better really. I'm just exhausted.'

'If you're sure,' Liz said, looking doubtful.

'Yes, I'm sure,' Sarah said.

'OK,' Dr Graham said, 'we'll see you again soon. I'm just sorry that something like this had to happen here.'

'I'll be with you in a second,' Carol called to them as they headed back to the office. 'Are you really OK now?' she asked Sarah quietly.

'Of course I'm not bloody OK!'

'I was telling the truth,' Carol asserted quietly. 'I didn't see who it was.'

'I'm going to call the police,' Sarah told her.

Carol was obviously appalled. 'Please,' she whispered fearfully, 'you don't know what you're dealing with.'

'Tell me then! Tell me what the hell we're dealing with!'

Carol shook her head. 'This was just a warning,' she said.

'This was attempted murder!'

'If you call the police then . . .' Carol didn't finish the sentence, leaving it to hang heavily in the air, adding to the feeling of fear and foreboding.

'And if we don't?' Sarah demanded. 'If we let this escalate further?'

'I don't know, Sarah, but it frightens me. Calling the police might make things worse.'

'Listen,' Sarah said, 'I know how to handle this.'

'Let's stop now,' Carol managed to say. 'I wish I'd kept my mouth shut now. Can't we call this off, please?'

There was no way that it could be called off. 'No,' Sarah stated flatly. 'There's someone in the police who can help us. Someone I can trust, I promise.'

'No, no, no,' Carol said, her voice hinting at tears to come.

'His name's Anthony Vallance,' Sarah said. 'We can trust him completely.'

'You can't be sure . . .'

Something hit home suddenly, with an appalling clarity that made Sarah's stomach turn. 'You saved my life,' she whispered.

Carol seemed as surprised as Sarah. 'I suppose I did,' she said, managing a nervous smile.

'I meant what I said,' Sarah said, taking Carol by the arm. 'I can trust Tony Vallance, and I'm going to call him before this thing gets any further out of hand.'

Sarah's calm and confidence seemed to do the trick. 'If you're sure,' Carol agreed quietly.

'I'm sure,' Sarah said.

FOUR

Vallance stared grimly at the crime-scene photographs. The dead woman lay stretched out on a patterned rug splattered with blood, with one arm thrown over her head and the other clutching at her throat. The knife was still embedded in her neck, stuck deep, the handle encrusted with dried blood. Her eyes were open but lifeless, the fear and the horror expunged for good. The next photograph was a close-up: the handle of the knife, dark wood with steel bolts through to the blade. A kitchen knife, a good one too by the look of it, and clearly imprinted in the dried blood a set of smudged fingerprints. Not that there was much need for forensic evidence.

Other photographs showed the rest of the scene: up-turned furniture, a room in utter disarray, a trail of blood, the body again. It was a sad and bloody end to a life. Her name was Jean Wilding, aged 46, a mother of two teenage children, one of whom was going to be charged with her murder. Vallance had interviewed the girl late the previous evening, and then again first thing in the morning. In between he'd suffered a long and sleepless night.

What was it that made a child snap like that? Where had that murderous rage come from? Angela Wilding was a sweet-looking fifteen-year-old, with no previous record of trouble, good reports from school and by all accounts a good kid.

According to her own statement, which was in accord with the photographic and forensic evidence, she had chased her mother from one room to the next, stabbing her repeatedly until, finally, she had plunged the knife deep into her mother's throat.

And the reason? A trivial argument about clothes. That was it. That was what cost Jean Wilding her life, and which had effectively destroyed Angela's too. There were, inevitably, going to be psychiatric reports, but having spoken to her teachers and to some of her friends, Vallance was convinced that she'd be found clinically sane. Her defence, though, were sure to attempt to come up with a plea of diminished responsibility or insanity.

He put the photographs down, trying to clear the darkness from his mind. No matter how much he tried to work it out, it made no sense, and he knew that it never would. There were few times in his career when he had felt such total despair. On the one hand his instincts were to protect the child, to try to help the poor little kid who'd done something so totally monstrous. At the same time he knew that what she had done put her beyond the pale. She would, always and for ever, be haunted by memories of the horrific act. And, if that were not enough, she would never forget the lurid headlines which were splashed across most of the tabloids.

He looked up sharply at the knock on the door. He was in no mood to talk, and, thankfully, most of CID had worked that out for themselves that morning.

'Yes?' he called, sitting back from the array of photographs spread across his desk.

DS Cooper came in. He had a teenage daughter the same age as Angela Wilding; his reactions to the murder were tempered by the realisation that the child he was arresting was no different to his own. He looked haggard, and Vallance recognised that he wasn't the only to have had a sleepless night.

'You look knackered,' Vallance said, indicating that Cooper should take a seat.

Cooper dragged a chair over to Vallance's desk. 'I am,' he said wearily. 'You know, last night I got home and all I could do was sit and look at Gail. I mean she's fifteen, she even looks like Angela. You know, it just makes you wonder.'

'It does,' Vallance agreed, knowing that it was a trite and useless thing to say but unable to come up with anything better. 'Any more from her family?'

'The sister's still under sedation, her dad's still in shock. Jesus, fancy coming home to that. There is one new development though. Some bloke's got in touch to say that his son's Angela's boyfriend.'

A boyfriend? Angela hadn't mentioned one, nor had the couple of girls that she went to school with. 'Is he for real or a wind-up merchant?'

Cooper shrugged. 'He says he'll come in with his kid to make a statement but he's worried about the press. He also wants a solicitor.'

Given the media interest – and their bloodlust was at a frenzy – the man's requests were more than reasonable. On the other hand the media interest meant that all sorts of low-life were ready to crawl out from under the woodwork. How much money was there in a sex and sleaze revelation about the girl?

'Get a car to pick them up,' Vallance said. 'In the meantime I want a PNC check on him and his son. Oh, and try her school friends again. Mention the boy's name and see what reactions we get.'

'Yes, sir.' Cooper stood up, pushing himself out of the chair like an old man. 'Who do you want to tackle the school kids?'

For once Vallance had free choice to pick the officers to handle the case. Even Riley had been shocked by the murder, so shocked in fact that he hadn't bothered to keep the best detectives off the case. 'Anne Quinn and Karen Greenwood,' he decided, picking two of the best of the detective constables. They were both capable officers and he knew that they'd relate well to the teenage girls who were still in shock.

'Yes, sir. Oh, there is one thing, sir,' Cooper added as he got to the door.

Vallance looked up expectantly. 'Yes?'

'There was a phone call from Sarah Fairfax, sir.'

Sarah? Vallance had declined to take calls: he hated dealing with the vultures from the press. 'She's not interested in this, is she?' he asked, unable to believe that she would be.

Cooper half-smiled. 'You know what she's like, sir,' he reported. 'She still hates my guts from the Ryder case. When I refused to put her through to you she hit the roof.'

That figured. Sarah had a volatile temper that was spectacular to behold, and he could clearly remember the antagonism between her and Cooper. 'So what did you say?'

Cooper smiled fully. 'I just told her you had a little matter of a mother stabbed twenty-three times by her daughter to deal with.'

Vallance smiled too. It was easy to picture Sarah's brown eyes narrowing as she fought between anger at Cooper and horror at the crime. 'When's she going to call back?' he asked, knowing that if she were determined to talk to him then nothing, not even a gruesome killing, would stop her.

'She just asked me to pass on the message, sir. She said it was important.'

'Sarah Fairfax doesn't make unimportant calls,' Vallance said. 'She's going to have to wait. Let me know as soon as you get the boyfriend in, and for Christ's sake keep the news out of the canteen. The last thing we want is the papers getting to the kid before we do.'

'Yes, sir.'

Vallance waited for Cooper to go before standing up. Sarah Fairfax? He hadn't spoken to her for a couple of months, not since the end of the Good Neighbours case. She had been instrumental in solving the case, just as she had been in the Ryder case before that. Not that it did her much good: in the eyes of his superiors she was still a meddling journalist, a troublemaker of the first order in their opinion. At the end of the Good Neighbours case he had been warned about his relationship with her. They had refused to believe that he had no say in whether she involved herself in a case or not.

Improper disclosure of information. That was the charge that had been threatened. And for what? Because she was better than most of the people in CID? Because she was serious about her work? Because she was a woman? In any case he had been warned by both Chief Superintendent Larkhall and Superintendent Riley: keep her away from any investigations. As if he had any control over her whatsoever. That was the worst of it, that they imagined there was something between them. A relationship. Fat chance.

Relationships. Vallance exhaled slowly then headed out for some coffee. He and relationships had become mutually exclusive terms. The divorce with Mags had finally gone through, though there was still a strong feeling between them. Hatred, anger, resentment . . . Lots of strong feelings. And since then? A string of sex-only relationships, nothing emotional, nothing social, just pure physical lust. And, now that Anne Quinn was keeping her distance, even that had stalled.

The coffee machine was a hive of activity as usual. The conversation buzzing animatedly between the three detective constables lapsed into guilty silence as soon as they saw him.

'Anything wrong?' he asked, reaching for a polystyrene cup to capture the thick, dark, coffee-flavoured sludge that leaked from the machine.

Alex Chiltern, dressed in his favourite dark blue suit, decided to answer for them all. 'Nothing, sir, just discussing the case.'

Vallance straightened up. The stuff in the cup looked lethal. 'Yes? That's what I like to see, young coppers taking their work seriously,' he said smoothly. 'Well done, lads.'

'Thank you, sir,' Chiltern said, suppressing the grin that Matthews was unable to keep hidden.

'And what, exactly, were you talking about?'

'The motive,' was Chiltern's answer. Unfortunately it was muttered at the same time as Terry South's answer: 'DNA blood typing.'

Vallance nodded sagely. 'What was it?'

'Sir?' Chiltern asked, speaking like a guilty school kid.

'Come on, I know what the hell goes on. What was it and who lost?'

They all looked guilty, heads down and staring at their feet, hoping that one of the others would speak up. Vallance knew what they'd been up to, it was a game they always played. 'What was it?' he asked sadly. 'Whether she'd get sent to a psych ward? How long it would take before the papers dug up dirt on her? What?'

Chiltern finally spoke up. 'The number of stab wounds, sir. The pathologist's confirmed twenty-three of them.'

'Karen Greenwood's the winner,' Matthews added. 'She was spot on.'

So that was what they'd found to bet on. 'You people are sick,' he said.

The sunshine of the previous day had been replaced with a blue sky shielded by thick grey cloud. The first rain of the day had already fallen, splashing down on the scorched earth just after dawn. It was cool too, and Sarah did not make the mistake of imagining that the day would brighten up. After the oppressive heat she was glad of the rain, glad of the greyness and the cool breeze that reminded everyone that the summer had yet to arrive.

She felt restless, as though the confines of her office could no longer hold her. She had told no one about the incident at the Science Park. There was no point, and her verbal report to Lucy that morning had been even more terse than usual. Had the car been a warning or a real attempt at murder? Her fear had been real, and the car near enough for her to feel the slipstream as it tore past them. If it was meant to scare her off then it had failed dismally. The fraud story was going to be uncovered no matter what happened.

She looked at the newspaper headlines again; it was horrific. The angelic-looking girl in the grainy picture accompanying the story looked barely old enough to walk home from school on her own, and yet she was alleged to have stabbed her mother to death. Twenty-three times according to Detective Sergeant Cooper, who had delivered the information with ill-concealed glee. He remembered her of course, and she him, but that was really no surprise given his negligence during the Ryder case.

She put the newspaper away, realising that she was being distracted. Her plan had been to meet with Anthony Vallance at the first opportunity, to explain the situation and if necessary to get him to talk to Carol. She had checked earlier that morning and both the university and the Science Park were within his divisional boundary. This time there was no way he could squirm out of helping her, the way he had with the Malik Alibhai story a few months previously.

The telephone buzzed as she sat down at her computer. She picked it up absently, her attention still on the screen. 'Sarah Fairfax,' she announced.

There was a moment of silence and then: 'Keep out of it.'

The harsh voice and the threatening warning jolted her. 'Who is this?' she demanded, but there was nothing but static in reply. 'Who is it?'

She cut the call dead and quickly dialled back to see where the call had come from. The computer-generated voice, speaking slowly and smoothly, announced that the caller had withheld the number. It was no surprise, only a fool would call in a warning like that and leave a traceable number.

There was no time to waste. She dialled Carol's work number quickly and then waited impatiently as it rang and rang. Finally, after what seemed an age, the voice mail message kicked. Damn it! Why did no one ever answer the phone?

'Carol, this is Sarah,' she said, leaving a message, 'please ring me as soon as you get in. It's urgent.'

Who next? She felt impelled to ring Vallance again but knew that it would be futile. He was not taking any calls, everything was being routed through the incident room investigating Jean Wilding's murder.

She stared at her computer screen for a second, her mind racing with ideas. What could she say about the voice? Adult male, that was all. He had half whispered his warning, making it sound more menacing but also carefully covering up any trace of accent or intonation. If only she'd recorded it, the hoarsely whispered threat would make the perfect soundtrack to the film of the decaying university campus merging into the high-tech modernity of the Science Park. She smiled at the idea of using the threat as part of her work, turning it from a warning to her into an invitation to her audience.

The phone buzzed again. She hesitated, wondering whether she'd have time to reach her tape recorder. 'Yes?' she demanded, snatching the phone from its cradle.

'Sarah?' Carol said. 'It's me, what's wrong?'

'I've just had a phone call telling me to keep out.'

'Shit!'

'You've had one too,' Sarah guessed.

Carol ignored the statement. 'What are you going to do?'

There was no doubt whatsoever in Sarah. 'Carry on of course,' she said.

'Have you talked to your friend in the police?'

Was Vallance really a friend? Wasn't he more of a colleague? She put the thought out of her mind. 'No, not yet,' she replied.

'Are you still planning to?'

'Of course. Look, I'm going to do some checks on Brian Quigley, the Newman brothers and Adam Taylor. Is there anyone else I need to check out?'

Sarah could almost see Carol's smile coming through the phone. 'Why don't you check out Gerry Graham?'

'Cut that out, Carol,' Sarah warned. 'This isn't a game. Someone tried to kill us last night, how can you sit there and –'

'Sarah! Come on, I need to joke, it stops me from going mad. Please, I'm here all the time, remember?'

Sarah decided to let it go. Carol was right, she was there on the Science Park all the time and the strain was probably hard to take. 'I'll spend the rest of the morning checking up on these people,' she said. 'I'll try and come up later on this afternoon. I think it's time I met Brian Quigley.'

'Should I let Liz know?'

'No,' Sarah decided. 'I'll give her a call myself later.'

'OK, I'll see you later then.'

Sarah put the phone down. Perhaps Carol was right after all. She reached for her pad that listed the names of the people she was going to check up on: Brian Quigley, Grant Newman, Gavin Newman and Adam Taylor. She grabbed a pen and added two more names to the end of the list: Dr Gerald Graham and Liz Farnham.

Cooper waited for Vallance outside the interview room, sucking hard on a last smoke before he and the boss would go in to interview Angela's boyfriend. Jake Coleman had been on the verge of tears when he'd been brought in, though his father, Ted, had been feeling more confident. The duty solicitor had been called as soon as they had arrived, but there was no need really, no one was planning on giving the lad a hard time.

Where was the boss? Cooper dropped the fag on the floor and ground it down hard, stamping it out decisively. Jake looked no older than twelve or thirteen, though in fact he was nearer sixteen than fifteen. He didn't look like a bad lad, certainly not like some of the young bastards that came to police attention often enough. Only some of Angela's friends knew of him, from what Quinn had discovered, though as he went to a different school none of them had met him.

'Everything ready?' Vallance asked, walking briskly down the corridor towards the interview room. The crappy weather meant that he was back in his uniform of dark trousers and black leather jacket. It was good to see that all the flak from the Chief Super made no difference to Vallance's dress sense.

'Yes, sir, they're all here,' Cooper reported. 'Old man Patterson's on duty this morning.'

Vallance smiled. 'It's too early for the booze to have worked into his system,' he said. 'At least there's no chance he'll fall asleep on us.'

Cooper smiled. 'I'm sure that the boy's dad'll keep him awake. Anyone would think that we're accusing his son of doing it.'

A frown replaced the smile on Vallance's stubbled face. 'Hostile is he?'

'Hostile or over-protective, I can't tell which.'

'They're both clean as far as the computer checks out,' Vallance said. 'Let's keep it simple for now.'

Cooper nodded and opened the door to the interview room. He waited for the boss to go in then followed. Jake was sitting forward, both arms on the table, a thick mop of hair falling across his forehead and half covering his eyes. He still looked pensive, his eyes darting nervously to Vallance and then to Cooper. In contrast, Ted Coleman was sitting with his arms folded across his chest, his guts bulging over tightly belted trousers and a dark look across his cleanly shaven features. Jake probably took after his mum, Cooper decided.

Vallance leant across the table and offered his hand to Ted first. 'Mr Coleman, Jake, I'm Chief Inspector Vallance,' he announced. 'I'm heading this investigation. Sergeant Cooper you've already met.'

The duty solicitor, Alan Patterson, was sitting well back, behind his clients, and he nodded curtly to Vallance and to Cooper. With his dark grey suit, steel-rimmed glasses and undertaker's expression he looked suitably sombre for the occasion. No one had ever owned up to seeing Patterson fall asleep on the job, but everyone was aware of his fondness for the juice and more than once his slurred speech had caused comment, not least with the poor bastards he was assigned to help.

'My son's done nothing wrong,' Ted stated coldly, setting the tone before Vallance had had a chance to make himself comfortable.

'No one's accusing him of doing anything,' Vallance replied easily, his voice calm and collected.

'We don't have to be here,' Ted retorted, as though there were any doubt.

Sitting beside Vallance, Cooper made himself comfortable, knowing that it was going to be one of *those* interviews; needlessly difficult, messy and likely to get loud.

'And we're very grateful that you are,' was Vallance's soothing response. 'Now, Jake, we just want to know as much as we can about Angela. That's all.'

The boy looked up, the soft green of his eyes making contact with Vallance, and then he looked down at his hands again. 'Did she really do what the papers said?' he asked softly.

There was no beating about the bush. 'Yes she did,' Vallance said. 'What we need to do now is to understand why she did it, that way we can help her. That's how *you* can help her, OK?'

The boy nodded. 'She had a temper, that's all,' he began, quietly. 'I mean, you know, she could go ballistic sometimes. I . . . I still can't believe it, I mean Angie . . .'

'Tell them about the time she hit you,' the boy's father suggested when his son subsided into a disbelieving silence.

Jake looked pained, as though embarrassed by the information his father had so casually blurted out. 'It's all right, Mr Coleman,' Vallance said. 'Let Jake tell us in his own time. Jake?'

'It's not like she beat me up, or anything,' he said. 'I mean she was well stressed out that day, you know, hyper. We were listening to music and I said something and then wham! She just kind of lashed out, you know, wham!'

'She blacked his eye,' Ted Coleman added, with a kind of brutal relish so at odds with his son's nervousness.

Cooper could see that Vallance was getting pissed off. Each time the father said something you could see Jake shrinking back into himself. It was bad enough having to be there, to have his dad going on all the time was probably making it worse for the kid. Why didn't he just shut up and let the kid get on with it?

'Had she done that sort of thing before?' Vallance asked softly.

'Sort of,' Jake admitted. 'It was getting worse, sort of. I mean, she was always a bit strung out, but when it was, you know, that time of the month, she was manic.'

'That's just an excuse,' Ted muttered under his breath.

That was it as far as the boss was concerned. 'Mr Coleman, this is difficult enough as it is,' Vallance said, fixing Coleman with a look that said 'don't fuck around any more'.

Patterson finally decided it was time for him to make a contribution. 'It would be preferable, Mr Coleman,' he said, 'if young Jake were allowed to speak for himself.'

Coleman looked at Vallance and then at Cooper. He had hard, blue eyes that radiated anger and aggression. 'I was just saying that all that premenstrual crap is an excuse, that's all.'

'And since when have you been an expert on premenstrual tension?' Vallance demanded. 'I didn't know you were a practising gynaecologist, Mr Coleman.'

Jake sniggered and even Patterson was smiling behind Coleman's back. 'We don't have to be here,' Coleman repeated.

'No you don't,' Vallance agreed, 'but if you want to help then let your son tell us what he knows.'

Coleman was struggling to think up a smart-alec reply; you could see it in his eyes as he sought in vain for some clever retort. 'Jake, you were telling us about her temper,' Cooper said, deciding to put Coleman senior out of his misery.

'Yes, she was all over the place when she was having her period. Like, she wouldn't go to school because she couldn't trust herself. She said it hadn't always been like that, but it just seemed to get worse each time.'

Dates? Cooper looked at his watch, wondering whether the boy would remember when her last period had been.

Vallance twigged it too. 'When was the last time she was so bad?' he asked.

Jake shrugged. 'I can't remember, weeks ago.'

There was a pause while the boss considered his next question. He was cool like that, Cooper thought, picking up on things that other people easily missed. That was why working with him was so useful, sometimes.

'Was she off school yesterday or the day before?' Vallance asked.

Jake looked towards his dad before answering. 'I don't know,' he admitted.

Vallance looked at Ted Coleman and then at his son. 'Jake,' he asked quietly, 'when was the last time you saw Angela?'

The look of pain crossed the boy's face again. Something was wrong. Cooper could see it in Jake's expression and in the way his father shifted uncomfortably in his seat. 'When?' Vallance repeated.

'About three weeks ago,' the boy mumbled.

'She belted him in the eye,' Ted said, leaning forward aggressively. 'I said he couldn't see her no more. What sort of a girl is it that does that? Eh?'

The boss was livid, his fists were clenched and it was obvious that he was going to go for Coleman. 'Mr Coleman,' Cooper said, hoping to put a stop to anything developing, 'will you please keep your opinions to yourself. The sooner we finish then the sooner you can go home. Understand?'

Vallance was seething. 'How did Angela take the news?' he asked, directing his attention exclusively to Jake.

He shrugged. 'Not too good,' he said softly. 'It wasn't my fault, I mean, I didn't want to chuck her . . .'

'When did you last speak to her?'

'Two days ago,' Jake said. 'She phoned but I told her that I couldn't see her any more. You know, it wasn't my fault.'

'How did she take that?'

'She was screaming and crying down the phone,' Jake said. His eyes were full of tears and his voice trembling. Beside him, Ted Coleman sat looking with grim disapproval at Vallance.

'And you've not spoken to her since?'

The boy shook his head. 'I put the phone down on her,' he whispered, and then, unable to hold back any longer, he buried his head in his hands and wept.

Sarah arrived at the Science Park later in the afternoon than she had hoped. The grey rain that sweated down from the sky did nothing to make the journey from London any easier, and by the time she pulled onto the slip road leading to the Park the day's feeble light was beginning to fade. In the dull light the Park looked bleak and isolated beside the muddy brown waters of the lake. Without the bright sunshine the tinted windows on the units looked black, effectively hiding the secrets of what went on inside each of the square blocks.

Liz would be waiting for her at Software Solutions, which occupied the last of the six units. Sarah hoped that Carol would do as asked and keep out of the way rather than spring any more surprises on her. Lying was hard enough but having to take on board another set of untruths would make life impossible.

As she drove onto the Park itself she glanced nervously in her rear-view mirror. It was no longer a reflex action: checking in the mirror had acquired a new importance. Paranoia. There was no other word for what she felt, but then it seemed to be the only attitude to take. All the way down from London she had been wary, glancing again and again, checking on the cars behind her to see who was following. A couple of times she'd caught her breath, convinced that this car or that was in hot pursuit, but in each case she had been mistaken.

There was a space directly opposite the Software Solutions building and she parked there, glad that there was no need to walk too far. The rain had started again, drumming softly on the windscreen as the sky darkened still more. She sat for a minute, watching the rain come down, observing the way individual droplets were caught in the soft orange glow of the street lamps. Behind her, on the other side of dense bushes, sat the lake, a dark pool of water that had sparkled invitingly the day before but which now looked cold and forbidding.

Liz appeared at the door to the office, a fixed smile on her lips. Sarah waved a greeting and then grabbed her things. There was no more putting things off. If Carol was right then Brian Quigley was at the centre of a scandal that needed to be uncovered. She opened the car door and the draught hit her suddenly, and with it the rain that came down harder at that instant. She ran across the car park, automatically looking to left and right in spite of her wish not to remind everyone of the previous evening's events.

'The weather's awful, isn't it?' Liz said, holding the door open as Sarah rushed into the lobby.

'Terrible,' Sarah agreed, brushing a hand through her shoulder-length hair. It wasn't too wet, thankfully.

'I've briefed Brian on our discussion yesterday,' Liz explained, 'and he seems very keen on the whole idea.'

'Good,' Sarah said simply. She needed Quigley to be as co-operative as possible, at least in the beginning, before his suspicions were aroused. Did he suspect Carol already? According to her he didn't, but someone, somewhere, clearly did.

There were sofas and a coffee table to one side of the lobby, with glossy trade magazines neatly laid out on the table and big, colourful posters on the wall. Potted plants stood sentry at strategic points leading to the entrance to the office, and at the door itself an entry-phone system and an electronic keypad. Liz tapped in the code and the door clicked open.

'They've made good use of the space,' Liz said, leading the way in. 'Mind you, if they carry on expanding at this rate they'll have to take on a bigger unit.'

The office was a maze of partitions, dull grey in colour and used to mark off different areas in what would otherwise have been a single open area. Muted voices and the tapping of keyboards floated over the tops of the partitions, the only clue that behind the grey barriers people were working. Sarah gazed at the scene for a second, looking with distaste at the impersonal warren of cubicles and alcoves. From where she and Liz stood, just by the entrance, she could see where people had tried to personalise their space. But the posters and humourless funny signs were swallowed up by the overriding sense of claustrophobia.

'Brian's office is upstairs,' Liz said, perhaps picking up on Sarah's disquiet.

'It must be stifling in the summer,' Sarah remarked, following her up the flight of stairs to the first floor.

'There are plenty of fans in the building,' Liz assured her. 'Besides, don't you just get that feeling of quiet industry down there?'

Sarah didn't. The quiet had a different quality to it, as though it were imposed by the geometry of screens and partitions rather than arising from intensity of concentration. 'Yes, I suppose so,' she said, preferring to keep her feelings to herself for the moment. 'How many people did you say Brian employs?'

'Thirty-two at the last count,' Liz said as she stopped at the top of the stairs. 'That's an increase of twenty-five per cent since they moved to the Science Park.'

'Is he still taking people on?' she asked. 'I mean with these big defence contracts to complete he must be in need of skilled specialist staff.'

'To be honest most of the staff here have come straight from the university – recent graduates mostly. That's a good angle, isn't it?' she suggested hopefully. 'It's a clear example of the way the university and the Park synergise.'

How could recent graduates have the experience and the skills to complete defence projects? From her earlier research Sarah knew that most software houses were interested in experience rather than in academic achievement alone. It was a small point but perhaps indicative of a deeper truth. She decided not to share her doubts with Liz, who was still waiting for an answer. 'Yes,' she agreed, 'it's a good angle.'

Liz seemed to detect the hesitation in Sarah's manner. 'It was only an idea,' she said.

'And I might use it,' Sarah assured her.

'Up here,' said Liz, pointing to the stairs that led to the upper floor. 'Come on, Brian's waiting for us.'

The first floor seemed roomier than the ground floor, though the grey partitions still divided up the space into different working areas. With more room to move the atmosphere was less claustrophobic, though the muted ambience of computer keyboards and lowered voices was still there. Quigley's office occupied one side of the room, marked off with floor to ceiling wood and glass screens and a glass door which was firmly closed. He sat at his desk, peering intently at a computer screen while he spoke into a phone cradled under his chin.

He was older than Sarah had anticipated, with greying hair that was seriously thinning on top and a face deeply lined and starting to sag. If she had to put an age to him she would have said early fifties, though it was possible she was out by five years either way. The sleeves of his off-white shirt were rolled up and his dark tie slightly skewed, making him look tired and harassed as he finished his call. As she and Liz approached he looked up, his eyes meeting hers for an instant. Light blue eyes touched with grey and which regarded her with a surprising intensity.

'Brian, this is Sarah,' Liz said, guiding Sarah into the office.

He was up and leaning across his desk, a welcoming smile on his face and his thick, podgy hand extended in greeting. She smiled back and shook his hand firmly, trying to work out what was going on behind his smile. There was something about him that didn't quite square up. There had been something quite wary in the way he had first looked at her. Had it been imagination? Or perhaps it had been a recognition of the caution that she herself felt so strongly.

'Please,' he said, 'take a seat. Coffee, tea? Liz?'

'Not for me, thanks,' said Liz, declining with a slight shake of the head as she sat down.

'Sarah?' he asked, raising his eyebrows hopefully. 'You must be parched after your long drive.'

He was right, she was thirsty and hungry. 'Tea would be fine, thank you,' she said, taking the seat next to Liz and directly opposite Brian.

'Good, good.' He walked to the door and called to one of

his staff, someone named Audrey. His instructions were delivered without humour or good grace, as though he were accustomed to barking orders and being instantly obeyed. He waited a second to see that Audrey was doing as she was told and then he walked back to his desk.

If he had been taller then his weight would probably have been fine, Sarah noted, but as he was only a little taller than she was he looked as though he had the start of a problem. His shirt was too tight around the middle, and the tightly cinched trousers did nothing to flatter his figure. Not that it mattered; he was far from obese and if anything he looked powerfully built.

'Liz has told me all about your project,' he began, sitting comfortably. His hands were together on the desk and he was leaning forward in a businesslike manner.

'And how do you feel about it?' Sarah responded, still trying to gauge how to handle him.

'In two minds about it, of course,' he said. 'Liz thinks it's a great idea: raise our profile, get a good bit of free publicity and the like, but . . .'

'But?' Sarah repeated when he failed to finish the sentence.

His smile broadened. 'I ask myself what can we gain from this? Liz gets a name for herself as a publicist who can deliver the goods. Do you not?'

'There's more to it than that,' Liz objected.

'I'm sure there is,' he agreed, 'but you can't deny that you would do well out of this.'

Sarah was certain that Liz was going to object again. 'Let's just accept that for now,' she said, not wanting to get bogged down in a detail that was patently true.

'And the Science Park gets a name for itself,' he continued, 'and hence can attract more venture capital and more companies when Phase Two is complete. Isn't that right?'

'Yes,' Sarah agreed quickly, wanting to head off yet another objection from Liz.

'So that leaves me,' he concluded. 'What do I get out of it? What's in it for Software Solutions?'

'You get publicity,' Liz pointed out. 'Publicity generates sales and contracts, Brian.'

'Only if you're in the market to sell things or are looking for new contracts,' Sarah said, hoping that she had correctly guessed the root of Brian's objections.

He looked impressed. 'Spot on,' he said. 'What we do here is specialist work. It's of no interest to the man in the street, no interest whatsoever. So I repeat my question, what do I get out of it?'

Liz looked at Sarah, as though she had no answers of her own and hoped that Sarah would provide them. 'It's a good question,' Sarah conceded.

'I know it is,' he agreed smugly. 'Ah! The tea's here. Leave it on the desk there,' he told the young girl who had brought the tray in.

'Thank you,' Sarah said softly as the girl backed out of the room. No one else felt moved to thank her, not even Liz, who had lapsed into an uneasy silence.

Brian sipped his tea noisily, keeping his eyes on Sarah all the time. She was determined to take her time with her answer. He was too intelligent to insult with some half-baked reply, and nor would he be fobbed off with vague generalisations.

'We all need a good public image, Brian,' Liz stated quietly. 'Where's the harm in that?'

Brian laughed, a hint of derision in his throat. 'The harm is, Liz, in having cameras and journalists disrupting things here. The harm is that the documentary becomes an end in itself. Think of Audrey preening herself for the cameras! What good does that do to anybody but the film company?'

Damn Carol! Why the hell had she suggested such a stupid idea? Especially when Quigley was more switched on than anyone else at the Science Park. 'You make us sound like a plague, Brian,' Sarah interjected, hoping to buy time.

'Present company excepted, of course,' he said, his charming smile returning. 'I take it then, Sarah, that you've nothing to convince me?'

It was time to sidestep the question. 'You're an interesting man, Brian,' she said, 'and that's what this film will be about. The Science Park and the individual companies are really just the back-drop; what I'm looking for is human interest.'

His eyes brimmed with amusement. 'Human interest,' he

repeated, as though trying out the words for size. 'Doesn't human interest usually cover fluffy pets, adorable orphans and personal tragedy? In which category am I?'

Sarah laughed. He was right of course, she hated the phrase 'human interest' too. 'I'm sorry,' she said. 'I was using the phrase human interest in its non-tabloid form. I imagined that I was here so that you could convince me to include you in the film; I didn't realise our positions would be reversed.'

'I take it I've convinced you?'

'You have,' she admitted. 'Unfortunately I don't seem to be having your success at the moment. Are you saying that you definitely don't want to be in the film?'

He hesitated for a second before answering. 'I'd say you had a long way to go still.'

'Brian's a tough negotiator,' Liz said, rather superfluously in Sarah's opinion.

'May I ask a little about your company?' Sarah asked.

'Still looking for an answer to my question?' he said. 'Yes, fire away.'

'You're obviously in no hurry for publicity. Does that mean you've got no interest in new business?'

'No, I'm always looking for new clients,' he assured her. 'But they have to be the right sort of clients. Our skills are very narrowly focused, we can't afford to lose sight of that.'

'And apart from the Ministry of Defence, who are your other clients?'

He leaned back in his seat. 'Most of our clients are government agencies,' he said. 'Other than that I can't say.'

'That's not a very satisfactory answer,' Sarah remarked, not bothering to mask her disappointment.

'I dare say it's not,' he agreed. 'It does nothing to convince me . . .'

'What about foreign governments?' Sarah asked.

He raised his eyebrows. 'I'm not really at liberty to answer that question either.'

Perhaps that was the way in, she decided. 'Would it not help you get more foreign contracts if you had a promotional film to show people?'

Liz saw the changed expression on his face too. 'That's not

a bad idea, Brian,' she said. 'You know we don't have the resources for that, and I doubt that you have either.'

'Why don't you think about it?' Sarah suggested.

'Of course,' he agreed. 'But I have to say that I'm still worried about the degree of disruption to my operations.'

'We'll minimise it,' Liz promised, as though she had any say in the film that was never going to be made.

'We can talk about it,' Sarah said.

He looked at her gravely, his eyes suddenly intense with suspicion. 'So long as I retain complete control,' he said, making it sound like a warning.

FIVE

The rain had stopped by the time the meeting with Brian Quigley had finished and Sarah and Liz walked back to the PR-Tech office together. The damp tarmac glistened under the street lamps which imparted a warm orange glow to the blackness. It was late and the car park had emptied considerably, though there were enough cars around to suggest that working late was not unusual on the Science Park.

'You're not too disheartened, are you?' Liz asked as they walked. Her diminutive figure and quiet voice seemed more pronounced out in the open, as though earlier, in the confining space of an office, she had grown in stature.

'No, it was a useful meeting,' Sarah said. It was true: it confirmed that Quigley was indeed an interesting character and it suggested that he did, after all, have something to hide. It also revealed an unashamedly mercenary streak, though in itself that was no proof of guilt.

'You see now why I thought Software Solutions was a poor choice? I know what Brian's like.'

They stopped at the door to the PR-Tech unit. 'I don't think he's a poor choice at all,' Sarah said. 'In fact I'm even more convinced that he's the perfect choice. He's intelligent, determined, difficult, mercenary...'

Liz smiled. 'He's also as stubborn as hell.'

'All the more reason to use him in the film.'

'OK. Are you coming up?'

'Yes, I need to talk to Carol.'

The lights were out in the G–Man Software office on the ground floor of the unit. That was the next port of call, Sarah decided. She'd tackled the biggest company on the unit and so, hopefully, the smallest company would prove more amenable. Gavin Newman had seemed friendly enough judging by the few words she had exchanged with him.

Carol was on the phone when Liz and Sarah arrived. She mouthed a 'hello' to them both and then quickly finished her call.

'How did it go?' she asked.

'Brian was as stubborn as I expected,' Liz said, throwing her bag on her desk. 'I could do with a drink. Anyone else?'

Sarah shook her head. 'I'm driving,' she said apologetically.

'Carol?'

Carol made a face. 'Sorry, I'm off the booze for the moment.'

'In that case I hope you don't mind me having one,' Liz said, walking over to the fridge in the far corner of the office.

'It's my booze-free week of the month,' Carol explained to them both. 'You know, alcohol's fine and all that, but sometimes you just need to detoxify yourself.'

Liz laughed as she poured herself a glass of white wine. 'You and your detoxification! Honestly, do you really think it makes any difference?'

'Of course it does,' Carol said. 'We pump ourselves so full of poisons that our bodies can't cope. What do you think causes disease?'

'Viruses and microbes?' Sarah suggested. She had already seen examples of Carol's food mania – no meat, organic produce, vitamin and mineral supplements – but this seemed even more extreme.

'Viruses and bacteria can only take effect when the immune system is compromised,' Carol asserted authoritatively. 'You should read up on this, Sarah, it's important. Alcohol suppresses immune response, that's a fact.'

Liz sipped a mouthful of chilled wine, savoured the flavour and then swallowed it greedily. 'That's true,' she agreed, slumping down into the nearest available seat, 'but then why drop booze for one week a month? Why not go the whole hog and give it up for good?'

Carol grinned. 'I will, one day,' she said, 'but for now fasting for seven days is good enough. It makes a difference, a real difference.'

Sarah was doubtful but the argument didn't interest her as much as talking about Quigley and the Newman brothers. 'It's late,' she said. 'I'd better be going. Liz, do you think you can arrange for me to talk to Gavin and Grant in a couple of days?'

Liz smiled. 'Gavin will be no problem. He'll be falling over himself to be helpful. Grant, on the other hand . . .'

'Grant can be helpful too,' Carol said, and her injured tone suggested an attachment to Grant which was in marked contrast to her feelings for Gavin.

'Good, let's make it early,' Sarah suggested. 'Say nine thirty?'

Carol laughed. 'If you want Gavin you'll have to make it nearer half ten.'

'I'll be here at ten in that case,' Sarah stated calmly, realising that it was possible Liz was about to spring to Gavin's defence. 'Come on, Carol, you can walk me to my car.'

Carol smiled. 'You mean you want me to save your life again?'

'That's not even funny!' Sarah snapped, her anger rising suddenly. How dare Carol be so flippant! They had almost been killed and all she could do was make a joke out of it.

'There's no need to bite my head off,' Carol said, looking surprised by Sarah's vehemence. Liz also looked surprised, but when Sarah looked at her she pretended not to have noticed.

'Are you coming or not?' Sarah demanded.

'Yes, sure,' Carol agreed.

The night was going to be cool again, in spite of the cloud cover which all but obscured the full moon. There were even fewer cars left in the car park as Sarah and Carol walked across it towards Sarah's car. Carol was lagging behind, quite deliberately in Sarah's opinion.

'Look, I said I'm sorry,' Carol said when they arrived at Sarah's car.

'What is wrong with you?' Sarah demanded, unable to keep her anger to herself. 'We could have been killed, both of us!'

'Is that really why you're angry?' Carol countered. 'Or are you just angry because you know I saved your life?'

'That's got nothing to do with it!' Sarah insisted. 'Nothing at all!'

'You're shouting,' Carol said quietly, peering up towards the Software Solutions building.

'I'm not!' Sarah said, spitting out the denial under her breath.

'Shall we start again?' Carol suggested, a placatory smile on her face.

Sarah breathed deeply. She had been shouting and she was angry because Carol had saved her life. The fact that Carol was so obviously right only seemed to make her angrier. She owed Carol her life and it rankled.

Carol was waiting. 'Please?' she asked softly.

'You've saved my life,' Sarah said, finally, 'and I can never repay that debt, but . . . but I don't want you to turn it into a joke. It's not, it's not that at all.'

'Sarah, let's not make a big deal of this, OK?'

'How can I not make a big deal of it? I owe you my life. Don't you think I spent all night thinking about that?'

'Really, I don't want us to get heavy about this,' Carol said. 'Come on, tell me what you thought about Brian Quigley. He's creepy, isn't he?'

'Creepy? I thought he was up-front and pretty smart, but not creepy, exactly.'

Carol shrugged. 'Maybe it's just me, then. He didn't agree to the film idea?'

'No, he said he was worried about us obstructing his operations. It seems like he keeps things tightly under control there. I couldn't believe the way he spoke to his secretary.'

'I told you, he's got something to hide.'

Sarah was startled by the sudden roar of an engine coming to life. They looked round to see someone pulling out of the car park in a mad rush of acceleration.

'Don't worry,' Carol said, 'it's another of the boy-racers.'

Sarah watched the car go, vowing to herself not to let

paranoia get the better of her. 'What's the story with the Newman brothers? Liz's favourite is Gavin, yours is Grant. What's going on?'

'Gavin's so shallow,' Carol explained, leaning back on the bonnet of Sarah's car. 'You've seen him; he's all braces and teeth and into making a million. You know the type, Sarah; he's another boy-racer who fancies himself.'

'And Grant?'

'Grant is sweet,' Carol said. 'He's shy, nervous and ten times smarter than his older brother. The company would have gone under by now if it wasn't for Grant's skills as a computer programmer.'

'But if Grant's so clever why is Liz so down about him?'

Carol smiled. 'Because Grant's got a weird hair-cut, listens to a lot of god-awful noise and has got a ring through his nose. He looks a million miles from the public image that Liz and Gerry Graham want to project for Epsley. Just look at it from their point of view: would you want some weird kid advertising your product?'

Sarah smiled. 'You called him a kid; how old is he?'

Carol shrugged. 'I'm not sure, twenty-two or twenty-three but going on twelve.'

'He sounds more interesting than his brother. God,' she exclaimed suddenly, 'I was just about to say that they'd make a good contrast for the film. I'm even starting to believe in this film myself. How do they fit in with Quigley's game?'

'Brian Quigley wants to poach Grant. Even though he hates the way Grant looks and acts he recognises that he's good at his job. From what I've heard Brian is getting deeper into trouble and he needs someone to pull him out.'

Sarah glanced up at Quigley's office but could see little through the tinted glass. 'What do you mean, trouble? I thought the whole point was that he was defrauding the MoD.'

'He is, but he's strung his contracts out for a long time now. He needs to deliver something and he needs to do it soon. Even the people at the ministry who are supporting him are getting jumpy. He hopes that someone like Grant can come up with the code required to keep people happy.'

It sounded less than convincing. 'That sounds more like

the action of an incompetent businessman than of a criminal,' Sarah pointed out. 'I need to know what he's really up to. Has he broken the law? Is he actively defrauding the tax payer or not? And who are these people at the ministry that you keep talking about?'

Carol had no doubt. 'He's broken the law and he's still doing it, Sarah. You've got to believe me, he's up to his neck in it. Why do you think we're getting so much attention?'

'I don't know. Come on, Carol, answer my questions with some hard facts. Who are these mysterious people at the Ministry of Defence?'

Carol was silent for a moment before answering. 'I don't know their names, really I don't. I do know that they're senior people and that they're working closely with Brian. They know what he's up to; they're in it together.'

'How do you know?'

Again there was a momentary pause before Carol answered. 'I was there one day to see one of his people about something and I could hear Brian bawling his software team out. The whole estate could hear him, he was really letting rip. They'd screwed up again on something and he was furious. Later on I went in to see him and he let me sit there while he took a call from the MoD. He was friendly and chatty and basically he admitted that he again would have nothing to show at the next meeting. They laughed about it and when he put the phone down he made a joke about sacking everyone in the company because it made no difference to whether he got paid or not on his contracts.'

'OK,' Sarah conceded, 'that sounds more like the action of an incompetent businessman. It doesn't sound remotely illegal.'

'But it is,' Carol insisted vehemently. 'They're in it together, it's a cosy little arrangement with all of them making money out of it. It's a conspiracy, Sarah, you've got to believe me.'

'Where's the proof?'

'Grant can help us get it, I'm sure. I know he's been going to see Brian in secret, behind Gavin's back. He's also had a look at what some of Brian's programmers are working on.'

'And?'

Carol shrugged. 'I don't know,' she confessed. 'I don't understand the technical stuff, but I do know he says that Brian's people are crap. The software they're working on is so full of holes that it wouldn't get through the first stage of testing.'

'Do you think he'll talk to me?'

'He might,' Carol said, smiling hopefully. 'I'll talk to him about it as well. Perhaps between the two of us we can get to the heart of what Brian Quigley's doing.'

'There is just one other thing: what have you got against Quigley?'

Carol smiled. 'What do you mean?'

'I mean why are you so keen to expose what he's doing?'

'Because I'm sick to death of the way people like him can get away with things. It's wrong, but he can get away with it because they use the excuse of national security.'

'And that,' Sarah said, looking at Carol directly, 'is your only motive.'

'That and the fact that he threatened me.'

'He did? Why?'

'Because he thought that I was trying to convince Alison Maybury to quit his company and to go over to work with Grant and Gavin.'

It was getting colder and Sarah suddenly had no heart to continue. The web of motives and relationships at Epsley was becoming harder and harder to fathom. Quigley wanted to headhunt Grant; Gavin wanted to steal away Alison Maybury; Liz hated Grant; Carol hated Gavin. Was there anything other than these petty jealousies and rivalries really going on?

'Alison is one of Brian's key employees,' Carol said, possibly mistaking Sarah's despairing silence for a wish for more information. 'He's got few enough decent people working for him, if he loses her –'

'Then who the hell is trying to frighten us off?' Sarah asked, interrupting Carol's apparently earnest explanation.

'I don't know,' Carol said. 'Sometimes I think it might be the security services – MI5 or MI6 – sometimes I think it might be some of the nasty people that Brian associates with. I really don't know, Sarah.'

'What nasty people that Brian associates with?' Sarah demanded.

Carol stepped back, suddenly cagey again. 'Keep your voice down,' she cautioned. 'I've said too much already; you know how frightened I am. Please, just talk to Grant and see what you can get out of him. He'll back me, I know he will.'

'Carol, tell me straight, is there something really going on here? This isn't a wild-goose chase, is it?'

'How can you even suggest that?' Carol asked, her face a picture of wounded dignity.

Sarah looked into Carol's clear blue eyes hoping that the doubts she felt would be swept away in a flood of confidence. Carol was lying, she knew it, but she also knew that somewhere, buried under the half-truths and the equivocations lay a truth that needed to be uncovered.

'Why don't you tell me everything?' she asked.

'Because I can't,' Carol replied simply. 'It's cold, I'd better get back. Will I see you tomorrow?'

Sarah nodded. She had no choice: she was already involved and could not back out until she knew what was going on. 'I'll be in at nine thirty,' she said.

The office was getting too much, Vallance decided. A day after the interview with the Colemans, father and son, and the place was still live with rumours and gossip. It would only be a matter of time before someone mouthed off to the press, and then there'd be hell to pay. Angela, like her sister, was now under sedation and looked likely to be kept under observation for a while. In the meantime the investigation was proceeding apace.

The girl's father was in a bad way too. Certainly he was in no fit state to give coherent answers to questions. And, in spite of the evidence, Vallance still wanted answers. He wanted to piece together every minute of Jean Wilding's last day. He wanted to know what it was that drove Angela to such rage, to such anger, to such obscene violence. No matter how harrowing, the truth needed to be uncovered, if only to salvage some peace of mind. And if along the way they helped Angela in some way then so much the better.

Cooper was still going through the day's statements as Vallance headed out of CID. 'It's getting late,' Vallance remarked, stopping by Cooper's desk and the cloud of cigarette smoke that surrounded it.

'I'm just going back over a few things, sir,' Cooper said.

'What're you after?'

Cooper shrugged. 'Not sure, really.'

Vallance smiled. He had the same feeling, that something fundamental had been missed. 'It's Ted Coleman, isn't it?' he said, guessing that Cooper felt the same antagonism to the man.

'Yes, sir. I don't know what, but there's something about him that makes me feel he's not playing straight.'

'I know, I get the same feeling. Part of me puts it down to the fact that he's such a callous bastard.'

Cooper sucked hard on his cigarette, making the end burn bright red under the ash. 'I know what you mean, sir, I wanted to smack him in the mouth too.'

'We'll try and get to talk to the Wildings' GP tomorrow,' Vallance said. 'We'll see how his view matches with the Colemans'.'

'Yes, sir.'

'Right, I'll see you tomorrow morning.'

Vallance headed out, avoiding the few remaining officers still working on the case. Already manpower was being diverted to more expedient cases. The command had come down from on high: Superintendent Riley had decreed that the case was effectively solved, Angela's confession counted as a result and therefore the investigation was being downgraded. People were being shifted away. Inspector Dobson was back looking at car crime, and with him went half a dozen detective constables and a sergeant.

As far as Vallance was concerned the Wilding case was still open, and it counted for more than any number of car thefts and cases of joyriding. For as long as he could he would resist the pressure to move on to something more politically acceptable, at least until he was satisfied that he understood what had really happened between Angela and her mother. Some cases were like that; even a desk-bound bureaucrat like Riley would understand.

It was cold and dark when he got outside. The whole day had been spent inside, moving no further from his office than the interview room. Lunch had provided no respite, soggy sandwiches being consumed as he pored over the morning's witness statements. Now, as he stood in the rear entrance to Area HQ, he breathed in the night air and marvelled that it felt so good. He walked slowly to his car, trying to decide whether it was better to pick up something to eat on his way home or to get home and then ring out for something. In either case he was too tired to do anything but eat and then slump in front of the TV.

It started to rain as soon as he got into his car, softly at first but soon picking up so that it drummed hard on the roof as he sat and watched it cascade down the windscreen. Cooper was right of course: there was something not quite kosher about Coleman. It was good to see that Cooper was willing to act on gut instinct, even though in the past that same gut instinct had led him astray. And this time?

He started the car, realising that the case was still playing on his mind. He needed to switch off for a while, to think about something else. It was a depressing thought, but with no one else for company he was more than likely to spend the entire night brooding about the case. Not for the first time he cursed himself for being so stupid as to mess things up with Anne Quinn. Like an idiot he'd allowed himself to be manipulated by Riley, and now Anne was deliberately keeping her distance.

Sarah Fairfax. He hadn't called her. She'd be angry; he could picture her fuming at the presumed snub, taking it as a personal insult that he hadn't dropped whatever he was doing to call her back. He smiled at the thought. The rain was still coming down hard so he pulled off the road at the next junction and then drove on until he found a convenient place to stop. He flicked through his address book quickly, hoping that she'd still be at work.

Of the three numbers he had listed for her he chose the mobile number. It rang for a while before the connection was made. The line was so clear as she announced herself, it sounded as though she were in the car beside him.

'Hello, Sarah, it's Anthony Vallance,' he said, waiting for the inevitable explosion of anger in response.

'Thank you for getting back to me, Mr Vallance,' she responded calmly, with perhaps even a hint of gratitude in her voice.

'I'm sorry I couldn't get back to you earlier,' he continued, feeling cheated of her histrionics. Why was it that when he wanted her to scream at him she was perfectly civil, and yet when he was being nice to her she'd hit the roof?

'It sounds horrendous,' she continued, the line suddenly spluttering noisily as she spoke. 'That poor girl, how is she?'

At least she wasn't following the rest of the world and assuming that Angela was evil personified. 'Under sedation,' he said.

'And her family?'

'Them too,' he said.

'I hope you didn't mind me contacting you,' she said, smoothly changing subject, 'but I think I need your help.'

Had he heard correctly? She was asking for help? He caught sight of himself in the rear-view mirror of the car, grinning inanely. 'How can I help, Sarah?'

'It's a long story,' she sighed, 'but myself and a friend are being threatened . . . She's already been attacked once and then someone tried to run us down in a car. We've also had threatening phone calls on a number of occasions.'

It was bound to be connected to a story she was working on. 'Who're you digging the dirt on?'

It came at last, the inevitable sharp breath that signalled her anger. 'I do not dig the dirt,' she stated coldly, enunciating every single syllable with crystal clarity that not even a burst of line noise could disguise. 'Why is it, Mr Vallance, that you cannot for one minute resist the temptation to disparage my work?'

He was still smiling as he spoke. 'I wasn't being disparaging,' he explained patiently. 'I guessed that you were investigating someone, why else would you be in trouble? Unless you've not paid your tax bill and the revenue are getting vicious.'

'I can see why you're a detective, Mr Vallance,' she said,

and he could easily picture the disdainful expression on her face.

'And I can see why people want to run you over,' he replied. 'Now, do you want my help or not?'

'Please, if it's too much trouble I'll go elsewhere,' she said. 'After all, I'm sure that one policeman is as good as another.'

For a second he was ready to put the phone down on her. She deserved it, the sarcastic bitch, but then he knew that she'd never forgive him. 'I said I'd help. What can I do?'

'Epsley Science Park is in your area?'

'You've checked,' he said, knowing that she would leave nothing to chance.

'Yes, I have. I'm working on a story connected with it. Do you think you could come out to talk about it?'

The Wilding case was his top priority. No matter what he felt towards Sarah, and it was a weird combination of irritation and respect, he couldn't take time out from that. 'I'm sorry, Sarah, but you know what I'm working on,' he explained.

'I understand,' she said. 'Perhaps Carol and I can come out to see you?'

The prospect of seeing Sarah again cheered him up. The fact that she'd have someone else along was less cheering. Not that he dared entertain the prospect of a meeting with Sarah that was not connected in some way with work. 'It's possible,' he said, deciding to hedge his bets for the moment.

'This is serious,' she repeated. 'You know I'm not prone to exaggerations, Mr Vallance, but my friend really does fear for her life.'

What harm would it do? Apart from causing more hassle from his superiors if they found out. Apart from possibly getting in the way of the Wilding case. Apart from . . . 'I'll call you tomorrow morning,' he promised. 'We can sort out somewhere to meet then. Unless . . .'

'Unless what?'

'Unless you want to meet me tonight?'

'I'll expect your call tomorrow morning,' she said.

It was the reply he had expected, of course. 'OK, I'll talk to you then.'

He was still smiling. He looked at himself in the mirror.

Things were worse than he had ever imagined. He was even looking forward to seeing her again.

The morning sky was as dark and as miserable as the previous evening's. The sun was out, somewhere, hidden behind thick grey cloud that seemed to have been painted onto the horizon. A sharp breeze caught at the bushes surrounding the car park opposite the PR-Tech offices, tugging hard at the dull green shrubs and buffeting Sarah's car as well.

Judging by the number of neatly parked cars, early starts were as common as late finishes at the Science Park. Except in Carol's case, Sarah noted gloomily. It was nearly 9.30 and she still hadn't turned up at work. Neither had Liz, come to that. In contrast Sarah had taken no chances; Duncan had complained sulkily as usual but she was out of bed and ready before eight. The early morning traffic had been bearable for a change and she had arrived at Epsley nearly fifteen minutes earlier than she had expected.

She sat huddled in her car, staring gloomily at the un-inspiring sky and the stark square buildings around her. The architecture was a little more intricate than was apparent at first sight; the tinted windows were framed in olive green, the clay tiles of the roof shaped in a pleasing wave, the heavy glass doors perfectly proportioned. The upper storey overhung a paved area around each building, providing a modicum of shelter for the poor souls who braved the elements for a quick smoke.

The lights were on in the offices of G-Man Software, so at least they were working. She hoped that they weren't busy putting together another tedious presentation for her to sit through. The thought of one more organisation chart made her heart sink. It was enough to make anyone scream. Brian Quigley's direct approach had seemed such a refreshing change. He might have been difficult but at least he wasn't trying to impress with flashy graphics and fancy fonts. Gavin Newman, on the other hand, seemed just the type to go for form rather than content.

Another car slotted into a space. Sarah craned forward to get a better look. Liz had finally made it to work. It was about time. She waited for Liz to emerge from her car before she got out too. The sharp breeze made her grit her teeth as she crossed the car park to the office.

Liz saw her and smiled a greeting. 'You're early,' she said.

'I've been here for a while,' Sarah said, following Liz into the relative warmth of the lobby.

'Does that make us look bad?' Liz asked, a defensive note in her voice barely masked by her smile.

It did, partly, but Sarah couldn't bring herself to say it. 'Not at all,' she lied. 'It's just that I was getting bored sitting in the car.'

Liz unlocked the office and they went in, a nervous silence between them. Sarah waited a moment then walked across to the meeting table and put her stuff down. Her tape recorder, pads, notes and other bits of stationery were all safely stowed. She sat in silence as Liz busied herself checking for phone messages and then putting some coffee on.

'Have you had any more thoughts on how you handle Brian?' Liz finally asked, turning to face Sarah.

'Very carefully, I would say. I'll need to go back and see him again soon.'

The door opened at that point and Carol came in. She was wearing dark sunglasses, the wide oval lenses completely obscuring her eyes. In the dismally grey weather they seemed utterly ridiculous.

'You're here already,' she exclaimed nervously.

Something was wrong. 'Take the glasses off,' Sarah said, realising instantly that she was not wearing them purely for cosmetic reasons.

'I bumped into a door,' Carol insisted, carefully easing the glasses off her face to reveal dark bruising around her left eye.

Liz ran over immediately. 'You poor thing,' she cried, gently touching her fingers to the bruising. 'Does it hurt?'

'Not as much as it did last night,' Carol said, studiously avoiding Sarah's eyes.

She was lying again; it was so clear that Sarah wanted to get up and give her a shake. However, Carol was saved by Liz's presence, which made it impossible to question her in detail. In the circumstances Sarah knew that she was expected to make sympathetic noises. But any sympathy she felt was swamped by her anger at Carol's refusal to admit the truth, or, more importantly, to act on it. 'The glasses make you look ridiculous,' was the only comment she felt able to make.

'Sarah!' Liz cried, suitably shocked by Sarah's apparent disregard for Carol's injury.

'It's all right,' Carol said, 'Sarah's only joking. Aren't you, Sarah?'

'Of course I was,' Sarah agreed coldly. 'And how did the door come out of it?'

Carol ignored the remark. 'I can't go out,' she complained. 'I know I look stupid wearing these things, but what can I do?'

'How did you do it?' Liz repeated.

'I got up in the middle of the night to go to the loo and forgot that I'd shut the door to my room. I think I must have been half asleep.'

It was crap, pure and simple. Sarah refused to believe that anyone could be taken in by a story so obviously a tissue of lies. 'Poor you,' she said, 'and to think you had no steak to put on it. A nut cutlet's probably not as good, is it?'

'Don't be horrible,' Carol moaned, pouting her lips like a spoilt child. 'It hurts.'

'Come on,' Liz added, 'don't be so mean to her.'

Someone had beaten Carol up; Sarah was willing to put money on it. The sooner that they got to see Vallance the better. 'I'm sorry,' she said. 'I'll make it up to you. Let me buy you lunch, Carol. How's that?'

'OK,' Carol agreed, attempting a smile that ended with a wince of pain.

'Good. Now, do you think we can make a start on some work?'

Liz did not look impressed. 'Yes, of course,' she said. 'I spoke to Gavin again last night. He and Grant are expecting us.'

'And me?' Carol asked hopefully.

Liz shook her head. 'I need you to man the phone this morning. Oh, and you've got to chase up the print bureau about the InfoSoft brochures.'

At least the blacked eye wouldn't be visible on the phone.

Sarah noted the look of disappointment on Carol's injured face and decided it was probably better not to voice the thought.

The two brothers were huddled around a computer screen when Liz and Sarah arrived. The contrast between the two young men was striking. Gavin was clean-shaven, well-groomed and dressed in a flashy double-breasted suit in a dark shade of green. Beside him Grant looked a mess: dirty jeans, a black sweatshirt which had seen better days, scuffed leather boots and hair which seemed at war with itself. But the resemblance was there: both were tall and had thick black hair and dark eyes, though in Grant's case there was none of the welcome that Sarah could discern in Gavin's expression.

'Hello, again,' Gavin said, striding across the room to shake Sarah's hand. 'Glad you could make it.'

Sarah responded with a 'hi' and a quick smile then looked beyond him towards his brother.

'Grant's just putting the finishing touch to our presentation,' Gavin explained. 'Ain't that right, Grant?'

'Yeah, that's right,' came the confirmation, muttered churlishly. He looked up from the computer briefly, making eye contact with Sarah for a split second before looking away.

'How about some coffee?' Liz suggested, stepping into the space between Sarah and Grant, as though she could shield Sarah from his resentment.

'Coffee's fine by me,' Gavin agreed. 'Grant's already on intravenous caffeine,' he added, laughing lightly at his own joke.

'Yes, please,' Sarah agreed. The wall above Grant was decorated with big dark posters of rock bands that she had never heard of, the images full of mock aggression and fetishistic violence. Directly above his computer screen a part of the wall had been taped over with sheets of white paper.

'Grant, coffee?' Liz called.

'Got some,' he murmured, tapping hard at the keyboard angrily.

'Told you, the man's a coffee demon,' Gavin said, still smiling.

Sarah stared at the blank white space, trying to work out

what was being covered up. At last, unable to resist the temptation, she walked over to get a better look. Grant kept his back to her, not even bothering to glance at her as she stopped by his chair. His hair was cut oddly, shoulder length on one side and shaved close to the skull on the other. Both ears were pierced too, though where Gavin sported a single stud Grant's ears were laced with steel and gold from the bottom of the lobe to the top.

'What're you hiding?' Sarah asked.

'Nothing,' he snapped back.

Sarah laughed. 'I mean there,' she said, pointing to the white sheets on the wall.

Gavin walked over too. 'It's just a gag,' he said, 'nothing special.'

Grant glared at him, then stood up and carefully removed the paper to expose the poster below it. The glossy image was distorted: leather, rubber, flesh and there, in the centre of it all, the stark words 'Fist Fuck'. A gag? In the sense that Gavin was desperately trying to gag his brother's behaviour.

'It's the name of a record,' Gavin said, and he sounded slightly embarrassed by his younger brother's taste.

'It's a fucking brilliant record,' Grant corrected him.

Sarah could see why Liz had been so loath to let her meet Grant. What was not so obvious was why Carol seemed so attached to him. 'I see,' she said, not quite knowing whether to act outraged or merely to nod acceptance. She suspected that outrage would have been the reaction he desired the most, but then she guessed it would only serve to confirm a picture of her he had already created in his own mind. Besides which, she felt not an ounce of outrage, nor even a hint of mild distaste.

'I could play it for you,' Grant suggested, his twisted smile matched at last by something other than foul humour in his eyes.

'Er, not now,' Gavin said, intervening quickly.

'Another time,' Sarah suggested. 'I'm intrigued to find out what a record with a name like that sounds like.'

'A horrible noise,' Liz said, arriving with the coffee.

'Since when do you know anything about music?' Grant demanded.

Gavin laughed. 'Come on, Grant, that ain't music and you know it.'

Grant shrugged. 'It's a fucking brilliant noise,' he told Sarah. 'I'll do you a tape of it if you like.'

'It's a deal,' she agreed. 'Now, about this presentation . . .'

'It's nearly done now,' Gavin assured her.

'Would you be offended if I asked not to see it?'

Liz seemed crestfallen. 'It won't be long,' she said.

Gavin too, seemed to be genuinely disappointed. 'We've spent ages doing it,' he added.

Grant smiled. 'Good,' he said, 'because it's a pile of shite.'

'In that case why don't we just sit and talk?' Sarah suggested.

Grant nodded. 'Yeah, sounds good to me.'

'If that's what you want,' Liz conceded and her reluctance only seemed to make Grant's smile deepen.

SIX

As Vallance pulled into the pub car park he saw Sarah Fairfax
and her friend still sitting in Sarah's car. One glance at Sarah's
strict countenance was all he needed to gauge the mood. She
was angry and having a real go at her friend, who was sitting
in grim silence looking straight ahead. He couldn't help
smiling. Was there anyone in the world Sarah Fairfax didn't
argue with?

He eased the car into the space next to Sarah's just as
she looked round. There was a moment of eye contact and
a flicker of a smile from her. Was that a welcoming one?
Just for once he hoped that they could be civil to each
other face to face, if only to set a precedent. He stopped
the car and looked round again. Sarah was saying something
to her friend, who was gazing directly at him. She was
wearing dark sunglasses, which meant she was either a
victim of fashion or was hiding something. He smiled at
her and was rewarded with a friendly, interested smile in
return.

He was out of the car before they were, the sharp breeze
making him pull his leather jacket tight. Did he look too
scruffy? The sleepless nights were beginning to get to him,
the dark rings under his eyes suggesting a debauched lifestyle
a million miles from the truth. Sarah's friend, despite the
pointless dark glasses, looked good. She had a round face,

with full lips, a small nose and a pale skin that was matched by her golden hair.

'I'm glad you could make it, Mr Vallance,' Sarah said, offering her hand in a gesture of formality that he found intensely annoying. She was making the point that it was purely a business meeting, just in case he got ideas above his station.

He shook her hand briefly. 'You know me,' he told her, grinning. 'I can never turn down a distress call.'

Humour – she could never handle being on the receiving end. He could see irritation in her blue eyes and tension around her mouth. 'Of course,' she responded on cue, 'that is what you're paid for, after all. This is the friend I spoke about. Carol Davis, Chief Inspector Vallance.'

'Pleased to meet you, Chief Inspector,' Carol said, and her smile suggested she really was pleased.

He shook her hand and smiled back. 'I just hope I can help,' he said.

'It's cold,' Sarah said. 'Shall we go inside?'

The pub was half empty, a log fire in one corner jealously guarded by a couple of old-timers staring morosely at the crackling logs while nursing pints of dark bitter. Vallance knew the type well enough: the pub was the central point of their existence and without it they'd be forced to sit at home and contemplate the horrors of daytime TV.

'Do they do good food here?' Carol asked, gazing through her sunglasses at the menu chalked up on the board above the bar.

'No, it's crap,' Vallance admitted, 'but it's better than most of the pubs around here.'

'I'm glad you've chosen so well then, Mr Vallance,' Sarah said.

He saw the slight shake of Carol's head and recognised the sympathy being extended. 'We can always nip back to the police canteen,' he responded. The suggestion was ignored. She was in a seriously bad mood, he realised. 'Let's order,' he suggested.

Carol dared to remove the sunglasses. The bruising around her eye looked fresh: still dark, slightly swollen and positioned perfectly. She half smiled at Vallance, as though in apology, and then stared hard at the menu again. He and Sarah ordered quickly, but a minute later her eyes were still glued to the menu.

'Hurry up,' Sarah urged impatiently.

'Do you have organic bread?' Carol asked the woman behind the bar.

'Sorry, love, it's brown or white,' came the reply.

'In that case can I have a salad sandwich on brown?' Carol ventured hesitantly.

The barmaid looked confused. 'What? Just salad?'

'Yes, please.'

'You don't want no pickle with it at least? Or a slice of cheese?'

Carol shook her head. 'No, thank you. Just some salad.'

'And a drink?' Vallance suggested. Sarah's gin and tonic had already arrived, and his bottle of lager was on the counter.

Again there was a pause while Carol carefully considered her options. Vallance could see that Sarah was fit to explode, patience not being one of her strongest points. 'Is the orange juice freshly squeezed?' Carol asked, her voice suggesting that she knew the answer was no but needed to ask the question anyway.

'No,' the barmaid said flatly.

'In that case I'll have a mineral water. Still, please.'

The barmaid did not look impressed. She grudgingly pulled out a bottle of still water and slammed it hard on the counter along with a glass.

'It's good to see that the art of customer service still survives,' Vallance said, leading the way to one of the tables at the back of the bar.

'She looked at me as though I'd insulted her,' Carol complained.

'You probably did,' Sarah said. 'Why can't you have processed cheese, unnatural bread and dead orange juice like everyone else?'

'Because it's unhealthy,' Carol replied earnestly.

'It was a rhetorical question,' Sarah said. 'Now, Carol, why don't you tell Mr Vallance what happened last night?'

Carol turned to Vallance and looked him in the eye for the

first time. She seemed nervous, her blue eyes filled with fear and indecision. 'It's OK,' he told her softly, 'just tell me what's wrong and I'll do my best to help.'

'It's not as easy as that.' She added, turning back to Sarah, 'You haven't told him what's going on?'

'No, I thought it best that you tell him.'

Carol turned back to him. 'I work at the Science Park,' she began. 'I'm doing PR work there. It's not very interesting to be honest with you, but then I've never found computer software especially interesting. That's what most of the companies do there, software. Some of it's normal commercial stuff, you know, applications and databases and so on. I mean that's –'

'Hurry up!' Sarah snapped. 'We don't have all day.'

Vallance was inclined to tell Sarah to keep quiet but he decided to hold back. She was right, time was of the essence, and furthermore there was something in Carol's indecision which suggested it was congenital and not directly linked to the case.

'OK, OK,' Carol said, looking to Vallance for sympathy. He smiled to her encouragingly and she smiled back before continuing. 'Some of the bigger companies on the Park are defence software specialists. They do contract work for the Ministry of Defence. It's all supposed to be top secret stuff, but a lot of it is just boring, mundane computer work. You know, little applications, databases, reporting software, that kind of thing. Do you know what I mean?'

Vallance smiled. 'No,' he said, 'but carry on anyway.'

'Well, from what I've discovered one of the companies is heavily involved in defrauding the MoD.'

'That's where you come in,' Vallance said, looking at Sarah.

'That's right,' she agreed. 'If these people are ripping off the taxpayer then we've every right to expose them.'

'The thing is,' Carol continued, 'that there are lots of people involved in this. Not just the companies on the Park but also people at the MoD itself.'

'Is that who beat you up?' Vallance asked.

Carol shrugged. 'I don't know. It might be. Last night I was walking from my car to my flat when someone jumped out of some bushes and belted me in the face, threw me to the ground and then ran off.'

'Was anything taken?'

'This is not a mugging,' Sarah remarked pointedly.

'Was anything taken?' Vallance repeated.

'No,' Carol said, sitting back as the barmaid arrived with their sandwiches.

Vallance looked at his ham and pickle sandwich and then at the sorry affair on Carol's plate. A salad sandwich consisted of two slices of wholemeal bread filled with damp lettuce, wafer-thin cucumber slices, mushy tomatoes and a scattering of cress. It almost – but not quite – looked good enough to eat.

'This is horrible,' Carol said, lifting the bread and looking distastefully at the sad excuse for a salad underneath it.

'Don't eat it,' Sarah suggested. 'We can stop off somewhere on the way back to the office and you can get something decent.'

Carol looked relieved. 'Thanks. It's just so hard to eat properly if you care about your food,' she said.

At that instant Vallance cared less about his food than about what Carol had been saying. 'Was last night the first time you've been attacked?'

'No,' Carol said quietly.

'She was also attacked in Lyndhurst recently,' Sarah said, evidently not satisfied with monosyllabic answers. 'We met up to talk the story through and someone jumped her in the car park.'

'Have you spoken to the police about this yet?'

It was a perfect cue for Sarah. 'No, Mr Vallance, we thought we'd talk to you instead.'

He ignored her snide remark, though God knows it deserved a comeback. 'Do you have any ideas who's behind the attacks?'

'No.'

'Well, who knew you'd be at Lyndhurst?' he asked.

Carol looked guiltily at Sarah before answering. 'Quite a few people,' she admitted. 'Apart from everyone at Sarah's office there was Liz at work, Grant, and Gavin probably, a few friends in that part of the world . . . I don't know, I'd probably mentioned it to half a dozen other people as well.'

'Is there anyone who didn't know?' Sarah asked sourly.

'I'm sorry,' Carol said. 'I didn't tell them what we were meeting for. I just mentioned to a few people that I was going away for the weekend.'

'Who knew you were meeting with Sarah to discuss your allegations?' he asked.

'No one,' she said, 'not one other person knew.'

'Except the people at Sarah's office,' he reminded them both.

Sarah shook her head emphatically. 'Don't even think about it,' she warned. 'The people I work with are not involved.'

'So who is it?' he responded instantly.

Again Sarah felt moved to do the talking. 'She suspects that it might be someone in the security services or perhaps someone associated with Brian Quigley.'

'He's the boss of one of the software companies,' Carol added. 'I'm sure he's the main person responsible for the fraud. I think that other people at the Park might be involved but he's the one with the direct links to Whitehall.'

'Evidence?'

Carol shrugged again. 'None. It might all be coincidence, it might have nothing to do with what's going on at Epsley.'

'Don't be ridiculous!' Sarah cried, her voice rising naturally to reach the tone of angry disdain which was so completely hers.

'How can you be so sure?' Vallance asked her.

'Because I've had threats made to me too,' she said. 'There's something dangerous going on here, Mr Vallance. How much longer do we have to wait for something to be done?'

'How can something be done if you've not reported it to anyone?' Vallance demanded. 'Carol, are you willing to make a formal statement?'

'I can't,' she said, looking away from him. 'It's too dangerous.'

'But how can it be more dangerous than letting them get away with it?' Sarah asked.

'Because if I complain to the police then Brian's going to

find out,' Carol said, her voice barely a whisper. 'He's got friends in the police, he'll find out and then . . .'

'Then what?' Vallance asked.

'I don't know.'

She was obviously scared but there was nothing that he could do without her help. 'Look,' he said softly, 'are you suggesting that this Quigley character is threatening your life?'

Carol refused to answer. 'Please, Carol,' Sarah said, losing for the moment her scornful attitude, 'you've got to tell the Chief Inspector everything.'

'But Brian's so devious, so clever . . .' Carol whispered.

'Is he dangerous?' Vallance demanded.

Carol closed her eyes. 'He does frighten me,' she admitted. 'You see, we . . . we had something going and I got to know him . . . That's how I know about the MoD stuff.'

Sarah looked as though a bomb had hit her. She obviously had not known that juicy little detail. 'Did he hurt you when you were together?' Vallance said.

'Yes, sometimes,' Carol admitted, avoiding the horrified expression on Sarah's face. 'And now he suspects me of plotting against him . . .'

'Did he attack you last night?' Vallance asked.

'No, he wouldn't do anything so obvious. I told you, he's devious.'

'He's not the only one,' Sarah remarked coldly.

There was going to be another row between the two women. Vallance could sense the cold fury that Sarah was aching to vent on Carol. It would have to wait, however. 'If you want my help then you've got to be straight with me,' he warned Carol. 'Tell me about Quigley.'

'He's clever, ruthless and totally fixated on money,' Carol said. 'He can be quite charming at times, you know, he's very bright and that makes him attractive to people. But I also know that he's got some very heavy friends . . .'

'Villains?' Vallance said.

'I don't know,' Carol said. 'It's hard to explain. They just give off bad vibes. I didn't know him well enough to meet them properly. He always got me out of the way when he was going to meet them.'

'Is this connected to the MoD fraud?' Sarah asked, coming into the conversation again.

'I'm not sure,' Carol said. 'I just know that if he thought I was doing this he'd do something to stop me.'

'She needs police protection,' Sarah stated, looking at Vallance as though she were giving an order.

'It's not that simple,' he said. 'Unless you make a full statement there's nothing we can do.'

'But you see,' Carol cried, 'I can't. If I make the statement he'll find out and it'll be too late.'

'Then what else can I do?' Vallance asked.

'You can help me,' Carol said quietly, a sly smile on her face.

'Oh, stop it!' Sarah cried angrily. 'There's no time for these stupid games, Carol.'

Vallance sat back. Carol was still smiling, her clear blue eyes fixed on him hopefully. 'Sarah's right,' he said, 'this is serious. At the very least you've got to report what happened last night.'

'I can't,' Carol insisted.

He turned to Sarah, who looked absolutely livid. 'Sarah? Will you report the threatening phone calls?'

'But it's not me at risk,' she pointed out. 'It's Carol. I can handle a few silly phone calls, it takes a lot to scare me, as you well know, Mr Vallance.'

He did know and it scared him. She was as likely to get herself killed in the course of the story as Carol was. 'I think you two should stop investigating the story now,' he said. 'Pull back before it goes any further. Report everything you know to us and then let us handle it. Please,' he added, hoping to pre-empt Sarah's inevitable hostility to the idea.

'This is a story of high public interest,' she said, 'and it's not your job, Mr Vallance, to tell us what we can and can't investigate. You know that I can't let this go now, I have to see it through.'

'Sarah, for Christ's sake, this could be dangerous.'

'Will you help us or not?' she demanded.

That was it, he'd had enough. 'What am I supposed to do? Arrest someone? For what? No complaint's been made. Give protection? To who? No one's requested it. Tell me, what can I do to help?'

'You're the policeman, you tell us what you can do!'

There was no point in continuing the slanging match. Carol had already given up and was merely watching the exchanges with a bewildered look on her face. 'What I'll do is run my own checks on this Quigley bloke,' he said. 'Don't worry,' he added, noting the alarm in Carol's eyes, 'I'll do these myself, just so that no one else can know about it. In the meantime if anything more happens, no matter how trivial, then you have to make an official complaint. Is that understood?'

Sarah nodded but said nothing more.

Carol searched in her handbag and then came up with a scrap of paper and a pen. She scribbled something down on it and handed it across the table to Vallance. 'I'd feel happier if you could call me some time,' she said.

'We'd better go now,' Sarah said.

'Sarah, you as well,' he added. 'If anything happens then you've got to make an official complaint. Call me if you need to, both of you, but unless there's something I can formally act on there's not a lot I can do.'

Sarah stood up to go, impatient and seething with anger. The meeting hadn't gone according to her plans, and he guessed that Carol was going to get the full force of a Fairfax explosion on the way back to Epsley. She was right to be pissed off though. The situation looked a lot murkier than she had probably believed, and the news that Carol had been in a relationship with Quigley had taken the wind from her sails somewhat.

Carol stood up too, throwing her bag over her shoulder. Her eye looked even worse under the pub lights, the darkness of the bruise contrasting with the whiteness of her skin. She had spoken of her relationship with Quigley in the past tense: did that mean she was currently unattached? The question had only just occurred to him and it made him smile again. Was that one of the reasons why Sarah was so angry? Was she jealous?

'Do you want me to call you tonight?' he asked, getting up too.

Carol's smile made an answer superfluous. 'If you don't mind,' she said.

'No, it'll be no problem,' he assured her.

'Come on,' Sarah said, her face totally straight, 'we've got to get back.'

Carol's dark glasses went back on as soon as they stepped out of the pub. They walked to the cars in silence, he following the two women. Sarah jumped into her car without a backward glance but Carol lingered for a second.

'Don't forget to call,' she said.

'I won't,' he promised. 'See you.'

'Bye.'

'See you, Sarah,' he called, but her response was to gun the engine to life. He stepped back quickly and the car accelerated forward with a roar.

Was that jealousy or just routine anger on her part? He watched her steer the car out onto the road and then zoom off at speed. Jealousy or not, he pocketed Carol's number anyway. There was no way he was not going to call her.

'And what do you think you're playing at?' Sarah demanded, keeping her eyes fixed on the road. Her hands gripped the wheel tightly, knuckles white and fingers digging into the soft leather grip.

Carol's face was impassive, her eyes hidden by the dark glasses. If there was an inclination to smile she controlled it well. 'What do you mean?' she responded, sounding for all the world as though she was totally mystified by the question.

'You know exactly what I mean.'

'I don't,' Carol insisted. 'Are you angry because he was interested in me?'

Sarah's grip on the wheel tightened and her foot pressed harder on the accelerator pedal. 'I don't care whether he was interested in you or not —'

'Don't you?' Carol cut in, smiling at last. She twisted round in her seat and her face was alive with excitement.

'No I don't,' Sarah stated flatly. 'What I do care about is being made a fool of.'

'Why didn't you tell me about him before? He's quite cute really, isn't he?'

The lights ahead switched to red and Sarah had to brake hard, making the tyres screech and jerking Carol forward in her seat. The driver of the car in front was shaking his head disapprovingly, looking at Sarah in his rear-view mirror. She glared at him, unwilling to accept his unspoken admonishment.

'Are you angry with me?' Carol asked quietly.

'Of course I'm bloody angry!'

'I won't see him if you don't want me to.'

Sarah turned and looked at Carol but the dark glasses and the blank expression on her face hid the truth. Surely she wasn't that stupid? It had to be obvious even to her what was wrong. 'It's nothing to do with you and him,' she said. 'It's about what you've been keeping back from me. Can't you see that? How much more is there that you've not told me?'

'It's green,' Carol said.

'What?'

Carol pointed at the lights. Sarah turned and saw that the car ahead was already speeding off. She shifted into gear just as the car behind started beeping at her. 'All right, all right,' she muttered, moving the car forward with a satisfying roar of the engine.

'I couldn't tell you about me and Brian, not at first, anyway,' Carol explained. 'I mean it all sounds so . . . so involved.'

'You mean it isn't?'

Sarah glanced round to see Carol's apologetic smile. 'I'm sorry, Sarah, I knew that if I told you that right away you wouldn't have believed anything. You wouldn't have, would you?'

The answer was no, and they both knew it. 'Then why didn't you mention it later? Why keep it hidden until we were with Anthony Vallance?'

'I don't know,' Carol said vaguely. 'I could never find the right time. It wasn't deliberate, I promise.'

'Is there anything else I should know?'

'No.'

'Are you sure?'

Carol shrugged. 'There's nothing else like this. It wasn't a big deal, me and Brian, I told you. It only lasted a few months; we finished ages ago.'

'You told Vallance that he hurt you when you were together. Did he beat you up?'

'Not exactly,' Carol said, and there was a sly undertone to her voice that made Sarah want to scream.

Sarah could hardly keep her eyes on the road. She wanted to stop the car and to slap Carol – hard – to bring her to her senses once and for all. 'What the hell does that mean, Carol?' she stormed. 'For Christ's sake stop playing these stupid games! First you're telling us how frightened you are, then you're flirting with Vallance and now you're being all coy again.'

'So you *are* angry because of Vallance,' Carol, pointed out gleefully. 'I knew it, Sarah. I knew there was something going on between you, and you're accusing me of keeping things hidden.'

'That's it,' Sarah declared, 'I quit. I've had enough, Carol. You do as Vallance says; report what's happened to the police and let them deal with it.'

Carol's alarm was obvious. 'I said I'm sorry!' she cried. 'Really I am, how many times do I have to say it? What else do I have to do to prove it to you?'

They were already back on the Science Park, the car heading down the incline towards the office units. Sarah slowed and then finally stopped. She turned to face Carol. 'How did Brian Quigley hurt you?'

Carol looked away, though there was little need to as her eyes were still hidden by the dark glasses. 'He beat me with a leather belt,' she said quietly.

'Why didn't you report it to the police?'

Carol shook her head. 'It wasn't like that,' she whispered. 'It was what turned him on, it's what he wanted in bed.'

No wonder she had been keeping things hidden. 'And you let him?' Sarah asked, appalled by the very idea of it.

'Yes . . . You don't know what he's like . . .'

'You're right, I don't, and that's why I need you to tell me what he's like.'

'He's dangerous,' Carol said. 'I'm frightened of him, can't you see that?'

Sarah closed her eyes. It was a mess, the whole damned story. What if there was nothing going on at all? What if Carol had been dumped by Quigley? What if the entire story were motivated by nothing more than her need for revenge?

Adam Taylor, the managing director of Advanced Micro Technologies, was a slim, neat and thoroughly unremarkable character. He too, like all of Liz's clients, had a computer-generated presentation to hand when he met Sarah. The nuts and bolts of his company's work were beyond Sarah, though that did not stop him making valiant attempts to simplify and explain. The more she protested that she was not interested in his company's product the more he felt the need to go into detail. In the end Liz had to step in and prompt him to move on, though even then it was clear that he felt thwarted.

Carol had indicated that Adam was also involved with Brian Quigley's schemes in some way. However, thanks to their lunch with Vallance, Sarah hadn't had time to get more information before the meeting. Once it had progressed to a certain point, however, she had started asking questions but the replies had all seemed so boring and innocuous, much like Adam Taylor himself, that it was difficult to see what connection there could possibly be between Taylor and Quigley. They worked in different technology sectors, were not involved in any joint projects and, from what Sarah was able to ascertain, the two men barely knew each other.

The meeting fizzled out late in the afternoon, by which time it was clear to everybody involved that it had been a complete waste of time. Liz seemed the most embarrassed by it all, as though she were responsible. Sarah thanked Adam for his time and input, but it did nothing to detract from Taylor's disappointment. Of all the people interviewed he had been the most forthcoming, the most reasonable and clearly the most interested. The poor man saw the chance to appear on television as a great opportunity and seemed more than a little disheartened to be missing out.

'I guess you won't be including them in the programme,' Liz remarked afterwards, as she and Sarah walked back to the PR-Tech office. The sky was dark blue and lined with thick grey clouds that loomed ominously on the horizon. It was going to be another cold and wet night, more like the autumn than the beginning of summer.

'No, I don't think so,' Sarah conceded. The deception was wearing her down and she hated not being able to tell the truth; it rankled deep down inside her. It also seemed so unfair to people like Adam Taylor and ludicrous that the man should feel so disappointed.

'I did try and tell you,' Liz said. 'What Adam does is too technical for most people to understand. It's leading edge stuff; parallel processing is the way of the future, but it's boring unless you understand the technology.'

'Will you apologise to him for me?' Sarah asked. 'I'm really sorry that it didn't work. Tell him it's not a reflection on him personally, or of his company.'

'I'll tell him,' Liz agreed. 'What about the other company I mentioned?'

'InfoSoft?'

'That's right. I'm sure that'll be better for television,' Liz said hopefully.

Sarah shook her head. Enough people were involved already and there was no way she wanted to raise other people's hopes or involve them in Carol's complicated schemes. 'No, I think we'll just stick with Brian Quigley and the Newman brothers.'

'You're sure? It's just that I think InfoSoft are probably doing the most exciting work here.'

Sarah was adamant. 'No, we'll stick with two companies.'

'It's Carol,' Liz said, stopping at the door to the office. 'I wish she'd keep her mouth shut sometimes.'

Sarah smiled. She had the opposite wish: she wanted Carol to open her mouth a bit more to reveal all that she knew. 'She can be quite persuasive sometimes,' she said mildly.

'Don't get me wrong. Carol's good at what she does, I'll grant you that. But sometimes she's so impulsive. Once she'd decided that AMT were candidates for the programme she wouldn't let go.'

'It must make working with her quite difficult sometimes,' Sarah said, hoping to draw Liz on.

'I don't know,' Liz sighed. 'Sometimes I have no idea what's going on in her head. It's not as if I run a big company where I can afford to let people go off on tangents. PR-Tech stands or falls on the work we do here, and she doesn't make it easy when she gets so personally involved with the clients.'

Liz suddenly looked shocked with herself, as though she'd said more than she'd meant to. Sarah knew it was time to take a gamble. 'Are you talking about her and Brian Quigley?' she asked, lowering her voice to a whisper.

'You know about that?' Liz said, sounding relieved.

'Yes, she told me all about it.'

'I don't know . . . I think it's just unprofessional to get involved with clients like that. Don't you agree?'

Sarah didn't have time to answer. She and Liz both turned towards the door to see Carol rushing towards them.

'Sarah, something's come up at the office,' she reported breathlessly. 'They said it's urgent, you're to call them now.'

'What is it?' Sarah demanded. 'Did they say?'

'No, they just said to call in immediately.'

Sarah stepped into the lobby and reached for the phone in her bag. In seconds she was through to the office. 'Lucy, what's going on?' she asked urgently. Carol and Liz were standing a few feet away. She realised, too late, that there'd be no privacy: she would have to chose her words carefully if it was anything to do with the story.

'You've got to get out of there,' Lucy told her calmly – too calmly.

'I'll be on my way home soon,' Sarah replied.

'There's been a threat –'

'We can talk later,' Sarah said quickly.

'No we can't,' Lucy said. 'There's been a death threat, Sarah, you've got to get out of there.'

Sarah smiled at Liz and Carol, who were both standing by the door, looking at her expectantly. 'I can't talk now,' she whispered, turning her back on her audience. 'Is the threat specific?'

'What? Look, Sarah, everyone in the office has been emailed a message warning you off the story. It calls you a meddling bitch and warns that you'll suffer if you don't leave things alone. You've got to get out of there and we'll call in the police.'

'I've spoken to the police,' Sarah whispered. 'I'll call you later. OK?'

'No, it's not OK. You've —'

Sarah closed the call abruptly. She turned and smiled at Liz and Carol. 'It was nothing really,' she said. 'You know what things are like sometimes.'

SEVEN

Carol Davis had sounded eager to talk when Vallance had called her earlier in the evening. He hadn't intended a long conversation but she had indicated that without Sarah around she could relax a little more. Although she didn't say it, he felt that she was clearly intimidated in some way by Sarah, therefore it was understandable that she wanted a chance to speak to him alone. He hadn't had a chance to check on Brian Quigley yet, so an opportunity to find out more about what was going on was bound to be useful.

On the other hand, had it been a come-on? If it was it had been entirely successful. His proposal of dinner had been declined politely and then she had suggested that he come round to her place for a drink. There was something quite tentative about her invitation, as though she feared he'd turn her down flat and she'd sounded pleasantly surprised when he had accepted.

As he parked outside Carol's ground floor flat – a Victorian conversion by the look of it – he couldn't help contrasting Carol with Sarah. They were both attractive women, though probably Sarah had the edge, but the vibes they gave off were so utterly different. Sarah was angry, determined and totally focused on her work. Sometimes he liked all that nervous energy, all that focus, but sometimes it seemed designed to scare people off. Why couldn't she relax a little? Occasionally

– just occasionally – he imagined that she was interested in him, and that all the stand-offish behaviour was meant to hide it.

Carol, on the other hand, seemed a much simpler character. Judging by their first meeting, she was hesitating, confused and frightened by what was happening to her, yet she still managed to appear in a lighter mood than Sarah. There was something almost frivolous about her; she was clearly a woman who liked to enjoy herself. He smiled at the thought of what that might mean . . .

He stepped out of the car and stood on the kerb for a moment. Carol's flat was practically on the pavement. Wrought iron railings guarded a rectangle of paved stone that was home to a dozen large terracotta pots full of vivid green plants and shrubs; to one side a path lead to the front door of the two-storey terraced house. It wasn't a busy street in terms of through traffic, but both sides of the road were lined with parked cars and he could see that people were coming and going all the time. Which meant, of course, that there would probably have been witnesses to Carol's attack. If she changed her mind and reported it to the local plod there was a good chance that someone would come forward and make a statement.

'You found somewhere to park then,' were her first words when she answered the door. She had changed out of her dress into a pair of slightly flared black trousers and a tight white short-sleeved top. Thankfully the dark glasses had been ditched too, though the bruising around the eye was still visible.

'Yes, does that mean I'm lucky?' he said, following her into the flat. She led the way along a short hall and turned to enter the first room on the left.

'You either get lucky and get a space instantly,' she laughed, 'or else you spend an hour circling the streets looking for somewhere to squeeze in.'

The small room was home to a double sofa and a matching armchair along one wall; under a bay window looking out onto the potted plants in the front, a television and stereo sat next to each other along the adjacent wall, faced by a fireplace and mantelpiece. It looked cramped but homely, with odd little tables and shelves stuffed away in corners and between the sofa and the armchair. The television was on with the sound off and the pictures flashed light across the dimly lit room.

She gestured towards the sofa and he settled himself down comfortably while she hovered by the door. 'Would you like a drink?' she asked. 'There's tea or coffee if you like, or there's beer in the fridge, or something a bit stronger.'

Booze? He'd had the impression that she didn't drink, but perhaps that only extended to drinking at lunchtime. 'What're you having?'

She smiled. 'Promise you won't tell Sarah,' she cautioned, 'but I was just about to have a drop of brandy. Do you want one?'

'Brandy's fine,' he replied. 'But why be scared of Sarah? You're old enough to drink, aren't you?'

He heard her laughter as she went into another room for a second. 'She's so perfect sometimes,' she called. 'I made the mistake of telling her I wasn't drinking, so if she found out about my little moment of weakness I'd never hear the end of it.'

'Well, don't worry,' he assured her when she returned with a couple of wine glasses, 'we're not that close. I promise I won't tell on you when I see her again.'

She poured two generous measures of brandy and handed one over to him. 'I thought you two were good friends,' she said, sitting in the armchair and tucking her bare feet under her.

'Us? No, we're more like colleagues than friends,' he said, taking a sip of his drink. It wasn't the best cognac in the world, but it was better than the cheap supermarket stuff he had at home.

'Really? I thought you were much much closer than that. But then again she's got Duncan.' She was smiling mischievously.

'Have you met him?' he asked, intrigued to find out what was behind her smile.

'No,' she said, 'but from what I hear he's not long for this world. What about you, Mr Vallance, are you with anyone?'

He shook his head ruefully. 'Firstly it's Tony at this hour, not Mr Vallance, and secondly the last person I was with is now arguing about the alimony.'

'Oh, I'm sorry,' she said, looking away as though embarrassed. 'I didn't mean to pry.'

'Don't be sorry. What about you? I assume that you and this Quigley character are no longer an item.'

'That's right,' she confirmed. 'That was a mistake. I wish I'd never got involved with him. You know how it is sometimes, you know someone's wrong for you and yet you still can't help getting involved.'

'How was he wrong for you?'

She looked startled by the question. 'I don't know, I suppose I just let myself be overpowered by him. You know, some people have such strong personalities and you can't resist them. You must know what that's like.'

Now it was his turn to be startled. 'Why should I know what that's like?'

'Because you're like that too, Tony, you're a very forceful person. You must know that. It's probably what makes you such a successful policeman.'

He laughed. 'What makes you think I'm a successful cop?'

She shrugged. 'It's just a feeling I get from you. I'm good at that, you see, I can sense what people are really like. I can sense what people are thinking, even when they're trying to hide it.'

'And what am I thinking?' he challenged, looking directly into her bright blue eyes.

She held his gaze for a moment and then lowered her eyes. 'You're wondering whether you're going to spend the night here,' she said quietly.

She was right, but then it didn't take a telepath to work that one out. 'And am I?' he asked.

For a moment there was silence and then she lifted her eyes to him once more. 'Yes,' she whispered, 'I want you to.'

It was the quickest seduction he'd ever seen – though who was seducing whom was open to question. What next? Things had moved so quickly that he found himself at a loss what to do next. Kiss her? Take her by the hand and lead her into the bedroom? Screw her there and then on the floor? The last thing he wanted to do was ruin everything by grinning like an idiot.

'I suppose this is something you want me to keep from Sarah too,' he said finally.

She laughed. 'She'd probably hit the roof,' she said. 'Even though she doesn't fancy you she'd still get up-tight about the two of us.'

Sarah didn't fancy him? For a second he wanted to seize on the question, to question her closely to get to the truth of her remark. She'd said it so casually, as though he already knew, or as though he didn't care whether Sarah fancied him or not. 'Why keep it secret?' he said instead, trying not to let his disappointment show through. 'There's nothing between us; it'd be worth telling her just to see the look on her face.'

Carol laughed again. 'I know what you mean,' she agreed readily.

'Anyway,' he said, realising that it was time to make his move, 'that's enough about her. Why don't you sit here,' he said, making room beside him on the sofa, 'and tell me all about you.'

'No,' she said, 'why don't we go in the other room, it's cosier.'

No wonder she wanted to detoxify. Vallance watched Carol lean across and grab the nearly empty bottle of brandy from the chest of drawers by her side of the bed. She was on her third generous glass while he was still only just starting his second. Her laughter was growing louder and less restrained, the booze loosening her up in all sorts of ways. He just hoped that she didn't intend to get totally plastered, though she was so near to the end of the bottle that he hoped that she'd stop there.

'You want more?' she asked, holding the bottle up to the dim light in an effort to gauge how much she could get out of it.

The candles flickered, casting dark shadows over the walls of her bedroom. 'No,' he said softly, 'I'm OK.'

She looked at him and pouted. 'You don't think I'm an alchy, do you?'

'No, you're probably not,' he said, hoping his smile would be enough to make her put the bottle down. Having sex with someone who was too drunk to know it was no fun.

'I'm not drunk,' she insisted, sounding more positive. 'It's just that with everything else going on in my life I just need this sometimes. Don't you? Aren't all cops hard-drinking, manic-depressives with fucked-up lives?'

'Only the women,' he said. 'Why don't you lay off it for a while?' he added, more seriously.

She put her glass and the bottle back on the pine chest of drawers, making the candles which adorned it flicker once more. She said her room was more cosy, and it was, in an odd kind of way. The walls were decorated with framed prints of blue whales breaking the surface of a vivid blue ocean and with desert scenes watched over by crystal clear skies and a fiery sun. She didn't have much in the way of furniture in the room, just the bed, the chest of drawers and a sturdy wooden wardrobe which sat heavily in the far corner.

'You're right,' she said, sitting back on the bed beside him, puffing up her pillows so that she was comfortable again, 'there's no need for that. I'm sorry; it's the pressure, it gets to me sometimes.'

She was repeating herself, but he merely nodded sympathetically rather than point it out. If she was in a bad way he didn't want to make it worse. 'It's OK,' he said, 'we all have our bad days.'

'You as well? Aren't you working on that "devil girl" case?'

It was hard to think of Angela Wilding as a devil girl, but it was what the tabloids had taken to calling her. 'Angela Wilding's a poor little kid who's done something that's unthinkable. She's killed her mum, ruined the lives of her family and thrown her own life away as well. Anyone who thinks that makes her a devil girl is talking crap.'

She seemed taken aback by his vehemence. 'You're having a bad day too,' she said softly.

'You could say that.'

'I'm sorry,' she said suddenly. 'I've let you sit there and listen to me go on inanely and all the time you've had this on your mind. I'm sorry.'

'Don't,' he cautioned. 'You'll start me on the booze again too.'

'No I won't,' she whispered. 'Tony? Can I hold you?'

He had been waiting for a chance to hold her ever since they'd come into the room, more than two hours previously. Her coy invitation had not translated into immediate sex. Instead they had sat on her bed and talked, getting to know each other. She had been right, her room was a cosier place to be.

He turned towards her and looked into her wide blue eyes, finding a nervousness and a vulnerability that was there for the first time. It felt as though the barriers were down at last, and that the pretence and the subterfuge were over. She had lost her smile, and in its place there was an expression that mingled insecurity with a deep longing that echoed his own need.

Her face was soft, her skin smooth as his fingertips traced the line from her cheek to her chin. He leant forward and touched his lips to hers, kissing her softly, letting her warm breath touch his mouth. She made no response and he kissed her again, softly, letting his lips brush hers, his fingers still on her face.

'You will stay with me,' she whispered, her words brushing his lips as she spoke.

He kissed her again, more forcefully, before replying with a slight nod of the head. She closed her eyes and they kissed again, both of them. She moved forward, into his arms, and he held her close, enjoying the warmth of her body against his. He could feel her breathe, could feel her fingers sliding across his back. He kissed her face, and then moved her back against the pillows to kiss the soft, white flesh of her throat.

She was still wearing her white top and black trousers, the ultra-white of her blouse making her skin seem soft and creamy. He kissed her mouth again, pushing his tongue into the welcome coolness between her lips. She touched his face, stroking the dark stubble of his chin with her fingers as he kissed her again and again. He shifted slightly on the bed and he knew that she could feel the hardness of his cock against her side.

He sat back for a second and she looked at him with a half-smile on her dark, red lips, her eyes alive with excitement. She began to undo the buttons on her top, slowly working her way down to expose the ivory lace of her bra. He watched her for a second before sitting up completely to quickly undo his shirt, which he removed and let drop untidily to the floor.

She undid all the buttons but made no effort to remove her top; instead she lay back on the bed, her arms outstretched, pulling him towards her. His chest brushed against the silky warmth of her body as they kissed once more. Her hands moved across his chest, her fingers exploring the contours of his body while he began to bite her softly on the neck and shoulders.

He stroked her shoulder, delighting in the feel of her skin against his, before he moved downwards slowly, curving his hand over the fullness of her breast. Through the softness of the lace bra he could feel the hardening of her nipple, her evident pleasure whispered as a sigh in his ear as his fingers brushed across her chest. He kissed her harder, sucking on her breath, pushing his tongue hard and deep into her mouth as he teased her nipples gently. As they moved the bra straps were pulled down over her shoulders, making her flesh bulge over the cups and revealing the darker tones of her nipples.

She slipped her top off completely and then he pulled her forwards and reached behind her, continuing to kiss her on the throat and neck as he sought for the catch to release her bra. Damn it! The bloody thing seemed to be stuck hard and no matter what he did he could not get it loose. She moved away for a second and he let go, realising that he was making things worse.

'I hate those things,' he muttered as she reached back and unclasped her bra instantly.

She smiled and held her bra in place across her chest, letting the straps come loose on either side. 'Next time I won't wear one,' she said, and then let the bra go.

He looked at her for a moment, feasting his eyes on her full round breasts and the darkly erect nipples at their focus. She looked good and she knew it; the mock coyness in her eyes and the slight pout of her lips were meant to arouse and entice, and it worked.

He lay back on the bed and pulled her on top of him, making her breasts rub across the dark hairs of his chest. They kissed long and slow before he released her and she moved higher, as though she understood perfectly what he wanted. He held her breasts tightly, cupping them in his hands and gazing at her greedily. He kissed first one and then the other, flicking his moist tongue over each erect nipple before closing his lips over one. He held a nipple between his lips and lapped his tongue back and forth, making her moan softly and making the bud of flesh harden still more.

He sucked at her breasts for a while, teasing with his tongue and with his fingers, caressing her excitedly until she pulled away from him. He lay back and looked at her. Her face and chest were flushed with excitement, and her nipples were red and glistening where they had been kissed. She stood up, unzipped her trousers and tugged them down sharply, pulling her black panties along the way. She stepped out of her clothes and stood there, by the side of the bed, hesitantly.

'You look good,' he whispered, unzipping his own trousers. His cock was hard and glistening with silvery fluid that was smeared all over the glans and in the dark hair running down his abdomen.

She climbed onto the bed and reached for his half-clothed erection, touching his cock directly for the first time. He shut his eyes as she closed her fingers around his hardness, easing the stiff fleshy pole from the dark cotton of his boxer shorts. He lifted himself slightly and eased his trousers and shorts down together and then he pushed them off completely, kicking the bundle off the end of the bed.

'Sarah doesn't know what she's missing,' Carol whispered, kissing his ear as she lay naked beside him.

'Don't talk about her,' he whispered in return, sliding his arm around her waist and pulling her onto him. Her body was so pale besides his, and her curves wrapped sinuously around his muscular frame.

She responded by reaching down once more to wrap her fingers around his hard cock as they kissed. He echoed her actions by sliding his hand down from her waist to caress the firm curves of her backside. His thigh was between her legs and as she moved he could feel the moist heat of her sex. He felt so excited that for a moment he panicked, afraid that he would not be able to control himself.

'What's wrong?' she asked, looking up at him quizzically. Damn it! 'Nothing.'

She lay on her back, disentangling her limbs from his, her arms up on her chest, her fingers cupping her breasts sensuously. He moved towards her and kissed her on the mouth softly, at the same time trailing his hand down between her thighs. She closed her eyes and smiled, parting her knees and opening her thighs wider to him. The prickly hairs of her sex gave way to a silky smooth wetness that felt like heaven. She sighed deeply as he stroked her pussy, enjoying the sensation as he teased her pussy lips apart with his fingers.

'That's good,' she whispered, her eyes still closed, as he edged up towards her clitoris. He began to rub his fingers back and forth slowly, concentrating hard on finding the right rhythm for her. She moved languorously, moaning softly, shifting herself higher so that his fingers pressed down in the place she so obviously wanted.

'Like this?' he asked, moving faster.

'Yes . . .' she sighed, and then, opening her eyes at last, she wrapped her arms around him.

They kissed long and deep and then he moved over her, his cock brushing against her as he moved between her thighs. She kept her arms wrapped around his neck, holding him closer so that she kissed his neck and shoulder. He reached down between them and found the wetness of her pussy again.

'It's OK,' she whispered, 'you don't need to put anything on.'

That was good, because he hadn't brought anything with him. He knew it was wrong, but he needed her and . . .

She held him tight as he pressed his glans against her pussy lips. His heart was pounding as she moved onto him, sliding herself deliciously against his cock. She felt so good against him, each tiny flutter of movement was pure pleasure that pulsed through him. He pushed himself deep into her and held it, savouring the sensation for as long as possible. She lay back down, her arms across his back, eyes half closed.

They began to move together, tentatively at first but then with greater confidence. She moved with him, grinding her hips with each long stroke of penetration. God . . . It felt so good, her body under him was so responsive . . .

'Not like this,' she whispered suddenly as he started to move faster.

The sound of her voice broke through and he pushed himself up on his elbows and looked at her. He was inside her still, his cock deep in the velvety heat of her sex, their hips pressed together sweatily. 'Do you want me to slow down?' he asked, breathing hard.

'No, let me turn over.'

He eased his erection out slowly, luxuriating in the feel of her slippery pussy against his skin. He looked down at the last second to watch his glistening flesh slide out from between her dark labia.

'I like it like this,' she said, turning over to lie on her stomach. She curved her back, pressing her backside higher so that her bottom was pertly rounded, offering him a rear glimpse of her sex and the dark button of her anus. He stroked his hand up from her thigh, pressing hard against her smooth pale flesh.

He moved over her again, his jutting hardness pushing up between her thighs to nestle in the damp hair at the apex. He kissed her on the back of the neck for a moment as he sought to push his cock into her pussy once more. She reached down under her tummy and her fingers eased him into her. It felt like heaven all over again as his achingly hard cock slipped smoothly into the tightness of her sex. She responded with a murmur of delight and pushed her bottom higher, pressing the globes of her backside against his abdomen.

He couldn't hold back much longer, each movement of her body seemed to send tendrils of pleasure that pierced through his resolve to hold on. She moved so deliciously . . . He wanted to make it last for ever, to feel that pleasure for as long as possible. As he thrust into her she pressed back against

116

him, grinding her bottom against him so that it added to the blissful pleasure that he felt.

'Just a bit longer,' she begged, moving faster to match his rhythm. He closed his eyes in an effort to block out everything but the pleasure he could feel. She was close to climax, he could feel it instinctively, but he was closer. Her fingers were down between her thighs, stroking her clitoris as he fucked her blindly, madly.

He cried out, half in anger with himself and half with pure unbridled passion. He pushed his cock deep into her cunt and held the position as he orgasmed in a mad rush of excitement. She was whimpering, moving still even as his cock subsided inside her. He rolled away, sated, bathed in sweat and come and the juices from her sex. She climaxed even as he lay back, crying out her orgasm as her fingers plunged deep into her body to fill the space left vacant by his cock.

'I'm sorry,' he said, breathlessly, reaching out to touch her consolingly. It had been so long since he'd fucked that in the end there had been no way he could hold back. Only a few more seconds and she would have climaxed too, with his hard cock deep inside her. Only a few more seconds . . .

She turned over onto her back, and let out a long, low breath. She looked sated too, her face and chest were flushed pink with pleasure, and her body was speckled with jewels of perspiration. 'It's OK,' she said, finally, 'it felt good.'

'I just couldn't hold on any longer,' he said, wanting to explain himself away, afraid that he'd failed her or that she hadn't enjoyed it.

'Don't worry about it, I enjoyed it, really I did,' she said, and she took his hand in hers and squeezed gently. 'You will stay with me? Just for tonight?'

It was just after midnight. He had time to get back to his place but then what would he be going back for? 'I said I'd stay,' he said.

'Good,' she said, smiling, 'I'm glad.'

In the dim light of early morning Carol's room now looked less cosy: the soft flame from the candles had cast a glow that was comfortable and friendly, but the cold light that spilled in through the cracks in the curtains held no warmth. There was no warmth on the other side of the bed, either. Vallance turned over, suddenly realising that he was alone. He yawned and stretched expansively, making the most of the space while he still could.

'Is that you?' Carol called from one of the other rooms.

Vallance sat up. 'No, it's someone else,' he called back.

'I'm just doing breakfast,' she said. 'It won't be long.'

His clothes were strewn carelessly across the floor on his side of the bed; hers had been picked up and dumped by the door. It was getting on; if he went back to his place to change he'd be late for work, on the other hand if he went in on time he'd look a bigger mess than usual. He was also in dire need of a shower, and there was no way he could go into work without that.

He reached over and started to pick his clothes up off the floor, but half of his stuff seemed to have been kicked under the pine bed frame. There was nothing for it but to get up, even if it did mean leaving the relative warmth of the duvet. He yawned again as he climbed out of bed and then knelt down on the threadbare carpet to reach under the bed. He was glad to see that she had his attitude to tidiness too, though he guessed that there were fewer discarded newspapers under her bed than his. He pulled the rest of his clothes out and with them came a couple of magazines and a book.

'Nearly ready,' she called from the kitchen.

He put the bundle of things on the bed and then climbed back under the duvet. He dropped his clothes back on the floor, this time keeping them within easy reach, but the magazines and the book seemed more interesting. The hefty paperback was called *Hitler's War* by David Irving; one of the magazines was called *Radical Nationalist* and the other was *Rebel European*. Definitely not the sort of stuff he kept hidden under his bed. He flicked through the magazines quickly, but there wasn't much to work out about them, the headlines said it all: 'Smash the Zionist Super-State', 'White Pride UK', 'The Holocaust Myth Destroyed' and more.

'Where'd you find that?' Carol said, coming into the room

bearing a silver tray stacked with coffee, cups, a couple of cereal bowls and a colourful array of vitamins and pills. Her hair was wet and slicked back and she wore nothing but a fluffy white towel around her.

'I could ask you the same question,' he said, putting the Nazi magazines down next to him.

She padded barefoot to the bed and carefully put the tray down on the floor before jumping onto the bed to sit up on her knees beside him. 'Oh, these,' she said, looking at the magazines with an expression of profound boredom, 'they were posted through the door once. We get all sorts round here. Jehovah's Witnesses, Evangelicals, Mormons –'

'Nazis,' he added.

She laughed. 'I've never really looked at it,' she said, 'it's not my scene at all.'

'What about the book?' he asked.

She shrugged. 'A friend gave it to me to read, but to be honest it's *so* boring. I don't mind reading about history but really, not like this.'

It didn't add up. Vallance was no expert, but everybody knew that Irving was the leading right-wing historian in the world, the darling of the intellectual *Mein Kampf* set. The magazines alone were easy to explain away, the book alone similarly, but the magazines and the book together were too much of a coincidence.

'You don't go for all this stuff, do you?' he asked, flicking back through the magazines, full of pictures of flag-waving thugs, neo-Nazi symbols and bizarre headlines.

Carol picked the magazines up and dumped them unceremoniously back on the floor. 'I'm not into politics,' she stated simply. 'I'm more interested in what we're doing to this planet, to wildlife and to our bodies,' she declared earnestly.

The politics could wait, he decided. 'What we do to our bodies?' he repeated, smiling.

She grinned back. 'Do you think we've got time?'

He tugged gently at the thick white towel and it came away in his hands. 'We've got time,' he said, gazing at her naked body greedily.

EIGHT

Sarah stared uneasily at her empty cup of coffee and hoped that she didn't appear too disheartened. It wasn't easy; she felt bored and dispirited in equal measure. Instinct told her to pull out before she got sucked in any further; Carol's story was going nowhere, and if there was anything to uncover it was buried so deep under layers of lies and half-truths that it was impossible to tell what was going on.

She had ruthlessly rescheduled her work and was spending more time on the story than it really merited. Her workload was increasing but she knew that she had to reach her decision quickly, much sooner than the six-week deadline that had been agreed with the programme editors. The emailed death threat had spooked them more than it had her; it had taken quite an argument to persuade them that the threat should be ignored and she knew that they were more than likely to call a halt to the whole thing behind her back.

Liz was at her desk, speaking quietly into the phone; her back was to Sarah while she worked with a diligence that Carol clearly did not and could not possess. Why did Liz keep Carol on? What possible use could Liz have for someone as unreliable and as devious as Carol? Clearly there were tensions between the two women, but there was obviously something else going on. Sarah knew that in Liz's position she would have dumped Carol immediately, and if that meant ruining a friendship then it was a price that had to be paid.

Ditch Carol. It was probably sound advice, and Sarah knew that it applied to her as much as to Liz. If Brian Quigley was going to be exposed as a fraudster then Sarah had to do it alone. Carol was a liability; she muddied things rather than making them any clearer. Ditch him, Carol had said about Duncan. Now it was time to ditch her.

She stood up, having finally come to a decision. Liz swivelled round in her chair, covering the mouthpiece of the phone with her hand.

'I'm sure she'll be here soon,' she whispered.

'It's OK,' Sarah mouthed back, 'I'm just going out for a walk. When she gets in tell her to wait for me.'

'OK,' Liz agreed then uncovered the mouthpiece to continue with her long and tedious conversation with a print bureau. Sarah had only been half-listening in, but she guessed that it was something to do with some colour brochures that Carol had screwed up on. Liz needed to get rid of her, there was no longer any doubt in Sarah's mind.

She grabbed her notes, left the office and walked downstairs. So far every conversation she'd had with a potential witness or suspect had been mediated by Carol. She had either organised it or had sat in on it, but now was the time to get away from that completely.

The Newman brothers were the first place to start. Gavin because, according to Carol, he was trying to recruit one of Quigley's people. Or Grant because Quigley had tried to recruit him. The whole thing sounded remarkably petty, juvenile even, but then in an environment as enclosed as the Science Park petty rivalries could easily take on an importance they did not merit.

The door to the G-Man office gave as soon as Sarah pushed. There seemed to be no need for electronic keypads or alarm systems, in marked contrast to the security evident at Software Solutions. The place was silent but for the unsteady tap of a keyboard. She stepped further into the room to find that Grant was in residence, huddled up close to his computer screen and typing in sudden bursts at the keyboard.

Grant was the one that Sarah wanted to speak to the most.

Not having Carol or his brother around was a stroke of luck.

'Working on something good?' she asked, walking over to him.

He twisted round in his seat as though a jolt of current had just passed through him. His dark eyes met hers and she saw the apprehension clearer than anything else.

'Gav's not here,' he snapped.

She smiled. 'I can see that,' she said. 'I didn't imagine that he was playing hide and seek.'

The attempt at humour did nothing to soften the icy expression. He flicked a hand through his hair, brushing the long, dark locks from one side of his head to the other. 'He'll be back later,' he said, and it was clear he was telling her to leave.

Why was he so hostile? 'Actually, it was you I was hoping to talk to.'

He looked surprised. 'Me? Gav's the one who does the talking.'

'And you're the one that does the work,' she said, hoping to appeal to his sense of pride.

'Yeah,' he agreed. 'So what?'

He sounded more like a difficult teenager than a grown man. 'Can I sit down?' she asked.

'If you want.'

She walked back across the room and grabbed a tubular steel chair which she dragged back towards him. 'I don't bite,' she said, seeing that his hostile expression was still fixed firmly in place.

'I do,' he responded instantly. She laughed and, at last, he managed to smile.

'Can we talk now? Please?' she asked.

He shrugged, turned back to his keyboard and pressed a couple of the keys before facing her again. 'Just saving my work,' he explained, gesturing towards his computer.

'What are you working on?' she asked.

'Crap,' he said. 'One of the shitty little jobs that my big brother manages to con people into paying for.'

'You don't like working with him?'

'I didn't say that,' he retorted defensively.

'Then what did you say?'

He grinned. 'I said he cons people into paying for shitty little software contracts. This is crap. I mean any idiot with a machine and a manual can knock out a shitty little database like this.'

'And what would you rather be doing?'

'I'd rather be doing some speed and getting out of my head.'

More teenage bravado. 'If you were really like that you'd be doing it,' she pointed out, 'not sitting here writing software.'

'I do my best work on speed,' he insisted, sounding somewhat deflated by her scepticism.

'Wouldn't you rather be working for Brian Quigley?' she asked, deciding to shift gear.

Grant laughed, his thin facing cracking up suddenly. 'That fat bastard? Why should I want to work for him?'

'Because he's got some interesting contracts from the Ministry of Defence.'

He looked at her suspiciously. 'He's told you that, has he?'

What was the answer he was waiting for? 'Yes,' she ventured. 'But from what I hear he can't deliver. Isn't that right?

Grant was scathing. 'His people are crap,' he declared confidently. 'He doesn't have a single decent programmer working for him. Not one. The number of times I've had to help those bastards out . . .'

Sarah surreptitiously reached into her bag and switched the tape recorder on. 'I bet they don't pay you when you do help out,' she guessed, carefully placing her bag in front of her.

'Not a penny. He's tight, that's why no one who's any good would work for him. If you want to deliver the goods then you've got to pay properly.'

'Does that mean you'd work for him if he offered the right money?'

Grant looked pained. 'I'd rather trash my machine than work for him. The man's bad news. You know what I mean?'

'No, I don't,' Sarah admitted.

Unfortunately that failed to elicit anything but a sad shake of the head. 'So, what d'you want me to talk about?' he asked.

Sarah wanted him to carry on. 'Have you been helping him recently?' she asked.

'Helping who?'

'Brian Quigley.'

Grant shook his head. 'No way. I've never helped him out. I've only helped some of the people that work for him. You know, they get into trouble and they ring me up and I talk them through it.'

'Just like that?'

'Yeah, why not?'

She guessed that solving the problem was the only reward that he was interested in. It was what was most important to him, much more important than money, cars, or any of the other status symbols. 'You like being a guru, don't you? How many other people do you help?'

He grinned sheepishly. 'A lot,' he admitted. 'I'm good, you know, and that means a lot to me. I might look like a sack of shit but I'm smart.'

Sarah looked up at the posters behind him, at the violent images, at the distorted sexuality on display, and then again at him. He liked the idea of being scary, of being weird, but in the end all he craved was respect. 'So, what do you think of the stuff that Quigley's company produces?'

'It's crap,' was his very predictable reply.

'Why, exactly? I mean this is software that's going to the government; it has to be good, doesn't it?'

Grant snorted derisively. 'Just because they've got a shelfload of software standards and tests to meet, that doesn't make it good. Most of the stuff they've written is so full of holes that it falls over. What they've got looks good; it's all nice screens, pretty icons and that shit, but it doesn't work. There's no code under the pictures. User interface is the only thing they've ever done properly, and that's just to convince people to hand over the dosh.'

Sarah fervently hoped that his voice was coming across loud and clear on the tape. She wanted every word captured, every nuance of derision to come across with total clarity. 'But if it's so full of holes then how come he's got so many big contracts?'

'Don't ask me, I know fuck all about that sort of thing.'

Damn! Just when it had been getting interesting. 'But doesn't it seem odd to you that software that falls over so easily can win such large contracts?'

'It's a piece of piss if you ask me,' Grant declared, sitting back and stretching his long legs. His denims were coming apart at the seams and his heavy black boots looked like they'd been steamrollered. Did he make a convincing witness? A man in his middle twenties who seemed stuck in his middle teens, a weird-looking, foul-mouthed yob sitting under a poster that screamed 'Fist Fuck'?

'I am asking you,' she said. 'How do you do it? More to the point how did Brian Quigley do it?'

'It's easy. What you do is knock up some screens. You know, context sensitive help screens, lots of menus, fancy options, the works. And then . . .' He had stopped suddenly.

'And then?' Sarah urged impatiently.

'Sarah, you're here.'

Hell! 'Yes I'm here,' she snapped, turning round to find Carol at the door.

'We were just chatting,' Grant explained, his whole demeanour suddenly changed. His confidence had disappeared, and he seemed awkward and anxious once more.

'I'm sorry I'm late,' Carol said, smiling apologetically. 'I hope it hasn't put you out much.'

Not as much as her arrival had. 'I'll be up in a minute,' Sarah said. 'Can you give us a few moments?'

'No, it's OK,' Grant insisted hurriedly, glancing beyond Sarah to Carol, 'we're done.'

There was so much more that she needed to find out. 'But . . .'

'I'm busy,' he said, avoiding Sarah's eyes. 'You talk to my brother if you like, he's the one who wants to be on the telly.'

There was no point in trying to dissuade him; he had already turned his back on her and was pounding the keyboard with renewed aggression. Sarah reached into her bag and carefully switched off the tape recorder. Why should Carol's presence cause him to clam up so quickly and decisively? The look that had passed between them had been significant;

it was as though he'd been caught out doing something that he shouldn't.

'When will he be back?' she asked, deciding that perhaps she could get something out of Gavin after all. Surely Grant would have shared his withering views on Quigley's work with his older brother.

'Later,' he mumbled over his shoulder.

'Can you ask him to call me?' she said, standing up.

'Yeah, sure.'

Carol held the door open, smiling as though oblivious to the fact that she had ruined the interview. Her bruise had gone down, the swelling had sunk into a red and purple ring around the eye that would fade to yellow before disappearing completely. She was looking pleased with herself for some unknown reason.

Sarah stopped in the doorway and looked back at Grant. He was engrossed in his work, his hands flying over the keyboard as he sat hunched up close to the screen. From the back the strange haircut looked like the result of some major surgical procedure. The long dank hair of one side of his head contrasted with the close crop on the other, as if one side of his head had been operated on.

'See you later,' she called to him, but he didn't even bother to reply.

'Well? What is it?' Sarah demanded, striding out into the lobby angrily. Carol was bursting to share some bit of news, the grin on her face and her excited manner easy to read.

'What do you mean?' Carol responded playfully, wearing the sort of coy smile that Sarah always associated with precocious schoolgirls.

'You know damn well what I mean,' she snapped. Carol's games were becoming tedious and she was not going to allow herself to be seduced by them any longer.

Carol lost the smile. 'Why are you so serious all the time?' she whined.

'Because I have to be. Now tell me what it is you're dying to get off your chest.'

'It's nothing important . . . Nothing important anyway.'

'Then why ruin my interview with Grant? Why couldn't you wait until I'd finished?'

'I didn't know you were working,' Carol complained. 'I'm sorry. Look, it's no big deal, I just wanted to tell you about what happened last night.'

Carol had been in too good a mood for anything bad to have happened. That meant no threats, no attacks and no jitters. 'So, what did happen last night?'

'Oh, nothing much,' Carol sighed airily. 'Tony Vallance came round to my place . . .'

The mischievous smile could only mean one thing. How could she! How dare she sleep with Vallance! For a second Sarah wanted to scream and rage but she gritted her teeth and kept her mouth shut.

'Aren't you going to ask me what happened?' Carol suggested, her wide blue eyes filled with wicked glee.

'I know exactly what happened,' Sarah managed to say in a voice so calm it took even her by surprise. 'And quite frankly I'm not interested.'

Carol shrugged. 'That's what he said about you,' she said. 'It's a pity, you don't know what you're missing.'

He wasn't interested? Well, damn him too! Carol could keep him, she could fuck him all she wanted . . . To hell with them both!

'Sarah? Are you OK?'

'Of course I'm all right!' she said, her voice suddenly loud. 'I'm just angry because you broke in on my talk with Grant, that's all.'

'You're sure that's all?'

The answer was no, but she couldn't say so. All along she'd imagined that Vallance was interested in her. God, she wasn't blind, she could see the way he looked at her sometimes.

'Yes, that's all,' she lied. 'Come on, we need to talk about Brian Quigley.'

Carol looked bored already. 'Do we have to? Aren't you interested in what Tony's like? I mean, what he's *really* like?'

Sarah swallowed hard. 'No, not a bit. What I'm interested in is getting to the truth about this story. I'm warning you,

Carol, if I don't get some answers then I'm going to be dropping this.'

The boss was smiling as he came into the pit, though he looked a wreck. And he was late. Cooper knew what that meant and wondered who the lucky woman was. There'd been rumours about him and Anne Quinn for a while, especially after the Ryder case, but that seemed to have blown over. Had he succumbed to temptation and gone after one of the WPCs? Everyone knew that it was bad form for a male DCI to be screwing one of the WPCs, but then Vallance had nothing but bad form to his name amongst certain quarters.

'Things looking up, sir?' Cooper asked as Vallance passed by.

The unexpected question stopped him in his tracks. 'What?' he asked, as though snapping back to reality.

'Nothing, it's just a while since you've looked so, er, relaxed, sir.'

Vallance grinned. 'You're right,' he admitted, 'I do feel pretty good this morning. Clean living,' he added, 'that's what it's down to. Lots of vitamins, minerals and a good diet can do wonders.'

There was obviously some private joke there but it escaped Cooper completely. The boss's sense of humour was always a bit weird anyway. 'Yes, sir,' he agreed, smiling. 'Anyway, I thought you might be interested in this.'

Vallance took the single sheet of paper that Cooper handed to him. He read it quickly, his smile fading as the significance became apparent. 'When did it arrive?' he asked, handing the statement back.

'This morning.'

'Have you spoken to her yet?'

'No, sir,' Cooper said. 'I was waiting for you.'

'Give me ten minutes and I'll join you,' Vallance said, heading straight for his office.

Cooper looked at the statement again. All that publicity in the papers had paid off for once. An assistant in one of the trendy girlie shops in town had recognised Angela Wilding's photograph and phoned in. She'd seen Angela on the morning of the murder, in fact only a couple of hours before. Angela had been trying on clothes; she'd seemed fine, in good spirits and obviously enjoying herself; she'd bought something and then left the shop. The assistant wasn't sure, but she seemed to remember that Angela had bumped into someone just outside. From the statement the girl sounded almost apologetic; she hadn't been sure about phoning in, but her friends had persuaded her that it was important.

They were slowly piecing together Angela's movements, filling in the blank spaces and building up a picture of her day. So far there had been nothing out of the ordinary, but Cooper was sure that somewhere along the line the trigger mechanism would become clear. They needed to know what it was that had caused her to snap so violently and destructively. In her statement Angela had mentioned an argument about clothes, but she had failed to mention that it was something she had only just bought.

Kids were always buying stuff their parents disapproved of. It was a fact of life; his mum had hated his shaven head, knee-high Doc Marten's and black combat jacket. It was part of the appeal; what was the point of being a skinhead, or a punk, or anything else, if it didn't outrage your parents? Now that he was on the receiving end he understood that outrage. When his daughter Gail came home with skirts that showed her knickers he couldn't stop himself hitting the roof. He didn't care whether it was in fashion or out, she wasn't going to be seen wearing clothes like that.

Had that same scene been replayed at the Wilding house? Had Angela bought something that was too revealing, too short, too flimsy? And instead of arguing it out had she finally flipped and turned on her mother with murderous results? God, it made him go cold just thinking about it.

Vallance yawned into the phone, his mouth stretching over the receiver until it looked as though he was going to swallow it. Cooper was right, he did feel relaxed, so relaxed in fact that he fancied nothing more than a good long sleep. Either that or another session with Carol. He clamped shut the yawn and smiled to himself. Carol. There was something really odd about her, something deep down that was a bit strange but he liked that. It was hard not to think of her on the bed, naked, the towel discarded beside her, on hands and knees while she sucked deliriously on his cock.

'PR–Tech, Carol speaking,' she announced briskly.

Perfect timing. 'Hi, Carol,' he said, still smiling as though she could see it on the other end of the phone. He knew that calling her so early made him look keen. It would have been better to wait until later in the day so that he appeared more cool but then he was afraid that she'd make other arrangements. Carol didn't strike him as the kind to be lonely for too long.

'Hi, Tony.' Her voice was suddenly softer and more alluring. She sounded pleased to hear from him, which was a relief.

He decided not to beat about the bush. Cooper was waiting outside and he was sure that there was someone at her end who'd make small talk difficult – not that he ever found small talk easy. 'Listen,' he said, 'I was wondering about tonight.'

'Yes?'

'How about I take you out for something to eat?'

'I'm not sure,' she said. 'You know it's not that I don't like eating out, it's just that it's so hard finding somewhere that does food you can eat with confidence.'

Deep down, she was weird, there was no doubt about it. 'What about a veggie restaurant,' he suggested hopefully. The idea of lentil burgers made his stomach turn but if that was what she wanted . . .

'No way, most of those places make you suffer for your food. Look, Tony, I'm going into a meeting in a minute. Can you call back later? Say just after lunch?'

He couldn't help but feel disappointed. 'Sure,' he said. 'I'll call you later.'

'Good. I'd better go, OK?'

'Yes, I'll talk to you later.'

Damn! He should have sorted it out before leaving her place. Everything had been such a rush after they'd had sex. There had hardly been time for breakfast; he'd downed a coffee and half a toast and she'd swallowed half a dozen pills with her coffee.

He looked at his watch. There was still time for some

breakfast. Cooper could stop off at a caff somewhere and get some bacon and tomato sarnies before they interviewed the shop assistant.

The day was going badly, far worse than Sarah had ever imagined. First her interview with Grant had been scuppered at precisely the point it had become interesting, then Carol had followed up with the news that she'd bedded Vallance, and then a lunch date had been sprung on her and there had been no way out of it. Liz and Dr Graham had descended on her and refused to take no for an answer. To cap it all Carol had been called away urgently on business, so that Sarah didn't even have the opportunity to interrogate her further on Brian Quigley.

Although Sarah suspected that lunch was Liz's idea, Dr Graham naturally took command of the situation. He had decided on the restaurant, a family-run Italian place a few miles from the Science Park, and had driven them down in his car. On the way Sarah, sitting in the passenger seat, had been sneaking glances at him. He had a good profile, the neatly trimmed beard covered a sharp, clefted chin, with a strong nose and deep-set eyes. He kept his eyes on the road as he spoke, handling the car with consummate skill so that she hardly noticed where they were going.

The restaurant was busy, the buzz of conversation attesting to the good atmosphere and, hopefully, a sign that the food was going to be good too. Dr Graham held the door open and Sarah followed Liz into the welcoming warmth. They were greeted with a pleasant and familiar smile from the waiter, an elderly Italian with a paunch and thick-rimmed spectacles. He had to weave his way through the closely packed tables, pressing in his stomach with one hand a couple of times.

'It's good to see you again, Dr Graham,' he cried heartily, 'very good.'

The recognition made Dr Graham smile. 'Hello, Mario, we're down to three I'm afraid.'

Mario winked at Sarah and Liz. 'It's OK, Dr Graham,' he decided, 'I sit with you and these lovely ladies. Come, I show you to the table.'

'The food here's wonderful,' Liz whispered as they followed Mario through to the far end of the restaurant. Glancing down at the other tables seemed to bear her out; the food looked delicious.

'Thank you, Mario,' Dr Graham said, waiting for the women to sit down, 'we'll be just fine here.'

The table was in a corner, nestling between a table on one side and an over-full coat rack on the other. The toilets were on the other side, but at least they were well out of the way of the sharp blasts of cold air nearer the door. Sarah took the seat nearest the window, glancing at the miserable weather waiting for them outside. The day looked autumnal, the grey sky heavy with dark cloud, the wind cold and unforgiving. It felt as though summer had been and gone in the space of a few days earlier in the month.

'At least we can eat meat without feeling guilty about it,' Liz said, looking down greedily at the menu.

'Carol still on at you to change your diet?' Dr Graham asked, not even bothering to glance at the menu.

Liz shared a knowing smile with him. 'Her and her manias. It's alcohol now, though we all know what she's like when it comes to the booze.'

He turned to Sarah, still carefully perusing the menu. 'What about you, Sarah? Are you a vegetarian or do you wickedly consume the flesh of your fellow creatures?'

She looked up and smiled. 'I eat meat and feel guilty about it,' she admitted, smiling.

'Why feel guilty about it?' Liz demanded provocatively. 'It's not as if animals don't eat other animals, is it?'

Even when she wasn't there, Carol's influence seemed to pervade the atmosphere. Sarah could feel herself being drawn into an argument, and she knew that she'd end up arguing against meat-eating even as she contemplated tucking into *Pollo alla Romana* or *Saltimbocca* or a meaty pasta dish.

'Come on,' Dr Graham said quietly, perhaps sensing Sarah's reluctance to get involved, 'let's not get on to this. What are people drinking?'

'Wine for me, please,' Liz replied promptly, her voice slightly too loud.

'Just a mineral water for now, please,' Sarah said. Something was wrong. Liz was edgy and it showed, her voice was too loud and her words ill-judged. Had she had an argument with Carol?

Dr Graham nodded sharply and Mario came over immediately. 'Two glasses of house red and a mineral water, please.'

'Still, please,' Sarah added. She noted the way that Dr Graham hadn't bothered to ask Liz what wine she wanted. Either they ate together frequently or else he was the sort of arrogant male who went ahead and took control of things regardless. It was hard to figure Dr Graham as that kind of arrogant bastard, ergo he and Liz were used to eating together. Was that significant?

'So, how did it go with Grant this morning?' Liz asked once Mario trundled off to get the drinks.

'OK,' Sarah said. 'He's an interesting man in lots of ways.'

'Man? I always regard him more as an overgrown adolescent,' Liz said.

'But he's technically very good,' Dr Graham interjected. 'Credit where it's due, he's an excellent programmer.'

Liz glared at Dr Graham. 'Come on, Gerry,' she said, not bothering to hide the irritation in her voice, 'we all know that's because he relates better to machines than to people.'

He smiled and turned to Sarah, his dark eyes meeting hers. He looked amused by Liz's annoyance and was waiting for Sarah's complicit smile. 'He *is* like an overgrown adolescent,' she said, picking her words carefully, 'but that doesn't stop him having some interesting things to say.'

'Really? Like what?' Liz scoffed.

Sarah had played badly. The truth was that Grant was interesting because of what he knew about Quigley's work, and that wasn't something she could share with Liz or Dr Graham. 'Well, when he talks about his work you get the sense of someone who finds problem solving a real kick and he's good at it. Underneath that silly haircut there's a real intellect at work.'

'He's self-taught,' Dr Graham added. 'Did you know that? His formal education is shot to pieces but he's taught himself to program.'

No wonder he had been so dismissive of the graduates that Quigley was taking on. 'I didn't know that,' Sarah said. 'That makes him even more interesting. What about Brian Quigley's background?'

Liz was about to answer when her mobile phone buzzed from inside her handbag. 'Shit! I'm sorry about this,' she muttered. The drinks arrived as she retrieved the phone from her bag. 'Yes? What? Hold on a second.' She covered the mouthpiece with her hand. 'I'm sorry about this,' she repeated, 'I just need to take this call. I'll be back in a second.'

She stood up and threaded her way round the table and then walked briskly to the toilets.

'It must be important,' Dr Graham said.

It was an understatement. Liz's face had lost colour the moment the call had come through. 'Do you think she's all right?' Sarah asked. 'She seems really on edge at the moment.'

Dr Graham smiled reassuringly. 'Perhaps things are getting a bit hectic for her at the moment. Anyway, how's your project progressing?'

'It's going slowly,' she said, and it was the truth.

'Is there anything we can do to speed things along? You know, I'm still keen to get our media people involved. This is a wonderful opportunity for us; it could really help to put Epsley on the map.'

He was right, though not in the way that he imagined. 'How did you come to be involved in the Science Park?' she asked, hoping to shift him onto safer ground.

'It's a long story and we haven't even ordered yet,' he pointed out. 'What do you fancy?'

Sarah glanced back at the menu briefly. 'I'll have the *Putanesca*,' she said, deciding not to go for a meat dish after all.

'Good choice,' he murmured. 'Do you know why it's called that? In English it would be called "Whores" spaghetti; the story is that it's so quick to make that a wife could go out to meet her lover and then come back and make dinner before her husband comes home.'

Sarah smiled. 'As I understood it, it was called that because a whore could rustle it up quickly between customers.'

He laughed, showing strong white teeth that contrasted with the dark black of his beard. Carol was right, he was definitely a good-looking man. Was he unattached? She looked instinctively at his hands resting on the table, but there was no wedding ring on display. His hands were like the rest of him, neat, well-kept, strong and deeply attractive.

'Here's Liz,' he said, looking over Sarah's shoulder. She turned and saw Liz rushing towards them, slightly hunched over, a worried look clouding her face.

'What's wrong?' Sarah asked her as she sat back at the table.

'I need to get back,' she said. 'I'm sorry about this, really I am, but something's cropped up that can't wait.'

'What is it?' Dr Graham asked calmly, though his eyes seemed to register alarm.

For a second she seemed lost for words. 'Gavin Newman's spitting fire,' she said, carefully avoiding Sarah's questioning eyes. 'It's something technical,' she added quickly. 'I'm sorry, Sarah, you'll have to carry on without me.'

Dr Graham hesitated for a second, his eyes flicking from Sarah to Liz and back again. He was worried too, but Sarah could see that he was making an effort to appear cool and collected. 'I'll get Mario to call a cab for you,' he suggested smoothly.

The worried frown on Liz's face didn't falter for a second. 'Thanks, Gerry, tell him to make it quick,' she said, though her manner indicated that the suggestion was not the one she had been hoping for.

Something major had occurred and instinctively Sarah knew that it was to do with her. Although Quigley's name had not been mentioned, she could feel that he was intimately involved in whatever emergency had come up. Had he finally found out the truth? Did he know that the documentary was an elaborate ruse to get at him? Her heart sank at the thought. And if that was the case, where did that leave Carol?

'I'm sorry,' Liz repeated when Dr Graham went off to organise a cab. 'You know how things get out of hand sometimes.'

'I understand,' Sarah said, trying not to let her own sudden rush of anxiety show. 'Perhaps we ought to come back with you? It'll be quicker than waiting for a cab.'

Liz looked and sounded relieved. 'You wouldn't mind?' she asked.

The prospect of lunch alone with Dr Graham – with Gerry – was appealing, but then the fear of being found out had already ruined everything. 'No,' Sarah said, 'I'd rather get back and talk to Carol.'

Liz didn't need much persuading. 'Yes,' she said. 'I'll just tell Gerry that we're all going back together.'

NINE

Vallance had made his concession to healthy eating: the thick slices of fried bacon, dripping with oil and thick with ketchup were sandwiched between two slices of wholemeal bread. It wasn't exactly the healthiest food in the world, but Cooper, on the other hand, had stuck to the canteen culture that they both knew and had gone for moist and mushy white bread for his dead pig sandwich. Vallance took a bite and reflected on his morning with Carol. She would be appalled at his choice of food; he knew that it would turn her stomach to tuck into a bacon sarnie, despite the fact that it tasted divine. She had taken at least half a dozen pills for breakfast, listing each one in turn as she took it. He recited the list mentally: beta-carotene, kelp extract, selenium, vitamin C with B-complex, folic acid, vitamin E and something called spirulina.

The windscreen of the car was starting to mist over as he and Cooper finished off their sandwiches. The tea that Cooper had bought had been strong and dark and perfect for washing down greasy mouthfuls of bread and bacon. They were parked not far from the shopping centre where Angela Wilding had gone shopping on the day of the murder. She hadn't gone to school that morning; the school register showed that it was an unauthorised absence, one of many according to her form teacher. Her friends had put it down to her having a period; she had been irritable and snappy for a couple of days previously. They also corroborated Jake Coleman's story that she suffered badly from premenstrual tension, and that it had been getting progressively worse.

Cooper wiped his mouth with his hand, looking as though he'd enjoyed every morsel and could probably eat a whole side of pig if given the chance. He was a man who liked his food in the traditional manner, and Vallance could no more see him sitting down to a plate of brown rice and tofu than he could of Carol in front of a meal of chicken or pork.

'Shall we get going, sir?' Cooper asked, wiping his mouth once more.

Vallance chased down the last mouthful of food with the last tepid drops of tea and then nodded. 'Yes, let's see what we can get out of this girl.'

Cooper started the car and switched the fan on to demist the windows. He waited for a few moments then carefully pulled out into the road, joining the steady flow of cars driving towards the busy shopping precinct. 'I asked my girl about this place,' he said, keeping his eyes on the road ahead.

'What did she say?'

'Says she's bought a few things there herself. A lot of the girls at her school shop there for their clubbing gear.'

Vallance smiled. It was hard to picture Cooper as a man whose daughter went clubbing. 'So it's all loud music, bright colours and lots of attitude,' he remarked.

'Something like that,' Cooper agreed, and the disapproval was writ all over his face.

He and Cooper were roughly the same age, but there was a world of difference between them. Vallance didn't mind dance music, loud clothes or clubbing, not that he did much of it. On the other hand he didn't have a teenage daughter to worry about. 'Do we know how Angie got here?' he asked, switching subject before it got uncomfortable.

'Not yet. It's a bus ride from her house, so we're assuming that's how she got here. When we get back I'll get someone to check on the bus drivers to see if anyone can remember her.'

It was a good line of attack, Vallance thought to himself. If she was travelling outside of school hours then there was a chance one of the drivers would remember her. 'None of her friends have owned up to see her that morning,' Vallance said, thinking back to the statements he had checked previously. 'We need to make sure she was on her own. If she met someone here then we have to talk to them. If this shop's got security cameras we might be able to get something.'

The shopping centre was a towering modernist affair at the bottom of a pedestrianised section of town. A glass and steel construction it towered over the cramped little streets full of shops on either side of it. In the dull grey light it appeared sombre, a miserable hulk that lacked warmth or atmosphere. It would be crowded, of course, but the crowds of shoppers would be as grey and as miserable as the weather and the building.

They parked the car near to the entrance and walked in silence through the dank streets towards a side entrance. The winding lane was lined on both sides with shops, but mostly they looked deserted, and the bright displays and the blaring music could do nothing to attract customers. Trendy clothes shops seemed to predominate, with the odd record shop competing on the noise stakes. Vallance had been shopping there before and he knew that on a weekend the streets were full of kids hanging around, there for each other as much as for the shops.

The side entrance of the centre led out onto a central plaza with escalators running up and down on each side and fountains and plants in the centre. The atrium ceiling was several storeys high and if there had been enough natural light it would have been impressively bright and airy. But there wasn't any and it merely felt cold and hollow, an empty shell of a building that made Vallance shiver.

'It's up on the second floor,' Cooper said, heading towards the up escalator.

Vallance followed, aware of the blank expressions on the eyes of the security guards patrolling in pairs. On a Saturday he knew that the guards spent all their time trailing after groups of teenage kids. Groups of teenagers spelt trouble; what the shopkeepers wanted was kids in pairs or on their own, ready to spend profusely and peacefully.

The shop was called Keg, and Vallance heard it before he set eyes on it. 'I hate techno,' Cooper remarked, his voice carrying the wearied tones of defeat rather than anything else.

'It's drum and bass,' Vallance informed him, listening out for the trademark cascade of breakbeats and percussion.

Cooper did not look impressed. 'It's still sounds like a lot of crap to me, sir,' he said.

The shop window was filled with mannequins in various states of undress, with bits of colourful material barely hiding erogenous zones. Vallance stopped and looked inside; the place was empty apart from two or three young women looking through the racks. The assistants were two teenage girls hanging around the counter, their expressions of profound boredom indicating that they worked there.

'Come on,' Vallance said, suspecting that Cooper was reluctant to go in.

The music blasted louder as they walked through the door but eased off closer to the counter. Both of the assistants looked up at the same time; they clearly knew that the two guys who had just walked in were policemen. They exchanged meaningful glances and then one of them stepped forward.

'You the police?' she asked, her voice raised above the music.

She was tall, slender, with long black hair and brown eyes that were all but obscured by heavy layers of mascara. If she was supposed to be a walking advert for the clothes she sold then she was doing a good job. Her short black skirt barely covered her backside, and her long legs were accentuated by platform heels that added three inches to her height. Her midriff was also on display and her ample breasts were encased in a skintight lime-green cropped top. Under her make-up she might have been pretty, but the bright lipstick, heavy foundation and pencilled eyebrows turned her face into a mask that was not at all attractive.

'You must be Marilyn,' Cooper said, showing once again his superb detecting skills.

'That's right,' she agreed. 'D'you want to go round the back?'

'Is it quieter there?' Cooper asked.

'Not really,' she said.

Vallance grinned. 'At least it gets us out of the shop,' he said. 'I don't suppose having two coppers in the shop's good for business.'

The girl grinned. 'It's not me,' she assured them, leading them towards a door at the back of the shop, 'it's what my boss told me to do.'

They all three walked through the door marked 'Staff Only' and then along a narrow passage to a larger room filled with boxes and clothes rails. The floor was filthy, and there were clothes dumped all over the place.

'I didn't know whether to call or not,' Marilyn said, leaning back against one of the big brown boxes, this one overflowing with belts and hangers. She crossed her legs in front of her and her arms crossed her chest; it was freezing.

'You were right to call,' Vallance assured her. 'We need to know exactly what Angela Wilding was doing and what her frame of mind was.'

She still seemed nervous, her eyes darting anxiously to Vallance and then down at her feet again. 'You know,' she said, 'it freaked me out a bit. You know, you just don't think that the people you're serving could be loopy. I mean, what if she'd flipped and stabbed one of us?'

Vallance bit his tongue. He felt the need to protect Angela, to tell people that she wasn't the monster the newspapers had created, but he also knew that he needed to get people to talk freely. 'At the time did she strike you as odd in any way?'

She shook her head. 'No. I mean she came in, spent about ten minutes looking at stuff then came over and tried on a top. She didn't want it then she went. Half hour later she was back and she tried it on again, this time with a pair of trousers. She liked it better with the trousers and bought it.'

'Did she buy the trousers as well?' Cooper asked.

There was no doubt. 'Nope,' Marilyn said. 'Said she already had a pair like it at home.'

'You've got a very good memory,' Valance remarked.

'It was a slow day,' she said. 'I remember because she came and went like that, and because she tried the trousers on.'

'What mood was she in?' Vallance asked.

She shrugged. 'Normal I suppose. I mean I didn't think she was dangerous or anything. You know, we get people like her in all the time. I just figured she was bunking off school that day.'

'How did you know she went to school?' Cooper asked.

The girl smiled. 'I don't know, after a while you just learn to guess. It's what a lot of girls do.'

Vallance smiled. 'It's what you used to do,' he suggested.

'That's right,' she agreed defiantly. 'So what?'

Vallance cursed himself silently; his comment had been meant as a joke. 'It's nothing. On the phone you suggested that she might have met someone outside,' he said, hoping that he hadn't put her off. 'Can you tell us any more about that?'

The scowl on her face disappeared. 'I'm not sure,' she said. 'I mean I think I saw her talking to some bloke outside but I could be wrong.'

'Did anyone see her?' Cooper asked.

'No. When I saw the papers I asked Trish if she remembered her but she didn't. I asked one of the guards who does this floor and he was gutted that he hadn't seen her.'

'Think carefully,' Vallance urged. 'Try and picture exactly what happened as she paid for her top.'

She looked down at her feet again, clearly concentrating hard on thinking back. 'I remember she paid cash,' she began. 'That's what they usually do when they're at school still. She didn't have any other shopping bags with her. I put her top in one of our carriers and then she walked out. I went over to talk to Trish and then I sort of looked over my shoulder and saw her standing in front of the shop window. I mean with all the display you can't see properly through it but I'm sure that she was there with someone. I couldn't see faces, I know that. Her and some bloke. I think he was wearing jeans and a leather jacket. Black, like yours,' she said, pointing to Vallance's battered jacket.

'Was he there when she came in?' Vallance asked.

She shrugged. 'Can't tell you.'

'Did they walk off together?'

'I don't know, I only sort of looked over my shoulder. I

mean I might be completely wrong, you know. I might have seen someone else or it might just have been the dummies in the window. I know I thought that she'd bunked off school to go shopping with her boyfriend.'

Vallance knew that they were going to get no further with her. It was amazing that she remembered so much given the succession of identikit teenage girls going in and out of the shop day after day. 'Thanks, Marilyn,' he said, 'you've been very helpful. And you were right to get in touch with us; we're grateful that you did.'

She smiled. 'You know, I thought what would they want with me? It's not like I saw a lot, is it?'

'There is one other thing,' he added. 'What time do you think she left?'

She needed little time to reflect on the question. 'Just after half eleven,' she replied, thankfully definite in her answer. 'That's the time I have my morning break.'

With a definite time to aim for, the surveillance cameras in the shopping centre could easily be scanned. Vallance made a note to get that organised immediately they left the shop; there was no point in delaying it.

'Which means she came in the first time at around eleven,' Cooper said.

'Yes, I suppose so,' she agreed, sounding less sure.

'Is there anything else you want to tell us?' Vallance suggested hopefully.

She shrugged once more, curling her glossy lips in an exaggerated gesture that she might have imagined was winsome. 'Oh, there is one thing,' she remembered. 'Will I have to go to court as a witness?'

Cooper raised his eyes to heaven but she didn't see him. 'Possibly,' Vallance told her. 'Thanks, and if you think of anything, no matter how silly it might seem, then call us immediately. OK?'

'There is one thing,' she said, grinning mischievously at Vallance. 'You could buy yourself a new pair of Levi's; you look like you've spent the morning crawling around on your hands and knees.'

Cooper looked dumbstruck but Vallance laughed. 'You

ought to join the police,' he said, 'you'd make a good copper.'

'No thanks,' she responded instantly, 'you wouldn't catch me dead in one of them uniforms.'

Vallance tried not to think of her in uniform. In vain.

Liz remained silent on the journey back to the Science Park. She sat in the back seat of Dr Graham's car, grimly looking out of the window, her teeth clenched tight as though reining in the anger that she obviously felt. Whatever it was that had happened it was clearly something other than a routine office emergency. Sarah could feel the tension in the car, and she knew that despite his outward calm, Dr Graham was as tense as Liz was. As tense as Sarah felt herself to be.

'You were asking how I'd come to be involved with the Science Park,' Dr Graham said, finally breaking the long silence that threatened to engulf them.

It broke through the long chain of consequences that Sarah had been imagining in intricate detail. 'Yes,' she said, glad for the chance for conversation but unable to think of anything to add.

Dr Graham chuckled. 'I saw it as my escape from academia,' he said. 'Don't get me wrong, there's a lot to commend the academic life, but these days there's a lot to be said against it. We spend too much time on bureaucracy, chasing bits of paper, desperately trying to cobble together enough funds to keep going.'

'It sounds depressing,' Sarah said, and thinking back to the depressing Epsley University campus, she could picture just how dispiriting it could be.

'It is,' he agreed. 'And, to be honest, Sarah, it's also a case that no matter how good you are you can only go so far these days. The public sector's so cash-strapped that new posts aren't being created and old posts are disappearing.'

She looked at his strong hands on the steering wheel and felt a surge of attraction for him. His voice was suddenly animated, driven by a passion and intelligence that she found immensely engaging. 'So you jumped at the chance to get involved with the Park,' she said.

He glanced round quickly, a smile on his lips, and then his

eyes were back on the road. 'That's right. It's a much more dynamic environment; there's room to grow here. We've worked hard to attract the funds from the private sector, and we've worked equally hard to gain a good measure of autonomy from the university. Good things are happening here, Sarah, good things.'

She wished that she could agree with him, but she couldn't. She looked away from his handsome profile, suddenly afraid that he'd see the guilt on her face or in her eyes.

'There's room to grow here,' he continued. 'When Phase Two comes on line we would have doubled the units and that means we can attract a few more medium-sized companies to our ranks. What I'm aiming for is a natural ecology here: large companies, medium-sized and a few good start-ups. With a mix and match in skills and technology this place could mushroom.'

He was becoming more excited, painting a vision of the future that embodied everything he wanted and needed. The contrast to his picture of academic life could not be stronger. 'You've made a good start already,' she said, inwardly hating the deceitful words that she had just uttered. What else could she do? Carol had driven her into a corner and now she was stuck.

'We have, we have,' he agreed. 'But there are still problems to overcome. Things still aren't quite right.'

'The ecology certainly isn't,' Liz muttered from the back seat.

Sarah turned round but Liz was still looking determinedly out of the window. 'In what way?' Sarah asked her, afraid of what the answer might be but unable to resist asking the question.

'We need a cull,' Liz said, whispering softly to the window.

Dr Graham laughed. 'Come on, Liz,' he cautioned, 'let's not get things out of proportion. Besides, you can take the ecology metaphor too far.'

Liz looked round, her eyes fixed on the back of Dr Graham's head as though she could pierce his skull with her eyes. 'You know as well as I do, Gerry, that some people have never fitted in here.'

145

Sarah saw him glaring at Liz through the rear-view mirror. 'This isn't the time or the place,' he said. 'I'm sorry, Sarah,' he added, looking towards her, 'but things have been tricky at times.'

'That's only to be expected,' she said, mouthing yet more platitudes. They were in sight of the Science Park, the buildings sitting glumly by the lake, an uninviting vista compared to the ideal that Dr Graham had been describing.

They parked outside the PR-Tech office and Liz was out of the car before the handbrake was on. Sarah's heart was pounding as she stepped out of the car and into the cold air. Things were coming to a head and she felt helpless, unable to assert control or stop things in any way. She knew that the best thing to do was to walk to her car and drive away, leaving the mess behind once and for all. It had been a mistake getting involved and she had been regretting it for too long without taking action.

Liz went in first, with Sarah and Dr Graham following close behind. Gavin Newman was there in the lobby, waiting for them. The pleasant, boyish smile was gone, now he was angry and aggressive.

'She's gotta fucking go!' he snapped angrily, his face a twisted sneer of violence.

'Calm down,' Dr Graham said smoothly, 'we can talk about this inside.'

'Don't give me any more of that shit!' Gavin cried. 'I've had enough. Carol fucking Davis is a slag and she's out to ruin me. You know that, I've told you a dozen bloody times and what do you do? Fuck all!'

'You're right,' Liz agreed, 'but this time we'll do something.'

'No you won't! You're all too scared of that bastard Quigley. Just 'cos he's got the biggest company here he thinks he can throw his weight around. Not with me he doesn't. I'll fucking chin the bastard.'

Sarah stood back, watching silently as Gavin's anger burst forth.

'No you won't, Gav,' Dr Graham said softly. 'Come on, you're up-tight and you've every right to be.'

'Don't patronise me!' Gavin stormed. 'I'm not some stupid

146

kid. Just 'cos I don't have all the chat like Quigley does doesn't mean I'm stupid. Understand? And you keep that slag away from my brother or there's going to be trouble. I mean it, there's going to be mega fucking trouble.'

Liz looked at Sarah and then back at Gavin. 'Gavin,' she said softly, 'I'm going to sack Carol. OK? She's no longer going to be working here, OK? I'll get rid of her once and for all.'

Dr Graham looked surprised but he held his tongue.

'Yeah? You better not be winding me up,' Gavin warned. 'You sack her now. She's up there.' He pointed up the stairs to the PR-Tech office.

'I promise you,' Liz said, 'that she'll be out of here by the end of the week. OK?'

'What about Quigley?' Gavin retorted. 'She's working for him not you, you know that.'

'No she's not,' Dr Graham said. 'She's a freelance, employed by Liz not Brian.'

'Bollocks. You both know that he barks and she jumps. You've just gone along with it because you're all scared of him upping sticks and pissing off to somewhere else.'

'That's not true,' Dr Graham insisted, but his voice lacked the hard edge of truth.

'Where's Grant?' Sarah asked suddenly, aware that the other half of the Newman team was notably absent.

'We had a row,' Gavin said, 'and he's pissed off home. Just 'cos he's shagging a woman for the first time ever he thinks he's a man now. But I told him, Carol's only fucking him so that he can go and work for Quigley. She's using him. I told him that and he didn't bloody like it.'

'Calm down,' Liz said softly. 'I've told you what I'm going to do. Why don't you go home too? Leave us to sort it out now.'

'It'd better be sorted,' Gavin warned, then he pushed past Dr Graham and marched angrily out of the building.

Dr Graham sighed; he looked shaken, his face drained of colour. For a split second Sarah had been convinced that Gavin was going to take a swing at him and she was sure that he had thought so too.

'This is all your fault,' Liz said bitterly, turning towards him with a look of pure venom in her eyes.

He held her gaze for a second and then looked away. 'I'm just glad your cameras weren't here to record this,' he told Sarah.

Sarah didn't know how to respond. Instinctively she wanted to spring to Carol's defence – they were friends after all – but in her heart of hearts she knew that Gavin's accusations had the ring of truth about them. She was the focus of the string of petty intrigues that had just come to a head. Carol had been manipulating everyone, and that included Sarah.

'I wish I'd never listened to you,' Liz said. 'She's been nothing but trouble.'

'Are you really going to get rid of her?' Sarah asked.

'I've got no choice,' Liz said. 'This can't go on any longer. She's pulling this place apart. You can see that, can't you?'

The answer was yes but Sarah could not bring herself to say it. She didn't answer. It was time to leave. She had the perfect opportunity; all she had to do was cite the bad atmosphere and say that it was impossible to make the film. A clean break. At least it would be clean from her point of view; no blame could possibly be attached to her. Except that there was still a lingering doubt in the back of her mind about Brian Quigley's activities.

Dr Graham looked at his watch. 'I'm sorry, Liz, but I've got to go. I've got an appointment with Peter Phillips at the Engineering Faculty office and I can't get out of it. I'm an external examiner this year and I need to be there for this meeting. I know this is bad timing,' he added apologetically, 'but I'll be back as soon as I can. OK?'

'How very convenient, Gerry,' Liz stated coldly. 'Why not let me clear this mess up, eh? It wouldn't be the first time, would it?'

He looked embarrassed. 'We'll talk later, Liz. Sarah, I'm sorry this had to happen. I hope that this doesn't mean you've decided to pull out.'

She almost made the break but the words would not form. 'I'll have to review the situation,' she said.

'Perhaps we can talk again,' he suggested hopefully.

'Yes, we ought to,' she agreed. The attraction that she felt for him had waned slightly; he hadn't come out of the scene too well. Liz's sharp comments suggested that his involvement ran deeper than at first appearance. And he was running out on Liz at a time when the situation demanded cool, decisive action. Was his urbane charm, calm manner and feeling of control really just a façade that ran only skin-deep? Damn it, for the first time in ages Sarah had been attracted to someone and now it seemed as though the qualities she liked in him were just for show.

Dr Graham departed silently, giving Sarah one last hopeful smile before he slipped out of the building like someone caught defacing the walls.

'You don't have to stay for this,' Liz said.

It was true but Sarah felt reluctant to go. 'Are you asking me to leave?' she asked, guessing that Liz would say no.

'It's your choice. I know she's a friend of yours, Sarah, but this is business. I just hope you understand that.'

Sarah appreciated the sentiment. And Liz seemed to have recovered her composure enough to sound confident and in control again. Perhaps she had been expecting worse. Or else she had decided that Dr Graham's presence was a hindrance rather than a help and was glad that he had gone. 'I do understand,' Sarah said. 'And if you want me to leave I'd fully understand.'

Liz thought for a second and then shook her head. 'Come on, let's see what state she's in,' she said.

The door to PR-Tech was locked from the inside. Liz peered through the window in the door but the office looked empty. Sarah peeped in too but there was no sign of Carol. Everything looked normal.

'Carol, open up, it's me,' Liz called through the locked door.

There was no answer. 'It's OK,' Sarah called, 'Gavin's gone home. It's just me and Liz here now.'

'Open the door now!' Liz cried angrily. 'I've had enough of this, Carol. We know you're in there. Come on!'

'Can't you open it?' Sarah asked, pulling hard at the door which hardly moved.

Liz tried but her key would not turn. 'It's latched from the inside. There's no way I can get in. Carol? You've got to face the music sooner or later! Open up, now!'

Sarah peered in again, straining on tiptoes to get a better look through the narrow rectangular window. The office looked empty . . . except for something in the far corner. It was hard to see. She tried again, pushing herself on her toes. A shoe. She looked again. A shoe, and with it a foot.

'There's something wrong,' she said, trying not to let herself be panicked.

'What sort of thing?' Liz asked, trying to look but she was shorter than Sarah and couldn't see as far.

Sarah tried again. In the far corner, protruding from under a desk, she could see a shoe and part of Carol's foot. Unmoving.

'We'd better call the police,' Sarah said, 'and an ambulance.'

TEN

The police arrived sooner than Sarah or Liz had anticipated. Two young constables sauntered in only minutes after Liz had called. Hardly out of their teens, clean-shaven and obviously keen on looking good in their uniforms, they both straightened up as soon as they found two women waiting for them. They flashed smiles at Sarah and Liz but the smiles were stashed away as soon as they realised what the situation was.

Sarah knew that Carol was dead. She could feel it; there was no other explanation that made sense to her. Instinct told her that not only was Carol dead, but that she had been murdered.

The policemen took it in turns to try the door, despite the fact that Liz had told them it was locked from the inside.

'Is there a fire escape?' one of them asked hopefully.

'No. The only other way in or out is through the windows. They lead out onto a sloping roof; can you see?' Liz walked across to the other end of the landing and pointed out of the window at the sloping tiled roof which provided a modicum of shelter around the ground floor offices. The tiles were in good shape, but it still looked a precarious way to get into the building.

The two constables looked at each other. 'Dave?' one of them said.

Dave looked at his partner and then at Liz. 'You reckon it's safe?' he asked.

'I've never had to try it. But there was a problem with the windows a few weeks ago and the glazier had no problems getting out there.'

'Oh well,' Dave decided, 'I might as well go for it.'

His partner smiled sheepishly. Perhaps they took it in turns for the mock heroics, Sarah decided. She watched them absently as they struggled with the window. Part of her felt impatient – she wanted them to hurry up and get into the room – but another part of her felt totally detached. Carol was dead and it made no difference whether it took five minutes or five hours to get into the room; it wasn't going to make any difference to Carol.

Dave managed to scramble out of the window and then stepped gingerly onto the tiled roof. He held on to the window frame and tested his weight on the tiles but there seemed to be no problem. He peered over the edge at the bushes below and made a face at his partner. It wasn't a sheer cliff face and a 300-foot ravine but you couldn't tell that from the expression on his face.

'Edge yourself along,' his partner cautioned.

'Yeah, I sussed that one out already,' Dave responded, reaching out to grab at the frame of the row of windows looking into the office.

Perhaps Carol had committed suicide? After all the door was locked from the inside and there was no other easy way in to or out of the office. But that didn't make sense. There was a lot about Carol that Sarah didn't know, but one thing she was sure about was her love of life. Would a woman who downed vitamins and minerals by the carton really kill herself? Would someone who refused meat, processed food and white flour because it was unhealthy take their own life?

'Can you see anything yet?' Liz called, her voice filled with dread.

'She's there in the corner,' Dave reported, peering in at the window. 'She's on the floor and she's sort of slumped over in a corner.'

'Try and get in through a window,' the other policeman suggested.

'They're probably all shut,' Dave said, trying the windows nearest to hand.

'It's this cold weather,' Liz explained; 'we've been keeping the windows closed.'

Sarah watched Dave edge along trying each of the windows in turn. They were all locked solidly. In which case that ruled out the slight possibility that someone had killed Carol and then made a clean getaway through a window.

'Don't worry, love,' the other policeman told Liz, 'I'm sure she'll be OK.'

'I hope so,' Liz said quietly.

Less than fifteen minutes earlier Liz had been spitting fire about Carol, now she looked genuinely concerned and not a little afraid of what they would find once the door was open. Did she really have illusions that Carol was still alive? Sarah herself did not. She was surprised at herself for feeling so calm, but then there was nothing else for her to do but remain in control.

In the distance they could hear the wail of an ambulance fast approaching. Again Sarah was surprised by the police response; she'd never known them to arrive at a scene so quickly. Was that significant? The thought disturbed her. Carol's paranoia no longer seemed like an act, nor did it seem to be unjustified. Suddenly Sarah felt a wave of guilt flood through her, making her stomach turn uncomfortably. She had come reluctantly to the conclusion that Carol was spinning an elaborate web of lies and that the stories of MoD fraud were either figments of her imagination or else a case of sharp business practice.

'I'm coming back,' Dave shouted, looking over his shoulder at the ambulance bearing down on them.

'We'll have to break the door down,' the other policeman informed Liz sadly. 'It's murder for paperwork though,' he added.

Sarah could hardly believe her ears. 'You're wasted in the police force,' she told him sharply.

'Huh?' he said, looking perplexed.

'Ever thought of a career as a diplomat?'

He looked at her blankly, an uncomprehending expression on his young, masculine face.

Dave came back in through the window. A thin layer of sweat glistened on his face, and his rolled-up shirtsleeves were covered with thick swathes of black dirt that continued up his arms. 'This doesn't look good,' he said sombrely. 'I think you ought to prepare yourselves for the worst.'

'Oh my God,' Liz whispered, covering her mouth with her hand. She was on the verge of tears, unable to handle the situation with her usual aplomb.

'We'd better get in, Dave,' the second policeman said, just as the door downstairs opened and the paramedics came rushing up the stairs.

'She's in there,' Sarah told them 'but the door's locked from the inside. I think we're just getting ready to put some paperwork into action.'

Liz looked at her angrily. 'How can you joke at a time like this?' she whispered, apparently appalled.

'Easily,' Sarah snapped back. 'Now, which of you two is going to do it or do I have to kick the door in myself?'

Both the policemen looked irritated by her remarks. 'I'll do it,' Dave volunteered. He looked around quickly, found a fire extinguisher and decided that it made the perfect implement. 'Stand well back now,' he cautioned. He waited until everyone was ready and then struck it hard against the glass panel in the door. It shattered spectacularly and then he reached in and seconds later the door swung open.

Liz stayed back but Sarah was in before the paramedics. As soon as she saw Carol's face she knew that she had been right all along. A thin trail of vomit leaked from her mouth, most of it splashed along the floor to her side. Her eyes were open and staring into nothing. Dead.

The phone rang as the paramedics hurried around the corpse, checking for a pulse that was non-existent, looking for signs of life that had expired. Liz was quietly sobbing in a corner, comforted by one of the policemen. No one rushed to pick the call up and suddenly the answerphone clicked into action. Sarah was only half listening when it started to record the message.

Sarah recognised the voice immediately. 'Hello? Er . . . Hi, this is Tony Vallance calling for Carol . . . I was just getting back to you about tonight. Er . . . Do you want to give me a call back, Carol? Thanks. Bye.'

One of the constables came over to Sarah. 'Excuse me, miss, but I think we're going to have to ask you to step outside.'

He clearly had not picked up on the phone message. 'Did you hear that?' she asked, pointing to the answering machine, now flashing that it had recorded a call.

'Sort of,' he said. 'Our CID people'll need to check it out.'

Sarah smiled at him serenely. 'I'm sorry, Constable, but that was one of your CID people.'

'Was it?'

'If I were you,' she said, 'I would call Chief Inspector Vallance back immediately.'

'Yeah,' he agreed, 'you're probably right.'

How many cameras does it take to monitor a shopping centre? And how many people does it take to monitor those cameras? Vallance had asked for six people to help go through the security recordings in an effort to establish precisely what time, and with whom, Angela Wilding had arrived to do her shopping. Aside from the cameras at the five entrances, security cameras also panned a number of escalators, the central lobby and the gangways connecting the different stores and levels of the centre.

More importantly, Vallance hoped that the cameras would confirm or deny Marilyn's suggestion that Angela had bumped into someone outside the clothes shop. Both he and Sergeant Cooper were convinced that it was a significant meeting. He was certain that the rage that led to Jean Wilding's death had been seeded earlier in the day.

However, the six people that he asked for had been whittled down to two, Sergeant Cooper and Anne Quinn. If that were not bad enough, Riley, skeletally humourless as usual, had insisted that Vallance take a break from the case too. There were other crimes stacking up: car thefts, burglaries, muggings, a sexual assault and more. As a senior CID officer Vallance was expected to take a lead; devoting himself to one crime –

a solved crime, according to Riley – was a luxury that the force could not afford.

There were times when it was worth fighting tooth and nail for things you believed in, and there were times when it was better to just sit back and accept orders. It went against the grain but Vallance knew that he needed to toe the line for a while, even if it was only because he needed to bide his time until the next occasion when he and Superintendent Riley locked horns.

While Cooper and Quinn had the tedious pleasure of sitting through hours of security footage, he had the equally tedious pleasure of ploughing through the crime reports that had been piling up on his desk. It was hard to concentrate on the minutiae of the routine reports; after a while it blurred and one burglary merged into the next. He initialled reports, made cursory notes and stared into space for ages.

He kept thinking about Carol. He'd blown it, she hadn't returned his call and it was getting late in the afternoon. She had sounded happy enough to hear from him earlier that morning. That could have been politeness on her part of course, but he was pretty sure it had been genuine at the time. What if she'd had time to think and had decided that he wasn't her type after all? Or perhaps there was someone else on the scene. Carol was the lively outgoing type; there was no way she'd sit at home on her own for long. If Quigley was history then surely she would have shacked up with someone else?

He stared at the paper in front of him and realised that he had been reading the same sentence over and over again. His mind was on other things. On the Wilding enquiry, on Carol's allegations, on Carol herself, on Sarah . . . Sarah. He hoped that Carol was playing things discreetly, despite what he'd said; there was no point in flaunting what they were doing. Even if Sarah wasn't interested in him, he was sure that she'd be pissed off about him and Carol. It was her way to be pissed off and he couldn't imagine her any other way.

The phone rang and he snatched it up greedily.

'Mr Vallance? This is PC Dave MacDonald, sir. I'm at a crime scene at Epsley Science Park.'

He swallowed hard. 'What crime scene?'

'A suspicious death, sir. We got your message on the answerphone a little while back, sir.'

'Who is it?'

'Carol Davis, sir. I've called it through to CID already, sir, but I thought you'd want to be informed directly.'

'Good man,' Vallance said, 'I'll be there as soon as I can.'

'Yes, sir.'

He put the phone down. He'd snatched it up hoping that it was Carol and he'd been right, in a weird, upside-down sort of way. Jesus . . . She was dead. A million questions ran through his head, a clamour of voices demanding answers. Was Sarah there?

He stood up, shaking. Sarah had been right all along. Why the hell hadn't he done more to check up on Carol's allegations? He'd done nothing at all about it. Damn it, if he had then perhaps Carol would still be alive.

Sarah waited in grim silence for Vallance to arrive. The ambulance had soon departed, there being no signs of life and nothing they could do but get in the way of the police. The two young PCs had ushered Sarah and Liz out of the office and then blocked the entrance to the building, ensuring that no one else got in or out. More police had arrived, and their presence soon attracted an excited crowd from the surrounding offices; statements were taken. Thankfully both Sarah and Liz were allowed sanctuary inside the building, away from the office workers peering in through the glass doors.

Who were the suspects? Sarah listed them in her head: Brian Quigley was top of the list, followed a long way behind by Gavin Newman and then Grant. Had Liz not been at lunch with her, Sarah would have classed her as a suspect too. The stairs were carpeted and clean, thankfully, and provided a good place to sit and think. From there it was possible to see the crowd outside, and she carefully noted that Brian Quigley's face was not among them. Curiosity alone should have called him out of his office; his absence from the scene was harder to explain than his presence would have been.

And Gavin? His anger had been raw and uncontrolled. Was it possible that he had killed Carol and then paraded his aggression in the belief that it would act as a decoy? After all his threats were all for the future; therefore he assumed she was still alive and therefore he did not kill her. Of course there was still the question of how the murderer had gained exit from the locked office. Gained exit, it was a neat reversal of the usual state of affairs. Gaining entrance was not problematic in this case, not at all.

She tried to block out the comings and goings of the police officers around her so that she could concentrate all her energy on thinking things through. Her notes were still in the office and she wasn't allowed back in to get them; for the moment they were still potentially evidence. She needed something to write on; it was hard to think straight without pen and paper.

Liz was sitting on the stairs further up. She had stopped crying and was staring blankly into space, her face colourless apart from red-rimmed eyes. She had wanted to get rid of Carol, but perhaps she hadn't meant things so literally. Or perhaps she had. Were the tears and the shock just a charade? There had always been something false, something overly controlled in Liz's manner, as though you were never sure what she was really thinking. Sarah tried to find keywords to describe her: secretive, controlled, efficient. Efficient? The air of efficiency so apparent on first meeting had slipped badly.

There was a commotion at the door and Sarah looked up. Vallance had arrived and was at the door, accompanied by Dave MacDonald. The young PC was delivering his report to an anxious senior officer, though in fact Vallance looked as though he was a suspect being given a caution. Scruffier than ever, his face darkened by thick untidy stubble, his eyes circled by dark bags of exhaustion. Even his clothes seemed worse than usual, as though he had dressed directly from his laundry basket.

He nodded curtly to MacDonald then his dark eyes met hers. She could see that his usual sardonic manner had disappeared and she felt sympathy fighting anger inside her. He had slept with Carol. The thought made her blood run cold. He wasn't her type, and Carol had told her that he wasn't interested but for a while she had been certain that he was definitely attracted to her. He had tried hard enough for sure, but then Vallance was probably the sort of man who was attracted to every woman he met. He shouldn't have done it! Why did he have to sleep with Carol? Why?

'Look, I'm sorry, Sarah,' were his first words to her.

God, he was suffering. For a man who came into contact with death and destruction every day he seemed genuinely moved. 'It's not your fault,' she said, losing the anger that had been raging inside her. She felt sorry for him, suddenly, and was willing to forgive him, just for the moment.

'Are you OK?'

The question surprised her. Of course she was OK, she wasn't the one who was dead. She swallowed hard and was surprised by the lump in her throat. Liz had succumbed to emotion, but there was no way she was going to let her guard down. 'Yes, I'm OK,' she said, knowing that her voice carried nothing but weariness.

'I'd better go up,' he said.

'Can I join you?' she asked.

He looked at her for a moment, weighing up the pros and cons and then nodded. 'You'd better keep out of the way,' he cautioned, 'and for Christ's sake let me do the talking.'

'Of course, Chief Inspector,' she said, hoping that her tone did not sound too mocking.

They walked up together, passing Liz who looked at them with eyes that were empty. The door was cordoned off and a path taped off through the office by the Scene of Crime Officers. One of them was carefully videoing the scene, filming every inch of the office in case it proved useful later on. Vallance walked carefully into the room, pointing down at the taped path to Sarah so that she'd not step out of it. He nodded curt recognition to the officer with the video camera and then walked on to the corner of the room where Carol's body was still on the floor, exactly as it had been earlier.

Sarah glanced at the scene, taking in the body curled in on itself, the vomit splashed on the dress, the glass of water spilled violently across the floor. Above her, on the shelf with the electric kettle, the tea and the coffee, half a dozen bottles of pills were carefully arranged in a neat row. If nothing else, Carol had always been extremely methodical in taking her cranky mixture of vitamins, minerals and herbs. Sarah had seen her do it half a dozen times: lining up the bottles, uncapping each in turn to take the pills, reciting the name of the pill as she took it then moving on to the next one. Given the sheer number of pills that Carol took the system was probably a wise move; it would have been easy to get confused as to what she had taken and what she hadn't.

A plain-clothes officer came over to Vallance immediately. His drab grey suit was matched by a drab grey countenance that Sarah had come to expect from certain members of CID. 'The doctor should be here soon,' he reported. 'Looks like poisoning to me, though. One of them pills I reckon.'

Vallance nodded agreement. 'You could be right. No one's touched the bottles, have they?'

The plain-clothes man looked pained by the suggestion of negligence. 'No, sir. The uniformed lads made sure that nothing was touched. We've been keeping everyone out,' he added, casting a quizzical eye at Sarah.

Vallance ignored the look. 'We need to get a list of everyone who's had access to this office,' he said. 'And I mean everyone, from the office cleaner upwards. See if you can find a list of visitors as well, say for the last couple of weeks or so. Sarah, do you know if she kept these here,' he asked, pointing at the pill bottles, 'or did she cart them from home every day?'

Of course Vallance knew that Carol had a supply of vitamins at home; he'd probably seen her with them. 'These were always here,' she said. 'I don't think I ever saw her putting them in or out of her bag.'

'Check her bag anyway,' Vallance decided. 'Her flat needs to be checked as well. If one of these bottles was tampered with then there's always a chance that others might have been too.'

'You're not reckoning on a suicide then, sir?' the CID officer asked.

'She wasn't the suicidal type,' Vallance told him. 'What about

160

door to door? We need to see if there are witnesses from the other buildings. There's always a chance that someone spotted something going on.'

'Yes, sir. I've checked her things for next of kin,' he added.

Vallance didn't hide the apprehension. 'And?'

'It looks like her family's up north,' he said, and Vallance looked relieved. 'Doncaster, according to the address book in her bag.'

'That's right,' Sarah confirmed. 'Her family moved up there while she was still at university. It occurs to me, Chief Inspector, that either the timing for this was extremely fortuitous or the murderer knew enough about Carol to know what pills she'd take in a given situation.'

'What do you mean?'

'I mean she was locked in here on her own when she died. That means there was no one around to help her, no witnesses and no one at the scene of the crime. Either that's a result of good luck or else someone knew that she'd take a particular pill in a particular situation.'

'You mean that someone knew that if she got into a stressful situation she'd take one of these,' Vallance pointed at the three open bottles, 'and that they deliberately made sure she'd get into a heated argument with someone.'

'Sounds a bit far-fetched to me,' the CID man remarked.

Vallance didn't look convinced either. 'We ought to check it out I suppose. It looks like she got through mega-dose Vitamin C, B-Complex and high dose Calcium. Anyone know what they're for?'

'They're for cranks with more money than sense,' Sarah snapped. She was irked that her theory was not being taken seriously. Carol was always expounding her pet theories on food and nutrition; anyone who was around her for a while would know that she took different combinations of pills in different situations. And given her complex of lies and deceits it would be remarkably easy to engineer a violent argument or other stressful situation.

'Maybe the doctor can tell us,' Vallance said. 'I know you've given a statement already, Sarah, but I want you to go through it again.'

161

They walked back out of the office, neither of them bothering to look at Carol again. When they were at the door Sarah turned to him. 'I've got a better idea,' she said. 'Rather than repeat myself I'll give you the list of suspects.'

His face broke into a thin smile. 'You mean you haven't solved it already? You must be slipping.'

'If you'd care to do this without me then I'd be more than happy to go home,' she said quietly.

He sighed wearily. 'No,' he said. 'Tell me who we should be going after.'

From the top of the stairs Vallance could see that the crowd outside the building had thinned out; there was nothing for the rubber-neckers to see and the grey weather was enough to put a dampener on most people's idle curiosity. MacDonald was still on the door, conscientiously guarding the entrance from the few people stupid enough to still be hanging around. MacDonald was young and relatively inexperienced but he'd done a good job, in Vallance's opinion, and was worth keeping an eye on. His partner on the other hand seemed to be along for the ride.

Liz Farnham was still sitting mutely on the stairs, hunched over, elbows on knees and her face cradled mournfully in her hands. MacDonald said she'd taken it badly; he'd also said that Sarah had hardly batted an eyelid. It was true enough; the death of a friend seemed no more than a mild irritant which she had overcome in a matter of minutes. God but she was hard sometimes.

'Let's go outside,' he suggested, realising that they couldn't speak with Liz so close.

Sarah looked down the stairs at Liz. 'Send her home first,' she suggested. 'There's no point in prolonging her agony, is there?'

'We've had her statement,' he said. 'She's been offered a lift home and MacDonald's already asked her if there's anyone she wants called. She says she's waiting for a guy called Gerry Graham. Is that her boss?'

'Sort of. He's the director of this place and her company works for him. He was with us at lunch but he got out of here soon enough when things started looking tricky.'

It sounded like good timing on his part. 'Is he on your hit list?' he whispered.

She shook her head slightly. 'I don't think so.'

He noted the element of doubt in her eyes. 'Come on,' he urged, 'we need to talk.'

The lake was on the other side of the car park, hidden by dense green bushes but still just about visible from the PR-Tech entrance. There was a chance that it was going to bucket down, but there was something about the water that attracted him. 'Down there,' he suggested, pointing to a narrow path threading through the bushes.

Her expression was one of pure distaste, as though he'd asked her to step into something that had just been expelled from a canine orifice. 'Do we have to?' she asked. 'The car's warmer.'

'No, you need the fresh air,' he said. 'When the doc arrives come and get us,' he added, turning to MacDonald still standing sentry at the door.

They walked down through the car park, the dark tarmac matched by a preponderance of blues and blacks in the cars, towards the bushes. He looked back at the uniform buildings of the Science Park, getting a good look for the first time. It wasn't a big place but there was money there judging by the cars.

The car park was bordered by thickly planted shrubs and bushes, dark green and thorny-looking. Up close they could see that there were paved paths down to the lake, but unofficial paths had been made through the thickly mulched borders.

'Through there?' Sarah asked. There was a gap between two of the bushes that wound down the sloping border and opened out onto a gravel path that circled the lake.

'Yes, it's quicker than going the other way.'

He went in first, his boots sinking into the soft mushy covering of bark and sawdust. The bushes briefly fought back, thorny creepers sticking to his denims, but Sarah, following, seemed to escape without a scratch. A few strides and they were down on the gravel path and looking directly onto the lake. It wasn't the most inspiring bit of open water that he'd ever seen, but it was better than nothing.

Wooden benches were parked at strategic points, and at one end the water narrowed and was crossed by a narrow bridge tacked on for decorative effect. A scum of dark green algae floated on the surface, and where that was broken it was possible to see the darker colour of the water underneath.

'She told me all about it,' Sarah announced, her heels crunching on the gravel as they walked towards the bridge.

'Told you all about what?' he asked, a horrible sinking feeling deep in the pit of his stomach.

'About you two,' she replied simply.

'You disapproved of course,' he said.

'Yes.'

He didn't want to talk about it. 'Can we talk about your list of suspects?'

She paused, looking down at her feet as they walked on. 'Yes, I suppose so. There's no point in discussing anything else, is there?'

It wasn't a question that begged an answer. There was no point. She didn't fancy him and Carol was dead. What else was there to say on the subject?

'Carol told you about Brian Quigley,' she began, her voice crisp and efficient once more. 'He remains at the top of the list of suspects. If, as seems likely, he was engaged in something shady and she knew about it then it gives him an excellent motive. We know that she was attacked repeatedly and that he had been violent towards her in the past. We also know that they were in a relationship for a while which means that he would have gained some insight into her behaviour.'

'This is back to your theory,' he said. It still sounded like a very hit and miss way of killing somebody but Sarah was right to pursue it.

'That's right, is there anything wrong with that?' she demanded defensively.

'No,' he hastened to assure her. 'You're right, he's got motive and he's got the knowledge to do something like that. We now need to know that he had access to that office or to her pills. Do you know anything about that?'

164

'We'll have to ask Liz, she'll know.'

He noted the way she said 'we'. It was always the same with Sarah; she assumed that she was investigating the crime. It sometimes felt as though he was merely tagging along as a spectator. 'Who else is on your list?'

'Gavin Newman.'

'This is the bloke she had the argument with earlier today?'

'That's right. His office is downstairs, so it's more than likely that he could have nipped in quickly and tampered with her pills. It might only take a few minutes. His brother, Grant, was also allegedly involved in a relationship with Carol, so he could have found out from him about her vitamin habit.'

Vallance winced. Another person involved with Carol. It was as he had suspected, she wasn't the type to be lonely for long. Were there others? He suddenly had visions of a long list of her lovers being read out in court, with his name the last of many. The newspapers would have a field day. He tried not to think about it.

'What about Grant?' he asked. 'How does he fit into all of this?'

Sarah let out a long, slow sigh. 'According to Gavin,' she said, 'Carol was having an affair with Grant on Quigley's orders.'

It didn't make sense. 'What? I thought that Quigley was public enemy number one.'

'So did I,' Sarah admitted. 'Basically Gavin was alleging that Carol was sleeping with Grant in order to lure him to work for Quigley's company. It makes no sense to me but Grant was quite adamant and a part of it does seem to fit in with what I know already.'

It was a mess and getting messier. 'In that case Grant Newman's also a suspect. If Carol was using him like that then that gives him ample motive. Christ, Sarah, this is going to be a nightmare to unravel.'

She smiled at last. 'Really, Mr Vallance, you must be losing your touch.'

'You're right,' he said sadly. 'OK, who else?'

'There's Liz I suppose. Basically Carol was causing so much

trouble that it looked like Liz's company was going to be destroyed in the process. After we came back from lunch and listened to Gavin's tirade she was ready to sack Carol on the spot. She even said she was going to get rid of her once and for all.'

'I don't think we can really count that as a serious threat,' he said. 'But she shared an office with Carol and I guess she knew her well enough. She doesn't seem the murdering type to me but then who does? Anyone else?'

Sarah shrugged. 'There could be a dozen more for all I know. You know, I don't think I've ever met someone so manipulative before. We weren't even proper friends at university; we were acquaintances nothing more. When she called me up it took a while to even remember her and then she acted as though we were best pals.'

Vallance had received the same impression; he had been convinced that Sarah and Carol were best friends that went back a long way. 'You think she was using you too?'

'Yes, I think so.'

Did that mean that he too had been manipulated by Carol? The thought was depressing. 'What about all this security services stuff? Do you think that's a load of crap?'

'I would except for one thing, an incident on the way to Lyndhurst.'

'You mean when Carol was attacked in the car park,' he said, stepping on to the wooden bridge over the dirty green water.

'No, not that. On the way down I was followed and harassed by someone in a black Mercedes car. It took a while but finally I managed to shake him off. When I got there I didn't tell Carol; she was jumpy and I didn't want to make it worse. In the end I never got round to it and she never ever hinted that she knew, so I guess she didn't know. There was also an incident in the pool of the hotel – someone was spying on me – but she was the one who'd told me to go swimming so I can't rule out her involvement in that. The car on the other hand . . .'

Vallance gazed at the green water lapping at the glistening timbers of the bridge. 'It's weird,' he said, 'but when I went to her place last night I had a look around her street. It's a busy sort of place, with people going in and out all the time. I couldn't figure out how she'd been attacked without there being witnesses. In a place like that I would have expected half a dozen calls to the local plod.'

Sarah didn't look surprised. 'You know, there's a part of me that thinks that Carol should be at the top of the list of suspects.'

He laughed curtly. 'She was suspect all right,' he said bitterly. 'But I still can't say that she struck me as the suicidal type. She was taking enough vitamins to live for ever.'

'It's just ironic that they killed her in the end.'

They heard footsteps on the gravel path and saw MacDonald jogging up towards them. The doctor had arrived and Vallance hoped that he'd be able to provide at least some answers quickly. He waved MacDonald to a dead stop before he got to the bridge. 'Tell the doc I'll be up in a minute,' he called.

MacDonald nodded an acknowledgement and then turned back the way he had come.

'What are you going to do now?' Sarah asked, leaning back against the bridge to stare across at the building site on the other side of the lake.

He had already decided on his first course of action. 'We're looking out for Gavin Newman now,' he reported. 'He'll be pulled in for questioning as soon as we get him. I'm not sure if Quigley's still around; if he is then I'll be up to talk to him as soon as I've got the preliminary report from the doc. I'll need to talk to the other Newman as well, but he can wait until I've finished with his brother. What about you?'

She closed her eyes for a moment and her face was revealed as a picture of exhaustion. She'd been playing it so cool that it had seemed as though Carol's death had not touched her. Maybe she wasn't so calm beneath the surface. 'I don't know yet,' she admitted.

'Look, why don't you go home?' he suggested softly, bracing himself for an angry rebuff.

'I do feel tired,' she said, looking away from him. 'But I'll be back again tomorrow. You'll need a fuller statement, won't you?'

'Of course,' he said, keeping his voice neutral in case she suddenly changed her mind.

ELEVEN

The doctor was still examining Carol's body when Vallance and Sarah entered the office. Cox, the CID man first on the scene, seemed to be disturbed by Sarah's presence once more. He looked at her with an expression that mixed curiosity with barely concealed hostility. Did he know who she was? Vallance had already been warned off from working with Sarah by both Riley and Larkhall, the unfunniest double act in the history of the police force.

'Any news on Gavin Newman yet?' Vallance asked, making a point of keeping Sarah beside him as he asked Cox the question.

'He's not gone back to his flat,' Cox reported stonily. 'His details have been circulated so it can't be too long before he turns up.'

The doctor – a slight figure in baggy white chinos, a tatty grey linen jacket and small round glasses on a face that looked barely old enough to need shaving once a month – straightened up suddenly.

'Chief Inspector Vallance?' he asked, his eyes darting nervously from Vallance to Sarah.

Vallance smiled. The doc clearly couldn't decide which of them was the DCI. Sarah, power-dressed and businesslike, looked the part, but then female DCIs were few and far between; he knew he himself looked less like CID than anyone else in the room apart from the corpse. 'That's right,' he said, putting the poor man out of his misery. 'What have you got for us?'

The doctor seemed to relax. 'I think it's a clear case of cyanide poisoning, Chief Inspector,' he said, smiling, 'an almost text-book case.'

'This must be your first,' Vallance guessed.

The doctor shook his head. 'No, I've dealt with a couple so far. Both of them were industrial accidents though, nothing like this. It's not much,' he added, 'but she would have lost consciousness fairly quickly, within a minute or so. Death would have followed a few minutes later, depending on the dose.'

Sarah listened in silence, her face betraying no emotion. Vallance expected that she would have questions to ask but there was nothing.

'Do you think that her vitamins could have been spiked with the stuff?' Vallance asked.

'Almost certainly. Sodium or potassium cyanide salts could easily be injected into some of those,' he said, pointing to a tube of vitamin E capsules. 'Once ingested the cyanide salts would have reacted with the hydrochloric acid in her stomach to release hydrogen cyanide gas, which almost guarantees death. On an empty stomach it would have taken a few minutes for the process to happen.'

'She missed lunch,' Sarah said.

The doctor smiled. 'In that case it would have been quicker. I would guess that if the beta-carotene capsules' – he pointed to the first jar in the row of vitamins – 'were taken first then by the time she'd reached half way through the rest of them the reaction would have been well under way.'

'How easy is it to get hold of the stuff?'

The doctor shrugged. 'There are dozens of industrial uses for cyanide salts. It's used a lot in plating and in metal working and I imagine that it wouldn't be too difficult for someone to acquire a few grains of it. But it's not the sort of thing you can walk into a pharmacy and buy over the counter.'

Vallance looked to Cox and to Sarah but they had no further questions. 'Is there anything else you can say at this stage?' he asked.

'Not really. I'm sure that my findings will be borne out by the autopsy. You might also suggest that your forensics people take extra care. If there's more cyanide salts in the other pills then they need to take precautions.'

Vallance thanked the doctor and then walked with Sarah to the door. 'At least it would have been quick,' he said. It sounded like a pointless thing to say. 'Are you OK?'

'Yes, I'm fine,' she insisted. 'I'm going to go home now, but I'll be back tomorrow. Will you keep me informed if there are any new developments?'

What did she expect? That Quigley, or either of the Newmans, would get down on their knees and confess? 'Of course,' he agreed, knowing that there'd be nothing happening until the next day, if then.

Sarah's feet felt like lead weights as she shuffled through the front door of her flat. She was exhausted, the strains of the day transformed into aches and pains that surged through her tired body in long, draining waves. The long drive up from Epsley had been the last straw. It had been a struggle to focus on the road ahead, and an even bigger fight to keep back the tears that kept welling up inside her. She wanted to cry, to let out the hot tears that burned her up, and yet she couldn't do it. There was something wrong with her – why else couldn't she let herself express the emotion that was a natural response to a friend's death?

She dropped her bag by the door and listened for a second. Silence. Thank God that Duncan was out. She couldn't face him, she couldn't face anyone. Her feet burned like fire when she kicked her shoes off, the carpet feeling cool in comparison. She knelt down to pick up her discarded shoes and then stopped. She was dog tired, too exhausted to do anything but slump into bed, and yet here she was tidying up. What was wrong with her? Why couldn't she let go? Why couldn't she just let go even for a second?

The shoes stayed on the floor by the door. To hell with it, Duncan could pick them up. No! They could stay there all bloody night. The idea made her recoil. She hated the idea of her shoes laying discarded by the door all night. It offended her somehow. No matter how bad she felt she couldn't cope with the idea of things being out of place. Out of place. She felt dizzy and reached for the wall to steady herself.

The front room was cool and dark, as though the evening sky had invaded through the big square window that dominated the space. She walked barefoot across the polished floor and dropped like a dead weight onto the sofa that accepted her lovingly. She curled her feet under her and grabbed a heavy cushion which she clutched tightly around her chest.

Poor Carol. How long had it taken her to form that thought? To mentally utter the words that should have been her first reaction? Hell, maybe she was the one that was weird, not Carol. At least Carol, for all her faults, had been able to express her emotions and to act upon them. Poor Carol. The doctor's report was brief and to the point: cyanide poisoning. It had to have been a high dose; Carol had died quickly, she hadn't even had time to call for help.

Vallance had accepted the news with outward equanimity, an attitude that mirrored Sarah's completely. It was a front in his case though; she knew him well enough to sense the anguish under the impassive exterior. What about her? They all thought she was a heartless bitch, Sarah knew that. It was how would she have described herself: cold, emotionless, detached, abnormal. All she cared about was work, all she was interested in was her precious career. It was what she thought and it was what everyone else felt about her too. No wonder Vallance had leapt into bed with Carol.

No! She wasn't going to think about that. She didn't want to think about that. She didn't want the anger rising up again. But it was still there, a livid, painful fury that she could not control. How could they? Poor Carol. Poor Vallance. Poor Sarah? No, not ever.

The tears began suddenly, flowing from her eyes as though they fell from outside of her. She inhaled in jagged bursts, unable to make a sound as the tears made tracks down her face. She felt wretched. Why did it have to be like this? She knew that if she'd wept in public, sobbing on the stairs like Liz, then everyone would have thought better of her. It was what they wanted, to see her cry, to prove to them that she was human too. To prove to them that under her business-like persona she was still a woman. A woman.

The silence was broken and she realised that the awful wail came from her. There, were they all happy now? She dug her long painted nails into the cushion as she tried to contain the pain. She felt so many things: anger, sorrow, regret, self-pity, self-loathing, hatred. She hated Carol. She hated Vallance. She hated herself.

Poor Carol. What a wretched, stupid, waste of a life. She didn't deserve to die. She was crazy, manipulative, deluded perhaps, but she didn't deserve to die. Sarah tried not to think of Carol suffering, but the doctor had spoken of violent convulsions leading to death and it was hard not to picture her writhing in pain on the floor. Had she called out? Had she, in the few minutes before losing consciousness, called out for help only to find that her activities had left her friendless and alone?

'Sarah? What's wrong?'

She looked up, startled by the unexpected appearance of Duncan. Ditch him. Carol's advice came through immediately. She could almost hear Carol's voice, loud and clear and without doubt. Ditch him. She looked at him and more tears tumbled from her eyes, unbidden and alien and yet inexplicably pouring from her eyes.

'It's OK,' he whispered, rushing over to sit beside her, a protective arm around her shoulders. She could smell the trace of the cologne he wore to work, a faint echo of it still clinging to his dark grey jacket. He drew her closer, his strong, masculine hands holding her with a softness and a tenderness that she did not deserve.

'What's wrong?' he whispered, his hot breath touching her ear. She tried to speak but couldn't, words would not form inside her skull. She felt too tired to speak, too weary to do anything but sob. God, she wanted to sleep. She wanted to sleep away the long, terrible day and all that had happened during it.

He kissed her softly on the cheek and she gave in to him, finally allowing her head to rest against his chest. She snuggled down in the folds of his jacket until she could feel his heart beating deep in his chest. He was alive. Carol was dead.

'Did something happen at work?' he asked, and she felt the words in his chest.

She closed her eyes and nodded. No more tears now, she told herself. Stop it now.

'It's OK,' he whispered, 'you can cry if you want to.'

It wasn't OK. He was wrong but she was too tired to argue.

For a long while he just held her, his warmth becoming hers, his heartbeat hers. She needed him, she needed to feel his arms around, protecting her, holding her, accepting her for what she was.

'Are you OK now?' he asked after what seemed an age.

'I'm tired,' she whispered.

'Let's go to bed,' he suggested.

Sleep. She longed for it. Slowly she disentangled herself from him, the sudden loss of his warmth making her shudder. She felt so cold inside. There was nothing left now, the emotion had been drained, like some awful wound that needed to bleed away the blood and pus.

She stood up and felt dizzy again but he was there to hold her and to guide her to their room. For once he was quiet, his inane chatter and constant whine of complaint completely silenced. It was what she needed from him and his unaccustomed silence only served to remind her how little she got it.

She sat on the bed and undressed quickly, her hands moving automatically of their own volition. She had stripped down to her knickers and bra before she realised that he was also undressing. Her eyes met his and he half smiled to her. He was naked, standing in front of her, his penis half erect and nestling in a bed of tightly curled blonde hair.

'Come on,' he said softly, 'let's get into bed.'

Vallance and Carol. Carol and Vallance. She felt the anger stir once more and she wondered why it had to be that way. What difference did it make to her if Vallance had fucked Carol?

Duncan sat beside her and softly kissed her on the shoulder, his lips cool against her pale skin. She turned to him and his lips were there, waiting for her, ready to capture her mouth. They kissed tenderly, without passion or excitement. Not a lover's kiss. But then not the kiss of a friend either. He put his arm on her shoulder and pulled her closer, pressing their bodies together and they kissed again. A harder kiss, more intent, more possessive perhaps.

'Carol's dead,' she whispered, pulling away from him suddenly.

His blue eyes registered shock and confusion. She saw him trying to work out what to do next. He didn't know. Desire thwarted, what next?

'She was poisoned,' she added.

'Jesus Christ, Sarah,' he said, looking away from her. 'Why didn't you tell me?'

She felt cold once more. Alone. Alive. She reached for his hand and curled her fingers in his and squeezed tightly. He squeezed back and then turned and kissed her again. This time she responded, kissing him back, opening her mouth to his tongue. They kissed again and again, his arms circling her and pulling her close to his chest. She held onto him tightly, her fingers stroking the smooth, warm flesh of his back.

He released her and she unhooked her bra before sliding into bed. It was cool under the duvet, the cotton sheet almost icy against her skin. She was alive. He climbed into bed beside her and embraced her again, his mouth planting moist kisses along her shoulder and neck before pressing hard against her lips. She rushed her hand through his thick mane of golden hair, luxuriating in the feel of it under her fingers. She was alive and she didn't want to be alone.

She moaned softly as his fingers brushed enticingly across her hardening nipples. He kissed her on the throat again and she knew that he would work his way down, the way he always did when they made love. She clung to him, wanting him to kiss her on the mouth again, to hold her longer and harder, to press his erection against her thigh, to wait for her desire to grow to match his.

He slipped from her arms and snuggled down deeper under the duvet, each hand cupping a breast, his thumbs poised like trigger fingers over her nipples. He kissed her once between the breasts and then began to lick and suck each nipple in turn, his hot mouth and wet lips sliding excitingly from one to the other. It felt good, her nipples bulging hard between his lips, but the pleasure lacked the edge of excitement and spontaneity that she secretly longed for.

She moaned softly and lay back, one arm outstretched above her head and the other stroking the back of his neck as he toyed with her breasts. Waves of pleasure flooded through her as his fingers and mouth alternated until her nipples were hard, erect points that seemed to connect with the wet heat between her thighs. Why didn't he kiss her on the mouth again? Why didn't he take her and push her down hard on the bed and kiss her on the mouth with a passionate, voracious violence?

With his mouth still on her breast his hand slipped down between her thighs, moving with practised precision to rub against her knickers at the opening of her sex. She parted her thighs a little, hoping that he would slow down, desperately wanting him to deviate from the strict routine that he always adhered to. He eased the lacy fabric between her labia, pushing gently so that her moisture rubbed onto her knickers, her heat suffusing through it.

'Slow down . . .' she whispered softly, but either he didn't hear her or he didn't care.

His fingers pushed her knickers aside, rudely exposing her sex for a moment. She sighed, excited by that simple act, aroused by it in a way that his rough ministrations could never hope to emulate. She parted her thighs, sliding them apart just as his fingers eased between her pussy lips. She was wet, open, her clitoris throbbing with a delicious ache of desire. His fingers slipped up and down slowly, teasing the wetness from within, becoming slippery with her juices and exciting her still further.

No! His fingers pressed into her, deeper, harder, a surrogate erection that sought to possess her when she wasn't ready. She squirmed away from him, trying to wriggle free of his invasive fingers but he mistook her action for pleasure and carried on. His thumb pushed higher, searching for her clit while he penetrated with his fingers. She was breathing hard, her pleasure disturbed by him rather than enhanced. At some point he eased off, deciding to concentrate on her clit, stroking it hard, coating it with the juices on his fingers. It felt better and she closed her eyes, letting the annoyance subside and the pleasure expand to take its place.

He stroked her lovingly, just the way she liked, teasing her with long slow strokes across her pussy lips up to the apex of her sex. She moved down further, opening herself to him, lying back to let the pleasure soar through her body. His breath was hot and fast across her chest, the slight stubble on his chin delightfully rough against her skin. She could breathe his animal scent, able at last to smell the sweat that bathed his body and which had been masked by his cologne.

'Shall I fuck you now?' he whispered hoarsely, but he was moving into place before she had a chance to answer. It was a formula, a question that he asked in order to excite himself rather than because he wanted an answer.

He moved into place between her thighs until they were face to face, his body pressed down on her, his hardness pushing against the top of her thigh. He kissed her on the mouth and she tasted the perspiration on his lips. He reached down and took his erect flesh in his hand and guided it between her pussy lips. She closed her eyes and gently he pushed into her, sliding his silky smooth hardness into the velvety folds of her sex.

She knew that it would be over soon. She wanted it to go on for longer, for him to give her the pleasure she needed so much. He began to move slowly in and out, his rhythm unmatched by her own movements. His eyes were closed and she wondered what he saw behind them. She was still wet, and each time he penetrated she sighed with a frisson of sensation that wickedly reminded her of the pleasure she was capable of enjoying. He was panting softly, fucking her faster, harder, deeper while she lay back and tried to match his stroke.

At last he slowed down slightly, and she relaxed too. She ground her hips against him, pushing herself into his downward stroke, pushing her pubis against his cock. It was better. She was breathing harder too, the pleasure building faster too, climbing to the peak she longed for. They were both moving together, faster and faster, a perfect match so that their pleasure was entwined, indivisible.

Carol was dead. She was alive, and so was Vallance. Vallance. His image filled her head, taking her by surprise. For a split second he was above her, his hardness pushing deep inside her . . . She cried out suddenly, the pleasure breaking through everything so that there was nothing but pure sensation. She clung tightly to him, tightly, her nails digging into his warm, sweaty flesh. His guttural cry was there, somewhere, and she knew that he had come too.

Duncan rolled away from her. Duncan.

She lay back breathing hard, her body still tingling with pleasure. Why did it have to end so suddenly? Why didn't he hold her? Why did he have to roll away as though she were nothing?

Ditch him. Carol's voice was there in her head. Ditch him. Carol was right, it was the only thing to do.

Vallance knew the rules. He was personally involved with the murder victim, therefore he should have nothing to do with the investigation. Not only was he a witness, he was also potentially a suspect. Common sense said that he should report everything directly to Riley, or even to Chief Superintendent Larkhall, and then make a formal statement to the investigating officer appointed in his place. It wasn't as if he could keep things hidden for very long; after all his telephone message to Carol had been heard by the two officers first on the scene. And if he did try to keep things hidden there'd be nasty stuff hitting the fan once the news got out.

Vallance knew all of that, but it was getting late and he felt no inclination to let go of the case. It was after nine but he wanted to hold on for a while longer to interview Quigley and the Newman brothers, and then, he promised himself, he'd write a preliminary report to hand over to Riley or the Chief Super the next day. There's still be hell to pay but he'd take the aggravation no matter what happened.

Now, as he sat at his desk, he looked at the reports still piled high in front of him. The routine stuff was still waiting, and it would carry on waiting for a while longer. He hadn't joined the police to push paper around, no matter what that meant in terms of his career.

There was a report that had come in from Sergeant Cooper but it was inconclusive. With hours of tape still to scan they had, finally, a definite time of arrival at the shopping centre for Angela, and, as expected, she had been on her own. She was seen on film going into a couple of shops but there were gaps in the sequencing. He and Quinn were still trying to get an exit time from the centre, and they were still searching for the elusive person she had met outside the clothes shop. Cooper had added a note to his report saying that he hoped that they would be finished by lunch-time the following day. Which was good for the Wilding case but it meant that neither officer would be available for the investigation into Carol's murder.

All of which meant that he needed to act and to act quickly. There was still no sign of Gavin Newman; he had yet to return to his flat, nor did his girlfriend know where he was. He had driven from the Science Park in a raging fury and then gone to ground. According to his girlfriend it wasn't how he behaved normally, but nevertheless she'd supplied them with a list of wine bars and pubs where he might be getting out of his head. The list had gone to Terry Cox, who, along with Karen Greenwood, was doing the rounds looking for him.

There was also no sign of Brian Quigley. The people in his office said that he'd left earlier than usual. His secretary had no idea where he had gone, his diary showed no appointments for that afternoon or evening, but she had also added that this was quite normal for him. He too had gone to ground. It was a pity because of all the people on Sarah's list he was the one that Vallance wanted to talk to first. It would have to wait until the morning, however.

Of the three major suspects one had been easy to track down. Grant Newman was at home, apparently blissfully un-aware of the police parked at the end of his road. It wasn't clear whether he'd been around when his brother had the argument with Carol, but at the very least he'd give them an insight into the triangular relationship between the three of them.

Vallance stood up and walked to the door. He took a look out into the pit but there were pitifully few bodies around. PC Matthews was still at his desk, diligently working at building up his overtime hours. Vallance needed a driver – there was no way he fancied driving around any more that day – but not Matthews. The young PC was still fairly new to CID and unfortunately he looked like he was going to take the paper-chaser's path to career advancement. Who else? At that instant PC Chiltern wandered in, looking as if he didn't have a worry in the world. He would do, Vallance decided.

'Coffee, guv?' Chiltern offered obligingly as Vallance approached him.

'On the way,' Vallance agreed.

Chiltern smiled as he stood up and grabbed his jacket off the back of his chair. 'On the way where, guv?'

Vallance stopped himself answering. There was no point in broadcasting the news; with PC Matthews about the story would go directly to DI Dobson and then on to Riley. 'Come on,' he said, 'you're on driving duty today.'

Chiltern fell into step, obviously happy enough to do as ordered. Vallance liked him, even if he wasn't the smartest cop in the world. Chiltern was savvy enough to understand the value of loyalty, a commodity that Vallance often felt was in short supply in his CID team.

The night sky offered hope that the following day would show some blue behind the clouds; perhaps they'd even get a glimpse of the sun again. There was still a good breeze but for the first time in days it looked as though the miserable weather was going to clear.

Vallance opened the passenger side door and threw the car keys to Chiltern on the driver's side. 'Right,' he said, leaning on the roof of the car, 'we're going visiting. Grant Newman's first on our list. He's got a flat in Tregarthen Place, not far from the Science Park.'

'Carol Davis,' Chiltern surmised. 'I saw the reports come in earlier, sir, and the details on the Newman brothers and the other bloke we're looking for.'

Vallance settled down comfortably in the passenger seat. Chiltern was the garrulous type, but he also had the nous to keep it shut when necessary. 'Good,' he said, 'don't forget the coffee on the way.'

The traffic was dying down, and what was left of it was mostly headed into town. Chiltern did the decent thing and grabbed coffee and food at one of the local takeaways before heading out south. He drove fast and efficiently, enjoying the power of the car without pushing it for the sake of it. He was learning, Vallance noted; there had been a time when every trip out with Chiltern had been an invitation for traffic division to settle scores.

Tregarthen Place was home to two rows of Victorian terraced houses, half of them in the process of gentrification and the other half going to rot. A railway track backed onto the houses on one side of the road, the line banked high above the tumbledown back gardens that were clearly visible as soon as Chiltern steered the car into the road. The other end was blocked off, a dead end that was home to a builder's skip overflowing with the inevitable detritus of home improvement and to an abandoned car going slowly to rust and oblivion.

Chiltern had radioed on ahead and their arrival was expected, and as soon as they parked one of the cops on sentry duty wandered across the street to greet them.

'He's in the house over there, sir,' the young WPC reported, indicating with a curt nod of the head to one of the houses with the railway line at the end of the garden. The front garden was a fenced-in square of nettles and thorns that guarded the entrance to a faded green porch and the downstairs windows were blacked out with thick drapes.

'Any sign that he's got company?' Vallance asked, scanning the parked cars in case Gavin had decided to make peace with his younger sibling.

Chiltern made the connection too. 'No sign of his brother's motor,' he remarked.

'There's been no movement in or out of the place since we arrived,' the WPC reported.

'In that case it's time he did have some company,' Vallance

said. 'I don't expect him to do anything stupid, but if you see him doing a runner then break his legs.'

The WPC smiled. 'With pleasure, sir. He looks like a right weird one. Hair cropped on one side and long on the other, and there's some god-awful noise blaring from the front room.'

Vallance crossed the road with Chiltern falling into step. The front gate was wedged open, the hinges had given up a long time ago and the weeds were growing between the mossy timbers which were rotting into damp soil. A paved path was fighting a losing battle with the nettles, dandelions and grass encroaching from the garden and pushing up between the cracked paving stones. The glass in the front door was cracked and taped over with thick brown masking tape.

The WPC was right about the noise. It was blasting out at full volume, an angry tirade of guitar chords, white noise, distortion and tortured screams that made Vallance smile. It was the sort of thing he'd listened to in his teens, the dark ranting and violent noise a perfect antidote to the commercial trash that most of his peers had listened to. What better way to cultivate an image as difficult and rebellious than by listening to a noise that rejected the embrace of the people you hated?

'He's never going to hear us,' Chiltern said, shaking his head.

'This? It's just a bit of easy listening,' Vallance replied. He waited for a moment, listening attentively to the thrashing electronic and guitar noise until it stopped suddenly, cutting away to a surprised silence. Perfect. He hammered on the door with his fist just as the next track started up. The noise started to build up again and then died.

Vallance faced the bay window, guessing correctly that Grant would look through the curtains rather than come to the door. The curtain was pulled back to reveal a thin, gaunt-looking young man with a wispy beard, clothed in black and wearing two hairstyles on the same head. His eyes widened a fraction and he mouthed a curse that Vallance could read without difficulty.

'This is the police,' Chiltern informed him in a voice loud enough to be heard right across the street. 'We need to talk to you.'

'About what?' Grant replied, the surly expression on his face belied by the nervousness in his eyes.

'We've got some bad news, Grant,' Vallance said, his voice lower, more serious. Grant hesitated and then nodded. The curtain went back and then there was nothing.

'He's hiding his dope,' Chiltern said quietly.

'You're probably right,' Vallance agreed, 'but we're not here for that now. It's not an issue unless he gets difficult. OK?'

Chiltern nodded. 'Yes, sir,' he agreed.

That was the trouble with the ambitious young officers: they felt the need to keep making arrests rather than solving crimes. It was an attitude that came down from the top – a good arrest sheet never hurt anyone's career, from a rookie on the street to a chief commissioner brandishing facts and figures in front of the press. Vallance didn't work that way, not any more at least.

Finally the door was opened and Grant made way for Vallance and Chiltern to enter. The floor was bare, unvarnished boards splattered with paint and bits of caked-in dirt. The air was still thick with the smell of cannabis, though now there was a suspiciously strong odour of pine straight out of an aerosol can. The stairs up to the first floor were to one side of the hallway, and on the other the door to the front room.

'In there,' Grant said, peering out of the front door before closing it.

It was easy to see where Grant's priorities lay. The house was falling to pieces around him, but the front room was home to enough electronic equipment to pilot a moon landing. One wall was lined with tables stacked with computers, keyboards, monitors, printers and other bits and pieces that Vallance couldn't recognise. Two of the monitors were switched on, one of them displaying swirling psychedelic patterns of colour that drew the eye. The chimney breast was flanked with massive black speakers that had obviously been the source of the bone-shaking music minutes earlier. The hi-fi, sporting a console of flashing lights and clever displays, was stacked high in one corner of the room.

The only concession to creature comforts was a shabby but comfortable-looking sofa under the bay window that faced a television with a screen that belonged in a cinema multiplex. The only other seats in the room were all parked under the computer tables.

Chiltern was gaping, first at the state of the room and then at the posters on the wall. One of them showed a beautiful young woman posing at the camera, her near naked body greased to a glistening, seductive shine that matched the chrome of her pierced tongue, nose, nipples and labia. The banner underneath it screamed 'Sex Love Death' in vivid red Gothic script on black.

'Put your tongue back in,' Vallance told Chiltern.

Grant almost smiled but stopped himself. He was faced with the police and he probably didn't quite know how to act yet. 'What's this about?' he asked, standing awkwardly in the middle of the room.

'Can we sit down?' Vallance asked.

'Sure. Look, you said you wanted to talk to me. What about?'

Vallance sank into the depth of the sofa; something so comfortable cost a packet. The dilapidated exterior of the house masked an appreciable income, in that sense at least Grant was probably typical of most of the people working at the Science Park. 'Why don't you sit down too?' he suggested, trying to work out the best way of breaking the news of Carol's death to him. And clearly it was still news to him: Grant gave no indication that he already knew about it.

The request seemed to make Grant even more nervous. He could tell that bad news was coming, his face was evidence of that. He grabbed one of the chairs from under the nearest computer table and parked it in the centre of the room, facing the two policeman comfortably ensconced on the sofa.

There was no point in beating about the bush. 'It's about Carol Davis,' Vallance told him. 'I'm sorry to have to tell you that she's dead.'

There was a moment of silence and then Grant drew in a sharp, jagged breath. He swallowed hard and looked at Vallance directly. 'How?'

It was better to keep details to a minimum for the moment. 'She was found dead in her office. We've not had a pathologist's report yet.'

Silence again and then Grant's face started to crack. 'I don't fucking believe this,' he whispered, his eyes filling with tears.

'I'm sorry to do this to you,' Vallance continued, 'but we need to ask you some questions.'

Grant swallowed hard again, as though the lump in his throat hurt like hell. Tears streamed down his face, his lips trembling as he tried to speak. 'No . . . She was so fucking beautiful, man . . . I can't believe it . . .'

Chiltern looked at Vallance but there was nothing either of them could think of to say. 'I'm sorry, Grant, but we have to do this.'

He nodded and wiped the tears across his face with the back of his hand. 'Sure, sure, I'll be all right.'

'Listen,' Chiltern said quietly, 'do you want a cup of tea or something?'

'Nah, I'll be OK,' Grant insisted.

'Grant, tell me about the argument with your brother this morning,' Vallance suggested softly.

Grant closed his eyes and sighed loudly, letting the emotion flow through him. He looked a wreck already, confirming that he and Carol had clearly been involved in some kind of relationship. 'It was Gav,' he said, 'he hated Carol. He fancied her like mad at first. You know, she was a real good-looking woman, but he could never handle the fact that she went for me and not him. You know, it's always been him with the babes, not me. But just for once someone fancied me and not him. He just couldn't handle it. Oh man, this is just so fucking hard to take.'

'So what was the argument about this morning, specifically?'

'He told me that I was being stupid and that Carol was still screwing that bastard Quigley,' Grant said. 'He's the fat bastard that runs one of the companies at the Science Park. I know he and Carol had something going a long time ago but that was dead. You know, she chucked him because he was such a bastard to her. But she's still got to work with him. It was her job, she had to see him.'

'How did you react to what Gavin was saying?'

Grant swept a hand through his hair, pushing the long locks right across to the other side of his head and baring his multiply-pierced ear. 'I told him he was talking bollocks and that he was jealous. I know that Carol wasn't screwing anyone else, we trusted each other.'

Vallance listened guiltily. Grant was being deceived by Carol; his brother was right about that. 'Was there anything else?'

'Gav also said that Carol was only screwing me so that I'd go and work for Quigley. I mean that's what his problem is, you see? He's crap at programming and he's scared that I'm going to piss off and work for someone else. Without me he'd be nothing.'

'And did Carol ever try to suggest that you work for someone else?'

Grant lowered his eyes. 'Sort of,' he said, softly.

'Did she suggest that you work for Quigley?'

Grant shook his head. 'No, never.'

He was lying, Vallance could sense it. 'Are you sure? She never once suggested that you work for Quigley?'

'Nope, never. I mean why should she? She hated Quigley even more than I did.'

'Why did you hate him?'

Grant smiled. 'Because of what he did to Carol and because the man's a fucking Nazi.'

Chiltern showed no sign of picking up on the point. Perhaps he assumed that Grant was using the term as a general pejorative. 'Do you mean he's just a shit,' Vallance asked, 'or do you mean that he's really a Nazi?'

'Both,' Grant confirmed. 'He's into this master-race shit, you know. The man's bad news, a real sack of shit.'

Carol's secret stash of fascist magazines and the David Irving book were suddenly explicable. Her relationship with Quigley was probably not as dead as Grant – and everyone else – had believed.

Vallance decided to switch tack for a moment. 'Was Carol there when you and Gavin argued today?' he asked.

'No. I got fucked off with Gav and decided to come home to do some work.'

'Did Gavin make any threats towards Carol?'

The question startled Grant. 'Sort of,' he said hesitantly.

'You mean he did?'

'Gav was always mouthing off about what he was going to do to people,' Grant said protectively. 'That's just what he's like. He's just all mouth, you know?'

'Has he ever directly made threats about Carol? To her face, I mean?'

Grant hesitated again. Clearly he was torn by feelings of loyalty towards his brother and a need to be honest. 'Look, I was there when he had a go at her before. You don't know Gav and you don't know Carol. She can give as good as she gets. She could put him in his place, you know? I mean she wasn't scared of him.'

'Was she scared of Brian Quigley?'

Chiltern looked up from his notes. 'Yes, she was terrified of him,' Grant said. 'She was really scared of him because she knew about his Nazi stuff. He likes to keep all of that secret. It's bad for business otherwise.'

'Do you know who attacked her recently?'

Grant looked away. 'No. No idea.'

He was lying again. 'What about you?' Vallance asked him. 'Are you scared of Brian Quigley?'

The idea made Grant smile. 'No way. Why the fuck should I be scared of him?'

'Because you know about his Nazi secret too,' Chiltern suggested.

'I'm not scared of anyone,' Grant stated with all the confidence of a ten-year-old kid.

Vallance leaned forward. 'Grant,' he warned, 'if you don't tell me the truth you're going to regret it.'

Grant looked nervously at Vallance and then at Chiltern. 'What you going to do?' he asked, and what was probably meant as a cocky taunt came out as a frightened question.

'Don't push me,' Vallance warned. 'I know that Carol was trying to get you to work for Quigley,' he stated flatly.

'She didn't,' Grant retorted automatically.

Vallance smiled. 'I think,' he said, 'it's time you took a trip in a police car. Oh, and by the way, your flat's going to be searched and your equipment impounded.'

'For what?' Grant asked.

'Because I feel like it,' Vallance snapped.

Grant looked at Chiltern, as though appealing to him for support. He didn't get it. Chiltern did his Rottweiler on a leash impression.

'You're bluffing,' Grant said, but it sounded more like wishful thinking than a firm declaration of belief.

It was a hackneyed response but it fitted the moment perfectly. 'Try me,' Vallance said.

When there was no response Vallance stood up. 'You're nicked,' he said, deciding to carry on with the quotes from the CID cliché library.

Grant's eyes filled with tears again. 'She didn't try to get me to work for Quigley, not directly,' he blurted out. 'She wanted me to set up shop on my own. You know, to ditch Gav and to work for myself. She reckoned that with my skills I'd make a fortune, especially as she said she could send a lot of work my way. That's what she wanted, for me to be a success.'

Vallance sat down again. 'Did she say that she could get work from Quigley for you?'

'Yeah. She said that she could guarantee a whole load of work from him. He'd be a client though, that's all. The first of many she said.'

'How much did she know about Quigley's work?'

'A lot,' he sniffed. 'She was smart, you know. She'd ditched Quigley but she'd got all the passwords for his files, all the names and addresses of people he dealt with. You know, she knew all about his fucking Nazi friends.'

'And what about his friends in the Ministry of Defence?'

Grant nodded. 'Yeah, she knew that he was ripping them off left, right and centre. She was smart, you know, and now she's dead. I can't believe it.' He looked up suddenly. 'You think someone killed her,' he said, and the sickness in his eyes suggested that the idea had only just occurred to him.

Vallance nodded. 'Who do you think would have wanted her dead?'

'Oh God, oh God . . .'

Vallance felt pity but he steeled himself to be hard. 'Who did it, Grant? Who wanted her out of the way permanently?'

Grant was sobbing, holding his face in his hands to cover

the tears and the pain. 'I don't know . . . Quigley . . . I can't believe this . . . This isn't true . . .'

TWELVE

Gavin Newman could hold his booze. He'd wandered out of a pub after closing time, staggered his way to his car and then driven carefully home, despite the fact that he could hardly stand up because there was so much alcohol in his bloodstream. He had been congratulating himself on getting home safely when he was nabbed by the uniformed WPC waiting discreetly near his doorstep. Half an hour – and one urine sample – later Gavin was sitting alone in an interview room sobering up fast.

Vallance downed the last dregs of his coffee with the hope that it – and the three others previous to it – would get him through the night. At the back of his mind was the knowledge that by the next morning he would find himself off the case and quite possibly facing a severe reprimand for what he'd done. To hell with that, though. Despite the complex weave of motives that he had to wade through, he was convinced that finding Carol's murderer was going to be a simple task. It had to be, it just had to.

The custody sergeant unlocked the door of the interview room and Vallance and Chiltern set eyes on Gavin Newman for the first time. He looked a lot less striking than his brother, though it was easy to see why Gavin had more luck with women. Even after a bellyful of booze he had the sort of boyish good looks that some women went for in a big way.

'They got you too, mate?' he slurred, looking up at Vallance standing in the doorway of the cell, with Chiltern glowering from behind him.

Vallance stifled the urge to laugh, though the grunt from the back suggested that Chiltern hadn't been able to. 'Yeah,' Vallance said, walking into the cell, 'sort of. I'm Chief Inspector Vallance and this is Detective Constable Chiltern.'

Gavin looked flummoxed momentarily but he recovered quickly enough. 'You bastards,' he spat truculently, 'you collared me after I got home. I mean what sort of a deal's that? I mean if I was as pissed as you say then how come you didn't get me on the way back from the pub?'

Vallance let the question hang in the air as he and Chiltern arranged themselves comfortably around the table. Gavin stared at them, his anger held momentarily in check, though from the look in his eyes he was just bursting to have another go.

Chiltern set the tapes going, intoning the sacred words to formally mark the beginning of the interview. 'May I remind you that you're still under caution,' Vallance added at the end – the formal caution had been issued by the WPC who'd arrested him outside his house.

Gavin took that as a signal to start complaining in a loud, whining voice. 'What's all this? I had a drink too many, what's the big bloody deal then? Why ain't you out catching real villains instead of chasing after people who've had one too many?'

'Real villains?' Vallance echoed. 'You mean like murderers?'

'That's right! And muggers and rapists. That's who you should be after, not people like me.'

Vallance smiled agreeably. 'I absolutely agree, Mr Newman, which is why you've been arrested.'

Gavin was about to launch into another tirade but Vallance had stopped him short. He looked perplexed, clearly trying to make sense of what he'd just heard through a fog of alcoholic confusion. 'What're you on about?' he asked, finally.

'Earlier today, Mr Newman, you had a violent argument with Carol Davis. Right?'

Gavin nodded. 'Right,' he agreed quietly.

'You made threats to her, in front of witnesses, and then stormed off, right?'

Gavin nodded again. 'Right.'

'A little while later Carol Davis was found dead. Murdered.'

Gavin inhaled deeply. 'You ain't fucking saying that . . .'

'We're not saying anything,' Vallance cut in quickly. 'You tell us what happened.'

'I don't believe this . . . I mean she was a right slag and I hated her guts but that doesn't mean I wanted to kill her. Christ . . . Where's my brother?' he demanded suddenly.

'Your brother's fine,' Chiltern assured him.

Gavin looked appalled. 'Does he know yet?' he asked, sounding less and less like a drunk. 'Christ, he had the hots for her. That woman was bad news, but he thought that he loved her. The stupid bastard couldn't see that she was taking him for a ride.'

'What happened today?' Vallance asked, anxious to get to the core of the story.

'My girlfriend, Alison, told me that Quigley and Carol were still having it off. They went off together pretending to work and that, but really they were still shagging. They're both bastards, well suited to each other. She's a slag who uses sex to get what she wants and he's a right sleazy bastard who treats people like shit. Anyway, Alison told me that Quigley was saying how Grant was going to come over to work for him. Carol was sleeping with Grant so that he'd do whatever she asked him to.'

It was familiar ground, though it sounded as though Alison – whoever she might be – could at least corroborate one side of the story. 'What happened after you and Grant argued this morning?' Vallance asked, keen to hurry things forward.

'He told me that I was jealous because Carol didn't fancy me and that he was going to leave the company. He said that I was holding him back, living off his work and that I never did anything but boss him around. That's the sort of stuff she used to tell him. She was poison, I tell you.'

It was the cue for a sick joke about Carol and poison but Vallance resisted the temptation. The fewer people who knew that details of her death the better. 'And then?'

Gavin rubbed his face with his hands. He looked ill, the drink catching up with him even if the drunkenness was wearing off. 'I told him I'd smack him in the mouth if he didn't shut up and then he pissed off.'

'What about Carol, where was she?'

'She was upstairs for some of the time,' Gavin said. 'I'd seen her come down with Liz and Gerry and that Fairfax woman but then she didn't go off with them. She must have heard our arguing because after Grant left I went up to talk to her.'

Chiltern almost choked at that. 'Talk? What, you mean you calmed down enough to talk to her?'

'All right,' Gavin admitted wearily, 'I was still screaming. She locked herself in the office and wouldn't come out. I tried to get in but she locked the door. I told her what I thought of her and then went back downstairs.'

'How did she react to what you were saying?' Vallance asked.

'She was sobbing and crying and telling me that I had her all wrong. She told me that she loved Grant and that if I loved him too I wouldn't stand in his way. Pure bollocks, know what I mean? I threatened to smack her in the face if she didn't keep clear of Grant and that was it.'

'Had you smacked her in the face before?'

Gavin recoiled instantly. 'I don't hit women,' he snapped. 'I just mouthed off at her, I was pissed off, you know? Even if she'd opened the door I wouldn't have laid a finger on her.'

That tallied with what Grant had said earlier. But there was still the unexplained attack that had left Carol's face bruised. 'Where were you two nights ago?'

'What?'

'Just answer the question,' Chiltern growled.

'At my mum's house with Alison,' Gavin replied. 'We went round to my mum and dad's place for dinner. Got there early, about half seven and stayed until just after eleven. What's all this got to do with Carol?'

'Nothing,' Vallance said. 'Tell me about Brian Quigley.'

Gavin leaned forward, resting his arms on the table in front of him. Droplets of perspiration were beaded under the hairline of his thick, dark hair. 'What's there to say?' he sighed. 'He runs the biggest company on the Science Park and he acts like he owns the place. They all jump when he tells them to because they're scared that he's going to bugger off somewhere else. And it's all fake, you know? Alison tells me what goes on; it's all just a front. He takes on these little kids, pays them a pittance to do crap work but still manages to rake in a fortune.'

'Then why would he need your brother?' Vallance asked. 'If he's as sharp as you say, why would he fork out the sort of money your brother would want?'

'What sort of money would my brother want?' Gavin asked. 'We just about make out, there's no big money coming in. Have you seen my brother's place? It looks like a squat, he doesn't have two pennies to rub together.'

'That stereo of his must have cost a fortune,' Chiltern pointed out. 'And then there's all those computers and things.'

'What computers? He's got a machine at home and one at work. Have you seen the motor he drives? It's a pile of junk that's going to fall apart soon and we can't afford to replace it.'

'You could sell your motor,' Chiltern suggested, referring to Gavin's flashy car.

Gavin looked affronted by the idea. 'That's for PR,' he said. 'I want clients to think we're doing OK. If they think we're skint then they're going to think we're crap, you see?'

Something didn't add up. It sounded as though Grant had more money coming in than could be explained by his work with his brother. The obvious source of that money had to be Brian Quigley, directly or indirectly. Talk about money was leading things off on a tangent though. 'Forget about that,' Vallance said. 'Why would an alleged crook like Quigley need your brother? It just doesn't make sense to me. Why wouldn't he just carry on raking in a fortune?'

'I don't know,' Gavin admitted. 'Maybe someone at the MoD's finally getting wise to him. Maybe he's finally got to meet a deadline and his people just can't hack the code together to fool people one more time. Why are you asking me? Why isn't Quigley here?'

'He'll be here soon enough,' Vallance promised. The more

he heard about the man the less he liked him. 'Is there anything more you can say about him?'

'Like what? He treats his workers like crap, Alison's worth twice what he pays her. He's the sort of —'

Vallance didn't want to hear it. 'Is there anything you know which you think might be relevant to Carol's death?' he interjected forcefully.

'Only that she reckoned she was scared of him. It was an act though, it used to make Grant feel all protective towards her. You know, like he was a big strong man there to protect his woman. God, talk about a sick joke.'

'Apart from what you've heard from Alison, do you have any other evidence that she was still involved with Brian Quigley?'

Gavin leant back in his seat. 'It wasn't just Alison, everyone in Quigley's company knew the truth. And so did Liz Farnham, she knew what was going on. They all did, Gerry Graham too. They knew she was two-timing my brother but not one of them would say something. In the end it made me look bad, you know what I mean? Like I really was jealous or something.'

Vallance paused. He knew instinctively that Gavin was telling the truth, from his allegations about Carol and Quigley to his protestation of innocence with regards to her death. His motives were probably mixed, his antipathy towards Carol driven as much by personal self-interest as by love for his younger brother, but still what he said had the definite ring of truth. Which hadn't been the case entirely with Grant.

'Can I go now?' Gavin asked.

'No, not yet,' Vallance decided. 'How do you think your brother would have reacted if he'd finally found out about Carol's relationship with Quigley?'

The question startled Grant. 'What do you mean? You ain't saying that Grant had anything to do with her death, are you?'

'I'm not saying anything,' Vallance said. 'Just answer the question. How would he have reacted?'

'He would have been gutted. Totally bloody devastated. You've got to know one thing about Grant: he knows all there is to know about machines but he knows shit about women. Carol was his first real girlfriend, ever. You know, at the age of twenty-four you'd expect him to have all that sorted but he spent more time with computers than with people.'

'And that's why you felt the need to protect him,' Vallance remarked cynically.

'Don't take the piss,' Gavin warned. 'He needs looking after. Do you really think that he could cope with things on his own? He used to talk about starting out on his own but without me to get the clients and then to keep them sweet we'd have nothing. Programmers are ten a penny, believe me.'

Vallance didn't believe him, but it wasn't important. 'Have you ever confronted Quigley with your accusations?' he wondered.

'Last time I did he warned me not to get in his way,' Gavin said. 'He just looked at me and told me not to mess with him. He said that things could get really heavy and it wasn't healthy to get in his way.'

'And what did you do?'

Gavin hesitated. 'To tell the truth I kept quiet,' he admitted, embarrassed. 'The bloke gives me the creeps. You know, to look at he's no big deal but he's got this way of looking at you. He gives off bad vibes, that's what Grant always said. He gives off bad vibes.'

'Did Grant ever suggest to you that he knew more about Quigley's activities than he was letting on?'

'No, not really. He just agreed with me that his people were no-hopers, except for Alison of course.'

Vallance glanced at his watch. It was just after midnight. He needed to speak to Grant once more before the morning. But not as much as he needed to talk to Quigley. It was time to suspend the interview for a while.

Sarah woke suddenly, the blaring of the car bearing down on her transformed into the insistent ring of the telephone. Her heart was pounding and her body was bathed with a cold sweat that made her shiver under the duvet pulled tight around her naked body. Beside her, oblivious to the telephone and to her, lay Duncan, sleeping soundly on his back. It had been so vividly real, the dark car screaming towards her, getting closer and closer, faster and faster, and always she was rooted to the spot, staring in mute horror at the monster roaring certain death towards her.

The phone. It was silent for a few seconds and then it started up again, demanding attention, screaming at her to get out of bed and answer it. She was cold and shivery but it was colder still out of bed. She turned to Duncan, hoping that her movement would disturb him but he was out for the count. She knew that nothing short of a hurricane would get him to wake up. It was the same every morning: he'd lie in bed soaking up the warmth while she was up and getting ready for work.

The phone. It stopped for a longer while, the seconds dragging into minutes and then it began again. This time she knew that she could not resist its call. She gritted her teeth and slid out of bed. The cold sweat on her naked body seemed to turn to ice. She reached for her robe and huddled into it as she walked through the darkness and out into the hall.

It had to be urgent. She snatched it up, afraid that it was something awful and unavoidable.

'Sarah? Sarah Fairfax?'

The voice was vaguely familiar. A half-whisper of sound that made her heart jump harder. It connected instantly – the same voice that had warned her off the Quigley investigation. More threats? Carol was dead, what more did they want?

'Who is it?' she demanded angrily.

'It's Grant. Grant Newman.'

She swallowed hard. She had been certain that it had been the voice behind the threatening phone calls, but now she wasn't sure. 'What is it, Grant?'

'Carol's dead,' he declared, his voice cracking, 'and they've got Gavin for it . . .'

Gavin? What was Vallance playing at? 'Has he been charged?'

'No, but they're keeping him in overnight for questioning. Look, Sarah, you've got to help us.'

He had been crying or perhaps he was talking through tears. 'Look, Grant,' she said softly, cradling the telephone under her chin so that she could wrap the robe around her more warmly, 'it's probably just routine questioning. That's the way the police work.'

'There's some hard nut of a cop called Vallance,' Grant informed her. 'I'm sure he's decided that Gav's done it. He and Carol had a right set-to today, and it looks like him, I'm sure it does. But he's not the one, it's not him.'

Where had he got her number from? Why had he called her up in the middle of the night? 'Please, Grant,' she said, quietly but firmly, 'why don't you let the police do their job?'

'Because they're all in with Brain Quigley. You don't know what he's like; he's a really dangerous guy. Carol trusted you, and now you've got to help her.'

He was raving, the poor man needed help. 'Where are you, Grant?'

'I'm at Epsley. I'm on my own. You've got to get down here.'

'Go home, you need to rest. I know you and Carol were close but –'

'It's not like that!' he snapped angrily. He sounded like the threatening phone caller again. 'Look, Quigley's here as well. He's trashing files, deleting things, covering up. You've got to get down here. Can you get a camera?'

'Grant, please, you need to get some sleep. So do I, I'm exhausted.'

'You never knew what was going on,' he said. 'I was there at Lyndhurst.'

Had she heard correctly? 'What?'

'I was there when you were having that swim. It freaked you out, remember? And I know that you don't work for who you said you did. You work for a TV programme called *Insight*. You're at Epsley to dish the dirt on Quigley.'

'Does that mean you were the one making the threatening phone calls too?' she asked.

'I'm sorry,' he said. 'It was Carol's idea. She was scared you'd lose interest or that you'd be taken in by Quigley. We had to do it, we had to keep you interested. But if you don't get here quick then it will all have been to waste. Quigley's clearing out. Please, Sarah, you've got to help.'

It was madness. Sheer lunacy. Even from the grave Carol was still exerting her strange influence, her schemes taking on a life beyond hers.

'All right,' she whispered, 'I'll be there as soon as I can.'

The phone went dead and she realised that she was no longer cold. She was numb. It was madness to go to Epsley. Grant was off his head. He was a murder suspect; what was there to say that he wasn't the one who poisoned Carol? He had already admitted to making the threatening phone calls and to frightening the life out of her at Lyndhurst. What else had he done?

She walked back to the bedroom and looked at Duncan, sleeping soundly, without a care in the world. What choice did she have? She had to go.

Damn! The house at Tregarthen Place was empty. The heavy drapes were still across the window but there were no lights on anywhere and there was no answer to Chiltern's hammering at the door. A few lights went on in the houses further up the street but that was it.

'I should have brought him in when we had the chance,' Vallance muttered, angry with himself for not having acted more decisively when he'd had the chance. He'd known at the time that Grant was being selectively honest, but he'd let that slide by. Hell, what was wrong with him? It was guilt. He'd had sex with Carol that morning and he'd been feeling guilty sitting in front of Grant, who really did believe that she was as pure as driven snow.

'Never mind, guv,' Chiltern said, kicking away the nettles that sniped at their feet. 'What could we get him for? His brother's the one that we needed to talk to first.'

'We could have collared him for the dope he's got stashed around the house,' Vallance replied. 'And before you say anything,' he added, 'I know I warned that going after the dope was a no-no.'

Chiltern grinned. 'I wasn't going to say a word, guv.'

They walked back along the narrow path and then out to their car, parked opposite. The clouds had cleared and a full moon shone brightly high up in the dark, milky sky. Where next? Gavin's parents had already been on the phone, the whole family knew that he'd been arrested. And no doubt Alison would be with them. And there was always a chance that they'd find Grant there too.

'Right, let's see what Gavin's girlfriend's got to say for herself. Radio in for the address, and see if we've got any word on Quigley yet.'

While Chiltern got on with that Vallance sat back in the seat and tried to stifle the yawn that forced its way out. He was knackered. And why? Because he'd spent the previous night with Carol. Just thinking about her made him feel cold. It hardly seemed real. There she was one minute, alive, healthy, frivolous and then the next she was dead. Why was it that life, so beautiful and precious, could be so easily destroyed? Why?

Chiltern finished with the call back to Area. 'There's someone called Liz Farnham back at base, sir,' he reported. 'Says she needs to talk to you straight away. Reckons that we've got the wrong man.'

'Christ, anyone would think we've charged and sentenced him. OK, forget going to see the rest of the Newman clan. Let's get back to see what Liz has got to say to us.'

The acceleration pushed Vallance back in his seat as Chiltern decided to take advantage of the empty roads back to Area.

'D'you reckon it is this Quigley bloke, sir?' he asked, keeping his eyes fixed on the clear road ahead. There were few other cars about but there was no point chancing it, a drunk driver was always a hazard so late at night.

'It might be,' Vallance admitted. 'But then it's hard to see why he'd do it. If Carol really was trying to get Grant to work for him then why kill her? Unless he'd found out about Sarah Fairfax and had figured that Carol was going to double-cross him. Even then, how could he be sure that she'd take the cyanide? Sarah's idea that he'd engineered the argument with Gavin strikes me as too far-fetched to be true.'

Chiltern thought about it for a while before coming back. 'What if all of the arguing was just coincidence? I mean, what if the poison was planted ages ago and it just so happened that she took the right pill today?'

'That's a good point,' Vallance agreed. 'It makes more sense than Sarah's explanation. But that still leaves us to work out who had access to the office, who knew about Carol's health mania and who had the motive.'

'Looks like there's a whole queue of people on the motive side of things,' Chiltern remarked. 'She was a bit of a stirrer, wasn't she, guv?'

Talk of motives triggered off a new question. 'What I can't work out yet,' Vallance said, 'is what she was after? I mean what did she hope to get at the end of all this manipulating and double-crossing? She must have had her reasons for all of this; it's hard to imagine anyone going to these extremes just for the sake of it. I'm sure that once we figure out what her angle was then we'd know who it was that needed her out of the way.'

The journey out to Epsley had taken on a silent, eerie quality that reminded Sarah of her dream. The darkness looming around the car as it sped down the motorway, the pale light of the street lamps flashing past strobically, drawing her ever onward. She needed to call someone. It was crazy otherwise. Duncan had not stirred even as she had dressed hurriedly with half a hope that he would open his eyes and try to stop her going. It was getting on for two o'clock, and apart from the few trucks on the motorway there seemed to be no one else around. Apart from Grant.

'Fist Fuck'. At the time she had accepted the violent images that Grant surrounded himself with as part of a defiant pose, along with the dirty clothes and the outrageous hairstyle. And now? She felt uncertain and nervous. What if the violence were for real? What if the psychotic imagery was not evidence of juvenile masculine posturing but an indication of something far deeper and more dangerous? Grant had more motive for killing Carol than anyone else. If it was true that she was using him then his violent rage would have been understandable.

The phone startled her. She steadied one hand on the steering wheel and with the other she fished the mobile from her bag.

'Sarah? How far are you?' Grant whispered urgently.

His voice was creepy, making her flesh crawl.

'I'll be there in a few minutes,' she said.

'Switch your lights off and leave the car near the building site,' he instructed.

If he planned something rash then he was asking her to make it easy for him. 'Why?'

His voice sounded louder; she could almost feel his hot breath in her ear. 'Because Quigley's men are down here now,' he said. 'They're loading stuff into a van. If they see you then God knows what'll happen.'

'What men?'

'Quigley's Nazi mates,' Grant said.

Had she heard correctly? It sounded absurd. 'Did you say nasty mates?' she asked, going for the nearest appropriate word.

'No, I said Nazi,' he confirmed. 'Didn't Carol tell you? I thought you knew about him.'

Another piece of the jigsaw fell into place. Carol had hinted at Quigley's dark associates, the heavy people who gave her the creeps. She hadn't mentioned Nazis but perhaps she had been saving that particular revelation until later. 'What are they loading up?'

There was a pause and all that Sarah could hear was the banging of the phone at the other end. 'I can't see,' he said, coming back. 'They've been using one of the empty units to store things. There's about five of them altogether, including Quigley.'

The prospect of coming face to face with a load of Nazi heavies was not immediately appealing – if it were true and not a figment of Grant's overwrought imagination. 'Grant, I think we need to call the police,' she said. It went against her instincts to make such a suggestion but the situation was too complicated and potentially too dangerous to tackle on her own.

'No! Quigley's got police protection,' he insisted. 'He's got lots of inside support; that's how he's got these contracts from the government . . . . Have you got a video camera with you?'

The question was so ludicrous that Sarah wanted to laugh. 'Of course I haven't,' she told him bluntly. 'Look, I don't know what Carol's told you, but I'm not the one that totes the cameras. I'm a researcher, nothing more, nothing less.'

'Shit! She told me that you'd have all that sort of gear. Look, get down here quick, before these bastards finish up and disappear for good.'

Was the whole thing an elaborate ruse? Perhaps Carol's devious talents had rubbed off onto Grant after all. Quigley as a neo-Nazi? It sounded bizarre. He had come across as hard-nosed, intelligent, not unlikeable and totally mercenary.

The phone was now on her lap. She glanced down at it then looked ahead to see the sign for the exit to the Science Park. Who to call? She suddenly felt paranoid again. What if Quigley did have police protection? There was only one person that Sarah could trust.

She slowed the car to a stop after coming off the slip road and then dialled Vallance's home telephone number. He'd probably be furious about being woken up, but she knew that within minutes he'd be back to his usual sarcastic self. How long did it take to rouse him? The phone rang insistently, again and again, but there was no reply. Anger swelled up suddenly. How dare he sleep when she needed him? Men! What was wrong with them?

She put the phone down angrily.

She looked up into the darkness as something else occurred to her. There was always the chance that Vallance had met someone in the course of the evening and gone to bed with her. The idea made her grip the wheel of the car tightly. She breathed in deeply. To hell with Tony Vallance. She'd go on without him.

Liz Farnham looked haggard. Her eyes were bloodshot, her skin sallow and her lips looked as though they'd been bitten to pieces. At least she wasn't crying; there was no way that Vallance could face that again. She looked up at him pleadingly as he and Chiltern came into the interview room.

'I'm so glad you could see me, Chief Inspector,' she said, standing up and offering her hand in greeting.

'It's no problem,' he replied, sitting opposite her. 'Now, you're here about Gavin Newman I take it.'

'That's right. I appreciate that it's probably not your doing,' she said, speaking quietly but firmly, 'but his arrest seems entirely inappropriate given these circumstances.'

Vallance smiled. 'You mean it's inappropriate to arrest a murder suspect? Or do you mean it's inappropriate to arrest a man who's so drunk he can't see straight but drives home anyway?'

The sarcasm didn't faze her at all. 'I think, Chief Inspector, that Gavin's a murder suspect purely for technical reasons. I'm sure that once you've examined the evidence you'll agree that he's innocent.'

Vallance agreed with her, but kept his reactions guarded. 'You sound totally convinced of his innocence, Ms Farnham. I'd just like to know who you suspect is the killer.'

She looked at him sharply. 'I think it's obvious, Chief Inspector. Carol Davis committed suicide.'

The answer surprised both him and Chiltern. 'You sound very sure,' Vallance said.

'I am,' she stated flatly. 'Don't forget that I worked with Carol for nearly three months. I saw her day in and day out, and I think I got to know her extremely well. I'd even say we were friends.'

Friends? Vallance wasn't so sure. 'And?'

'And I can tell you that she was mentally unstable. I know that sounds like a harsh thing to say about someone who's just passed away, but it's the honest truth.'

Vallance looked at her coldly. Although he hadn't known Carol for very long she had given every indication of being perfectly stable − except that she also seemed pathologically incapable of being honest with people. 'In what way was she unstable?' he asked.

'She was a compulsive liar for a start,' Liz said. 'And she lived in a fantasy world where people were always plotting this or that against her. She had a streak of paranoia about her, Chief Inspector, a real deep vein of it.'

'And you think she was also the suicidal type?'

Liz nodded. 'Yes. She liked to overdramatise everything. Do you know that she blacked her own eye to get Sarah Fairfax's sympathy? There was no mysterious attack. It was just her being the drama queen, spinning lies and trying to con people into liking her.'

Vallance had his own doubts about the attack on Carol, but he hadn't thought Carol capable of beating herself up. 'How can you be so sure that she did it herself?'

'Because I know her well enough and it's the only explanation that makes sense. I've seen what she's capable of. Do you know that she was having an affair with Grant Newman? And that she was still involved in a long-term relationship with Brian Quigley?'

It seemed more and more like the only person not in the know had been Grant. 'No, I've not heard anything about that,' Vallance lied. 'Tell me about that.'

Liz folded her hands in front of her. 'I'm not speaking ill of the dead,' she began. 'Carol harboured genuine feelings for Grant. Perhaps it was because they're both such strange and compelling personalities. For whatever reason she began to see Grant soon after she started with me at PR-Tech. However, she was still involved with Brian Quigley.'

'Did she know Quigley prior to starting at the Science Park?'

'Yes, she had been living with Brian for a while before she started with me. It was his idea, and Dr Graham was keen that I took her on too. I wasn't so sure, but Dr Graham was insistent and Brian indicated that he'd support me financially with Carol's freelance fees.'

The story was getting murkier again. 'When did she leave Quigley?' Vallance asked.

'Just after she started with me. They had a row and she moved out, or he kicked her out. I didn't want the sordid details to be honest. But they patched it up soon afterwards and their relationship has persisted during the time she was involved with Grant too.'

'Did Brian Quigley know about that?'

She looked embarrassed but whispered her answer. 'Yes, and I think that he was keen for it to continue until Grant joined his company.'

'Do you think that she started the affair with Grant at Brian Quigley's instigation?'

She shook her head. 'No, I know that she really was attracted to him. That's one of the things about Carol, Chief Inspector, she wanted to be loved. She would do anything to gain people's approval. Don't think badly of her; she really was a poor little sick girl.'

That didn't square with the Carol that Vallance had known. But then again he suspected that no one really knew what was going on in her head. It was probable that half a dozen different Carols existed, each one the 'real' thing, and each one a bravura performance for one person only.

'So you think it was suicide? Why now? Did she give any indication that she was planning to kill herself?'

Liz shrugged. 'I just think that things were coming to a head. She was afraid of losing Grant, afraid of losing Brian . . .'

'Afraid of losing her job?' Vallance added.

She looked at him sharply. 'I had no choice,' she said coldly. 'She was slowly tearing that place apart. Grant and Gavin were at each other's throats. Brian Quigley was making impossible demands on her. In the end it just overwhelmed her.'

'Tell me about Brian Quigley,' Vallance suggested. 'It sounds like he's an important client of yours. Gavin alleges that you're all frightened of him. Is that true?'

'No, not at all true. Gavin's got every right to be resentful though,' she added hastily. 'You see, Chief Inspector, his company's a very prestigious client of ours. He's a real catch, you see. We need companies like his in order to attract the right sort of client and to attract more private funding. Brian's an entrepreneur, and that means he drives a hard bargain. Sometimes when we have to make choices between our clients he gets the first crack of the whip and the biggest chunk of our resources.'

It all sounded so neat and plausible. Carol's suicide would suit everybody: Liz, Quigley, Gavin. 'What would be the impact on the Science Park if it was shown that Carol had been murdered rather than it being a case of suicide?'

'It wouldn't be good,' she admitted.

'And presumably that wouldn't be good for you, either?'

She glared at him. 'I didn't come here in the middle of the night to have you make snide remarks, Chief Inspector.'

There was a faint echo of Sarah Fairfax there, but Liz lacked

Sarah's vitriolic temper. 'No, you came here ostensibly to get Gavin Newman released,' he said. 'But instead you've spent more time trying to convince me of Carol's suicide than anything else. I'm afraid that the theory doesn't wash, Ms Farnham. Now, what I'd like to talk about is Brian Quigley.'

Liz shuffled uncomfortably in her seat. 'What about him?' she asked.

'Tell me about his politics,' Vallance suggested, smiling broadly as he saw the look of horror dawning on Liz's face.

THIRTEEN

Sarah stopped the car at the top of the road, switched off the headlights and stepped out into the cold night air. The Science Park lay below, a ghost town of square blocks huddled together and lit by pale orange street lamps. The lake opposite reflected the pale orange and the sharper white light of the moon. From her vantage point she could see the car park was almost empty, apart from a black Transit van and two dark-coloured cars parked close to the Software Solutions office. There was movement there too: she could see people carrying things from one of the units to the van.

She climbed back into her car, at once relieved and yet afraid. It wasn't all a figment of Grant's deranged imagination. On the other hand if Grant's explanation were correct then the men were probably extremely tense and likely to be dangerous. There was no turning back, she realised, it was too late to do anything but get to the truth. She released the handbrake of the car and let it roll forward, taking advantage of the slope to pick up speed without switching the engine on. Her lights were off and in the darkness she was scared that her car would roll off the road and onto the pavement or down into the ditch that ran parallel to the road, but she controlled the speed and kept her foot lightly pressed on the brake.

Instead of turning off onto the Park she let the car go

onward towards the building site. There were street lamps there, and arc lights blazing harsh glare onto the silent and immobile building site, catching it in an electric flash that lasted all night. She spotted a beat-up old car tucked away near the gates and guessed that it belonged to Grant. Her car had finally run out of steam but she dared not start the engine. She let it roll as far as it would then she stopped it dead. It was sticking out at an odd angle — as an example of how to park it stunk to high heaven — but it would do in the circumstances.

The bushes that surrounded the Park and shielded it from the lake provided good cover and she was grateful for it as she scooted out of the car and across the road. She kept low, moving stealthily closer to the first of the units. The lights were off, including those of the G-Man office, but Sarah was close enough to hear the hushed voices of the men as they worked shifting heavy white boxes into the Transit van. She listened for a moment, but the voices were muted and she couldn't make out Quigley's voice. But then Quigley was the type to give orders, not the type to stand in line and shift boxes around.

She chanced a look, peering from between the bushes, and saw that there were four men standing in line, moving the cardboard boxes from hand to hand. They didn't look like textbook Nazis; although they all had closely cropped hair none of them was a skinhead or a middle-aged beer-bellied yob. As they were clearly preoccupied with what they were doing, she took her chance and jogged across from her hiding place to the door of the first unit. She tugged at the glass door and was in before she had a chance to look round. She ducked down and listened but all she could hear was the sound of her heartbeat and the shallowness of her breath.

'Sarah?'

She looked into the shadows beyond the lobby and saw Grant peering through the half open door of the G-Man office. 'Yes, I made it,' she whispered.

'Come on,' he urged her, 'we haven't got long.'

She joined him in his office, keeping well down in case someone should glance in through the window. The lights were off but the computer screen that Grant had positioned on the floor cast a pale icy glow across the room. 'How did you know they'd be here?' she asked, suddenly suspicious of him again.

'I didn't,' he said. 'I came here to get the goods on Quigley once and for all but when I got here I spotted them from up on the hill. It made sense of course, Quigley's sharp like that, and he's not likely to leave stuff around if the Old Bill are going to be nosing around for a while.'

It did make sense, of course. She got down on her hands and knees and crawled along the floor towards Grant. She was glad that the cold weather meant she'd gone for jeans and sweatshirt; the idea of crawling around with a skirt on made her blood run cold.

'Look at this stuff,' Grant told her, pointing to the screen in front of him. He was lying flat on the floor, up on his elbows so that he could type on the keyboard positioned in front of the screen.

Sarah looked at the pages of text scrolling rapidly down the screen. She caught odd words but it was flying past so quickly that she couldn't scan it. 'What is it?'

'This is what the Science Park has been paying for,' Grant said quietly. 'They'd be sick if they knew that that cash was being spent on this sort of fascist garbage.'

The movement of words on the screen stopped and Grant typed rapidly, his fingers flying over the keyboard with practised ease. Suddenly the screen cleared and a graphic began to form, line by line, the blurred image becoming focused until she could clearly see what it was. The Gothic script announced a welcome to the 'Aryan Resistance Net', and below it was the stark image of a swastika and the slogan 'White Pride World Wide'.

'It's a computer bulletin board,' Sarah said. 'Is this part of the internet?'

Grant smiled. 'God, why does everyone think that the internet is everything? Quigley's smarter than that. This is a private access bulletin board system – a BBS. Only certain people can access this; it's invitation only, there's no way you could log on to this by accident.'

'And he runs this here?' Sarah asked.

'That's right. The host machine is sitting in the Software Solutions office right now. I reckon by the morning it's going to be vaped.'

'Vaped?'

'Yeah, wiped out, deleted, deceased. That's why I'm down-loading as much of it as I can. I want every single fucking word of it stored away.'

The screen image had cleared and in its place there was a menu of choices. She looked down the list, intrigued and appalled by what she saw. There were articles extolling the virtues of National Socialism, others denying the existence of the holocaust, more reports on 'actions' and events and more.

'Do you want to see something that'll really freak you out?' Grant asked, his fingers poised over the keyboard.

'I think I'm freaked out already,' Sarah murmured.

Grant chuckled and then clicked a mouse button. The screen cleared and was replaced by another that was headed 'Scum'. Under the heading there were more choices: Race traitors; Reds; Jews; Niggers; Anarchists; Renegades. Grant clicked again on the item marked 'Race Traitors' and the screen changed and a long list of names, addresses, telephone numbers and personal details began to appear. Some of the names were familiar, prominent names from politics and the media, church leaders, trades unionists and more. Other names were unfamiliar but the details were there.

'This is their hit-list,' Grant announced. 'These are the poor bastards who've got to look out for car bombs, death threats, random attacks in the streets. Do you know how many people log on to this list? Hundreds, from all over the world. There's a whole fucking network of these people and they're dangerous.'

Sarah didn't need convincing. 'Do you have the names and addresses of the people who use this system?'

Grant shook his head. 'You've got to be kidding. These people are security-conscious. I've been reading this stuff. They reckon they're engaged in a war, they see themselves as soldiers. They log on to this system using IDs and passwords that can't be traced. I doubt if even Quigley knows who's who. Leaderless resistance they call it. The less you know the less you can inform, and if one Nazi cell gets wiped out then another can still function.'

Sarah was suddenly conscious that there was a group of them outside. She swallowed hard. Damn it! Why hadn't she called someone?

'Look at this,' Grant continued, excited now by what he was revealing to her. His face was lit up by the glow from the screen, giving him a ghostly countenance that exaggerated the warped contours of his face and hair.

Sarah looked back from him to the screen. The top of the screen was headed 'Training' and below it, marked by tiny icons of bombs and swastikas, was the contents list for that section of the system. She felt a dark thrill of fear jolt through her. Training included details on how to make bombs, how to carry out surveillance, black propaganda, martial arts . . .

'What's that?' she said, pointing to one of the items.

'Chemicals? Probably how to make bombs I guess,' Grant said. He moved the mouse pointer to the menu item and then clicked the button.

'My God . . .' Sarah whispered, reading down the list of substances that scrolled down the screen. Some were explosives, others were home-made napalm, acids, poisons. Poisons. The list scrolled down quickly, each substance named and then followed the details on how to manufacture and use it. It was there. Cyanide.

'You're saving all of this?' she asked, hardly daring to believe what she had just seen. Grant had no idea that Carol had been poisoned with cyanide; the significance of what he had just downloaded was lost on him. But not on Sarah. Quigley not only knew how to manufacture the poison, his computer system gave explicit details on how to use it.

'Yeah, I've got all of this,' Grant confirmed. 'It's a terrorist's dream, isn't it?'

'Grant,' Sarah said, finally, 'we need to call the police. They're going to be finished soon. How long have you been here?'

'An hour I reckon. We can't trust the police. They're in with him.'

'How can you be sure?'

'Because Carol told me,' he assured her, speaking as one who could not doubt the veracity of Carol's word. She wanted to demand evidence but guessed that it wasn't the right time to get into an argument with him.

'Then what are we going to do?' she asked.

He was silent for a minute, staring at the screen as it unveiled page after page of deadly information. 'I don't know,' he admitted, finally. 'I sort of hoped that you could film them while they carried on loading up their stuff.'

For someone so intelligent he was either remarkably naïve or incredibly stupid. She controlled her temper though. There was no point in having a go at him, not yet. 'I'm going to call the police,' she said finally. 'I'm sure that they can't all be in Quigley's pockets.'

'Er . . . I think you'd better get on and do it, then' Grant whispered, his voice so low that Sarah could barely hear him. But she sensed his sudden panic.

She looked up but there was nothing but the sky visible from the window. She looked at him and saw the nervousness in his eyes. Returning her gaze back to the monitor she noticed a blank box covering up part of the screen. 'What's wrong?' she asked.

'It's a chat box,' he told her, as though that made any sense.

'What's that in English?' she asked, unable to hide her irritation.

'It means we've been rumbled. Someone's noticed that we're logged on to the computer and they've decided to talk to us directly.'

A dozen sick thoughts ran through her head. But it wasn't the time to give in to panic. The empty panel on the screen began to fill with words, typed in slowly as though each letter was being picked out individually. 'Can they trace who we are?' she whispered.

'If they're good they can,' Grant replied, smiling to himself. 'I mean they've only got to look at our IP address and they'll know that we're connected through the Science Park. On the other hand I doubt that any of Quigley's people know what an IP address is. I know he doesn't; he's got some smart-arsed Yank Nazi to set this up for him.'

Sarah read out the message that had been typed in: 'Hello, friend. Where are you logged on from?'

'How should we reply?' Grant asked.

'You could tell him to fuck off but I'm not sure that's the right answer. Make something up while I call the police, OK?'

'I'll tell him I'm dialling in from Louisiana or somewhere,' Grant decided. 'Maybe I can keep him on-line long enough for the Old Bill to get here.'

Vallance sat back at his desk and glanced at his watch. There was still no sign of Gavin or Brian Quigley and time was ticking by fast. Liz Farnham had been less than forthcoming about Quigley's sick politics. Perhaps she genuinely didn't know to what level he was involved, though it was clear that she suspected that there was something dodgy about his ideas. She also suggested that Carol's ideas were not so far removed, though for the life of him Vallance couldn't work out how a desire to save the planet and an obsession with health married with racism, violence and a desire for racial purity. Perhaps Carol and Quigley shared a fascination for purity that went beyond anything rational. Besides, wasn't Hitler a vegetarian and an animal lover? In any case he couldn't be sure whether Carol had or hadn't shared Quigley's politics.

It looked like there was nothing else to do but wait for the morning. There was no point in rousing Gavin Newman for more questioning: he clearly had no idea as to his brother's whereabouts, and still less about Quigley's. Chiltern knocked on cue, and came in bearing yet another dose of caffeine-flavoured sludge. Vallance took the cup gratefully, wondering what exactly Carol would have said about the poisons he was ingesting in such great quantities. Poisons. That word again.

Chiltern took a long, slow slurp from his cup before speaking. 'Are we going to call it a day, guv?' he asked.

Vallance couldn't tell whether Chiltern wanted to give up or carry on. 'I think we call it a day,' he decided regretfully. 'We need to get Grant and Quigley into custody as soon as poss. We also need to see this Dr Graham, the office cleaners, and also some bloke from a print bureau who was in and out a lot. Oh, and we need to chase details on the cyanide. We need to know exactly what form it was in and what the sources of it are. Like the doc said, it's not exactly an over-the-counter drug.'

The phone interrupted Chiltern's reply. 'Let's hope someone's got Quigley,' Vallance said, taking the call. He listened for a moment, hardly daring to believe his ears. 'Get everybody there,' he snapped and then put the phone down.

'Have we come up trumps?' Chiltern asked hopefully.

'No, Sarah Fairfax has,' he said. 'Come on, let's see how fast you can really drive.'

Chiltern looked like he'd just become a lottery winner. 'Where are we going, guv?'

'Epsley Science Park. Sarah Fairfax is holed up with Grant Newman and they're spying on Brian Quigley and assorted mates.'

The office was suddenly swept by a wide, bright beam of light. Sarah's heart skipped a beat but then she realised it wasn't a torch but the twin beams from a car. Above the steady clicking of the keyboard she heard the swish of a car pulling up outside.

'That can't be the Old Bill,' Grant whispered.

'No, I've only just got through to them. And we're in luck,' she added, 'there's an officer there that I know we can trust.'

'You mean this bloke Vallance? The one that's got my brother?'

'I'm sure he's only doing that for routine purposes,' she said, hoping that it would reassure him. 'He needs to eliminate Gavin from his enquiries.'

'Then how come they've not pulled that bastard in?'

It was a good question that Sarah could not answer. She looked at the computer screen. The chat box was still there and Grant was typing in yet another reply to the increasingly detailed questions being put to him. They were both assuming that it was Quigley at the other end; so far, however, he had only addressed himself as the 'sys-op' for the system. It meant system-operator according to Grant, who seemed unable to comprehend that such terms were not everyday usage for most of the population.

'Are we still downloading stuff?' she asked, anxious to get as much as possible saved on Grant's computer for later use.

'It's working as a background task,' he said, 'which means it's slower but at least it's still going.'

'Good, we need all the evidence we can get.'

Grant grinned. 'This is for Carol,' he said. 'D'you think you can dedicate your programme to her? I mean at least her death won't have been in vain, you know? She's like a martyr, killed by these Nazi bastards for trying to expose them.'

Sarah smiled but said nothing. Poor Grant was still deluded. Carol had been sitting on the story for so long that it was clear she had no real desire to expose Quigley's politics. She had to have had other motives. If she had wanted to get Quigley for real then she would have done things more straightforwardly: all she had needed to do was to sit Grant in front of the computer and a television camera and tell him to let rip.

'Grant, can I ask you something?'

'Hold on,' he said. 'Look, he's signing off.'

She looked at the screen and saw the last words appear in the chat box: 'Keep up the fight, friend. Bye. Logoff.' The chat box disappeared and the text scrolling underneath it picked up speed as it downloaded on to Grant's machine. It was a relief, but the feeling was tempered by the fear that it meant that the entire system was going to be shut down before Grant had finished copying everything.

He looked up from the screen. 'What did you want to ask?' he said.

She crossed her fingers and asked the question. 'Grant, who was it that attacked Carol in the street? Who blacked her eye?'

He grinned nervously. 'Look, I know it looks bad and all that, but it wasn't the way she said it was.'

Sarah knew precisely what was coming next. 'You did it,' she stated coldly.

He looked sheepish. 'Yeah, it was me. But there was a good reason for it, you know? It was necessary to keep you interested in what she was saying. We couldn't risk you backing out.'

'Grant, didn't you think it odd that she asked you to punch her in the face like that?'

'No way, I mean she was right on the edge,' he explained proudly. 'That's how we were alike, you know, living on the edge like that. I admired her for it; she was the coolest person I ever met.'

'And you didn't find it difficult to hit her?'

'Yeah, it wasn't easy but that's what we had to do. It hurt her but it hurt me too, you know.'

'If it was so important to keep me interested then why didn't she just come out and tell me the truth? Why didn't she give me all the information that she'd unearthed?'

He looked at her uneasily. 'Don't take offence or anything,' he whispered nervously, 'but we both agreed that we couldn't trust the media. She'd tried to get other people interested in the past but as soon as they figured what was going on they backed out. We couldn't risk you doing the same.'

She felt close to boiling point. It was a blatant lie. There was no way that Carol had tried to interest anyone else in the story. It was the sort of lie that only someone as naïve as Grant would believe.

'Oh, shit,' he muttered.

Sarah stared at the words on the screen. 'Hello Grant,' it said, 'so glad you could drop in on us.'

'I thought you said he didn't know what an IP address was,' Sarah whispered angrily. Her stomach was churning and she suddenly felt sick.

'How did you know?' Grant typed quickly.

'I ran an IP trace,' came the reply quickly, 'and you're logged in from the Park. There's no one else here who'd have the skill to hack this system, is there, Grant?'

Grant's proud grin was illuminated by the translucent glow from the computer screen. It was what he craved, recognition of his skills as a technician, no matter what the circumstances, no matter what the consequences. He seemed pleased by the exchange, rather than frightened of what it could lead to.

'Find out if it is Quigley at the other end,' Sarah said grimly, determined to have the confirmation of his identity stored permanently on disk.

The next message appeared on the screen before Grant could act. 'Take a look outside, Grant,' it suggested.

Sarah's heart was pounding and her hands were shaking as she dared raise her head slightly to look outside. The men loading the van had stopped and were standing by the door to Quigley's unit, all of them looking suspiciously across the Park. She could sense that the atmosphere had changed: they were alarmed now, which made them ten times as dangerous.

Grant risked a look too, just for a second, and then he ducked down again to pound at the keyboard. 'I'm not scared,' he typed, and the plain words on the screen somehow carried an echo of his adolescent bravado.

'We need to talk,' was the response. 'Now that Carol's out of the way we need to sort things out once and for all. How would you like a little escort?'

Sarah swallowed hard. There was absolutely no doubt about who was on the other end of the computer now. And if he'd killed once there would be nothing to stop him killing again. Especially with his gang of supporters with him – who knew what kind of bloody end they'd inflict on Grant. It suddenly occurred to her that they had no idea that she was here.

'There's nothing for us to say,' Grant typed.

'But there is, Grant,' was the response. 'I think we need to talk now.'

The chat box disappeared and the text scrolling underneath it picked up speed as it downloaded on to Grant's machine. It was a relief that it was going more quickly, but the feeling was tempered by the fear that it meant that the entire system was going to be shut down before Grant had finished copying everything.

'Look,' he said, nodding towards the screen. She turned and saw that another message had appeared, overlaying the text on the screen. 'He's shutting the system down,' she said.

'And it sounds like they've finished up outside too.'

Sarah crawled over to the window and risked taking a peek. The men loading the van were clustered by it, chatting quietly, the back door of the van open to reveal dozens of closely packed boxes. The car which had arrived earlier was parked on the other side of the van but Sarah recognised it nevertheless – it was Dr Graham's car. Was he involved too?

She felt disappointment mingled with apprehension. How many other people were involved in the conspiracy?

She ducked down and crawled back to Grant, now busy tapping at the keyboard with total concentration, the staccato rhythm of the keys filling the air.

'Grant, where does Dr Graham fit in all of this?'

'Wait a minute,' he said, 'I just need to get this . . .'

'It's important,' Sarah hissed. 'What's his relationship to Carol and to Quigley?'

Grant spoke without taking his eyes off the computer screen and without slowing the action of his fingers tapping sharply at the keyboard. 'The poor bastard's being blackmailed by Quigley. He's got so much of his poxy life wound up in this place and he knows that if it gets out that it's being used by Nazis then he's not only going to get a lot of bad publicity, he's liable to get the chop. It's bad for the corporate image to have a bunch of racists using the place. Besides, Quigley's been using some of the funds for the Science Park for his network and stuff.'

'You're certain of that?'

'Yeah, it got to the point where Quigley was calling the shots all the time. It used to piss off the other companies on the site but there was nothing any of them could do about it without Gerry's support. You know that Venture Capital International – the company that put the money up for this place – is owned by a Jew? Carol told me that it was a point of honour for Quigley that he was ripping off Jewish money to fund his network.'

'But Dr Graham's not a Nazi as such,' she said, trying to salvage some respect for the man.

'To be honest I don't think he's into politics. He's into his career more than anything else. That's what these people are like, you know? They don't give a shit, but we're not like that.'

Voices were raised outside and she knew that Grant's escort was coming for him. For him, not her. Part of her wanted to hide, to let them take Grant so that she might get away, but another part of her was appalled by the idea. They were in it together no matter what.

'They're coming after us,' Grant whispered, and his voice betrayed the real fear inside him.

Trying to keep hidden, she risked another look. Three of the men had fanned out and were walking slowly towards the unit. They were silent, intent, keeping watch in case Grant tried to make a run for it. Two of the men were smiling, leering aggressively, looking forward to the obvious violence they were planning. One of them had a flashlight and was panning it to and fro, a beacon that drew closer with every step.

'Oh fuck,' Grant whispered, 'they're going to beat the shit out of us.'

Sarah tried to answer but words would not form. She felt paralysed, her knees close to giving way and she didn't even have the energy to try to run.

There was a sudden call of voices, urgent shouts and the sound of engines being gunned into life. The police? Sarah took a chance and stood up, no longer willing to wait. She was right. In the distance she could see half a dozen police vehicles bearing down at speed. The Nazis were panicking, calling instructions to each other but unable to decide on what to do. There was only one way in or out of the Science Park and none of them wanted to get head to head with the police cars.

A flashlight caught herself and Grant, and she saw one of the Nazis glaring at her. She caught his eyes, saw the hatred and the aggression as he began to call the others. She stared back, finally unafraid to stand and face him. He looked for a moment longer and then ran back to the van. The first police cars screeched into the car park and the black Transit started forward. They were going to make a run for it. It swerved past the car and then veered off as a police van careened around the corner. The driver of the black van, losing control, swerved sharply before hurtling through the bushes and down towards the lake.

Sarah watched silently as several uniformed police officers poured from the cars and tore through the bushes in hot pursuit. More police cars arrived, the flashing lights and sirens filling the air and drowning out the shouting coming from around the lake. She looked back and saw Brian Quigley calmly surveying the scene, and there, beside him, stood a shocked Gerry Graham.

'Look,' Grant spat angrily, 'the police haven't even touched Quigley yet.'

'They will, I'm sure,' Sarah promised, turning back to the mêlée of police vehicles in search of Vallance. He was there, dressed all in black, looking more like one of the Nazis than Quigley did. At last he turned and smiled at Sarah, who managed a smile back. He waved and then, with his young sidekick in tow, he strode confidently across the car park towards Quigley and Dr Graham.

They eyed each other up for a moment and then the young CID officer took Quigley gently by the arm and led him towards a waiting police car. Quigley looked supremely calm, as though he had expected such an eventuality and was thoroughly prepared for it. Gerry Graham on the other hand had lost his composure completely: he walked stoop-shouldered to another car, looking for all the world like the guilty man.

'They've got him,' Sarah announced proudly.

'It's all for show,' Grant declared cynically. 'I'm not fooled by it all.'

'No,' she disagreed, 'I trust Vallance to see this through to the end.'

'Just so long as you don't forget that all of this is down to Carol,' Grant said.

Just before Quigley got into the police car he looked over at Sarah. He nodded an acknowledgement, a slight smile on his face. He said something to Vallance who glowered at him and then pushed him down into the car.

It was over. After everything that had happened she was willing to concede that perhaps Vallance wasn't such a dead loss after all.

FOURTEEN

It was just before dawn when Quigley's brief arrived. There was no duty solicitor or someone pulled from a telephone directory for him; he could afford someone in from central London, someone who evinced no shock at the early morning call to see his client. Like everything else to do with Quigley's arrest, it seemed as if the whole thing had been planned well in advance.

Vallance had interviewed Sarah first, wanting to glean as much useful information as possible before going in to see Quigley. The story that he got was so fantastic that it beggared belief – Carol revealed as the prime mover in the conspiracy that she had created around her. Nothing was as it appeared, everyone had been used, there were no innocent explanations, no insignificant acts. Even the punch in the face that had blacked her eye was her own doing, Grant Newman clearly going along with whatever she told him to do.

The interview with Quigley was just being set up when Vallance arrived. Chiltern was seeing to the tapes; Quigley, looking relaxed, was whispering to his solicitor. Vallance took a seat and flicked through the book that he'd taken from the boxes loaded into the van at the Science Park. It looked like an entire print run had been loaded up; one of the PCs had estimated that there were at least five thousand copies of the book boxed up and ready to ship.

Vallance looked up. 'What can you tell us about this?' he asked, handing the book across the table to Quigley.

'DCI Vallance hands a copy of the confiscated book to Mr Quigley,' Chiltern intoned into the tape recorder.

Quigley looked at it disdainfully and shoved the book back across the table. 'I've never seen it before,' he stated confidently.

Vallance picked it up. '*White Fist*,' he read from the cover, '*A Manual For Aryan Commandos*. You've never seen this before?'

Quigley smiled. 'No, never.'

'Then can you explain to me what you were doing helping to load a few thousand copies of this into a van at Epsley Science Park this morning?'

Quigley looked over at his solicitor who nodded. 'I wasn't helping to load anything, Chief Inspector. I had never met any of the men who were doing the loading before, and I had no idea what was in the boxes. As I said, I've never seen the book before and have no idea of what it contains.'

'Then what were you doing at Epsley?'

Quigley smiled. 'I was working late, Chief Inspector.'

Vallance was irritated by Quigley's total self-confidence. All of the men in the van denied knowing Quigley. They all said the same thing: they were drinking in a pub when some guy they'd never met before offered them cash to help him shift some boxes from an office. They also said that the guy from the pub had disappeared when the police had arrived, though all of them gave the same description of him: a big black guy they said, with dreadlocks and gold chains around his neck. It was such an audaciously blatant lie that none of them had been able to stop smiling as they reported it. Not even the charges against them – resisting arrest, obstruction and in one case an assault charge – had been enough to wipe the grins from their faces. And, like Quigley, they all denied knowledge of what the boxes contained.

'What were you working on?' Vallance asked.

'I was involved in doing some programming work,' Quigley explained.

'Do you realise what's in this book?' Vallance asked.

'Obviously I don't,' Quigley said. 'As I have never seen the book before, how could I possibly know what it contains?'

'It's a manual for terrorists, Mr Quigley. It contains details on how to make bombs, weapons, how to avoid the police, how to forge documents and more.'

'Really? That surprises me, Chief Inspector. I do hope that you catch the men responsible for publishing it.'

Quigley's smile made Vallance clench his fists and bite back the urge to belt him in the mouth. 'Do you have a key to the empty unit next to your office?'

There was a moment of hesitation before Quigley answered. 'Yes, I do,' he admitted. 'I had been interested in taking on the unit,' he added. 'My company's expanding and we need the space.'

'And when was the last time you looked at it?'

'Last week.'

'And were the boxes full of books stored there when you last looked?'

Quigley shook his head. 'No, Chief Inspector, they were not.'

'Did you open the door to the unit this morning?'

'Are you asking my client whether he allowed these other men to gain access to the unit, Chief Inspector?' Quigley's solicitor asked, his clear, well-modulated voice lacking any trace of emotion.

'Yes, I am.'

'In that case there's no need to answer,' the solicitor told Quigley.

'It's OK, George,' Quigley said. 'The answer is no, Chief Inspector. I have no idea who let them into the unit, but I wasn't the only one on the scene who had keys to it. Dr Graham, for example, was also around.'

'Are you alleging that Dr Graham let them use the unit?'

Quigley shrugged. 'I have no idea, Chief Inspector. Ask him yourself.'

'Did you see someone loading the books into the unit in the last few days?'

'No.'

Vallance could see that it was a fruitless line of enquiry. The men doing the loading were just hired hands; Quigley was an innocent bystander; the people responsible had mysteriously disappeared from the scene. Everything had been worked out in advance, the story so well-rehearsed that it could not easily be broken.

'You know that the computers in your office have all been impounded,' Vallance said. 'It's alleged that the information contained in these books is also stored on your computers.'

Quigley looked to his solicitor who made a slight shake of the head. 'I'll be fighting that in court, Chief Inspector,' Quigley announced. 'Until then I'll make no comment.'

'Do you deny that you ran a computer bulletin board system that was used to disseminate information useful to terrorists?'

Quigley grinned. 'No comment,' he said.

Chiltern glared at him but there was nothing that anyone could do. There wasn't enough evidence to arrest him, yet. The books and the information stored on the computer system would be passed on to the Director of Public Prosecutions to decide whether charges could be laid or not.

'Tell me about Carol Davis,' Vallance said.

Quigley leaned back in his chair, his heavy, powerful frame making the seat creak a little bit. He didn't look like a text-book Nazi; he looked as though he enjoyed the good life too much to be bothered by politics. Except that his eyes were animated by a fire that was part arrogance and part hatred. 'Carol Davis? I can honestly say, Chief Inspector, that I've yet to meet a more Machiavellian character. She was the most manipulative, untruthful and cunning woman I have ever met.'

At least Quigley was willing to talk about her. His description of her might have been damning but for the note of admiration in his voice. 'And what was the nature of your relationship with her?' Vallance asked.

'Purely sexual,' Quigley admitted.

Did she ever have any other sort of relationship? Vallance tried to banish the thought. 'And was this relationship on-going?'

'Yes.'

'When was the last time you saw her?'

'This morning.'

'Where and when?'

'I saw her this morning, just before she was going out for lunch. I called and asked her to see me immediately, I needed to talk to her about an urgent matter. She agreed to skip her lunch date and she came over as soon as she could.'

Why was he being so forthcoming? 'What did you want to see her about?'

'About Sarah Fairfax,' Quigley said.

Chiltern looked at Vallance quickly then looked back to Quigley. Vallance knew what Quigley's easy manner and willingness to speak meant. 'What about Sarah Fairfax?'

'As you well know, Chief Inspector,' Quigley said, 'Sarah Fairfax was pretending to make a documentary about the Science Park. She and Carol had convinced Liz Farnham and Gerry Graham, but I preferred to make my own enquiries about it. She works for a blatantly left-wing muck-raking programme called *Insight*. It was clear to me that I was the target of the film, not the Science Park.'

'Why would you be a target?' Chiltern asked.

Quigley smiled. 'Because Carol Davis was trying to blackmail me. She imagined that she could put pressure on me by having Sarah Fairfax around. No doubt she fed Ms Fairfax a pack of lies just to keep her interested.'

Vallance was momentarily floored. 'Back up a minute,' he said. 'What was Carol trying to blackmail you about?'

'She was a strange woman,' Quigley said, as though anyone connected with the case had any doubt on that score. 'She felt that because I gave her to Gerry Graham I ought to pay her.'

The stunned silence that greeted the remark was accompanied by a lecherous grin on Quigley's face. 'She had no compunction about using her body to gain favours from people,' he added, finally. 'I wanted her there at the Science Park, I felt that she would be a useful person to work with. I introduced her to Dr Graham and they seemed to hit it off immediately. I knew that she'd have sex with him, and it was no surprise when, a fortnight later, she was appointed to work with Liz Farnham.'

'That doesn't answer my original question,' Vallance said,

his head still reeling with the news. 'What was the secret she was threatening to reveal?'

'That's just it,' Quigley said, leaning forward as if to emphasise the point, 'there was no secret. She made up a pack of lies about fraud at the Ministry of Defence and then embellished it with whatever else her fevered imagination could come up with. She felt that just having Sarah Fairfax along would unsettle me enough to make me pay her.'

'What about her relationship with Grant Newman?'

'I encouraged that also,' Quigley admitted casually. 'As you see, she was completely amoral, Chief Inspector. She had that admirable quality that one sees so rarely in young people these days. There was no nonsense about it. Young Grant's a mixed-up lad but very talented. I think that under the right conditions he'd clean up his act and become a useful employee.'

'Did she threaten to tell people about your political activities?'

'I'm a businessman, Chief Inspector. Although I am a patriot — and I make no apologies for that — I'm not politically involved. There was nothing for Carol to reveal.'

Vallance found it hard to believe what he was hearing. Hardest of all was the idea that Quigley had nothing to hide. 'Are you saying that there was no substance whatsoever to the allegations Carol was making to Sarah Fairfax?'

Quigley smiled. 'None, Chief Inspector. Do you know that at one time she even threatened to get a senior policeman involved, as though that would frighten me.'

Vallance swallowed hard. At least he now knew what part Carol had assigned to him: second fiddle to Sarah Fairfax in an unsuccessful blackmail attempt. 'How did she react when you told her that you knew the truth about Sarah Fairfax's purpose for making the film?'

Quigley chuckled. 'She took it in good humour. She laughed and said that it didn't matter that I knew. She said that once she got her policeman along I'd want to cough up. She claimed that I owed her half a million pounds, Chief Inspector. I mean, really, sometimes she had no grasp of reality whatsoever.'

'Why did she think you owed her that?'

Quigley shrugged. 'I have no idea.'

Vallance suddenly saw why. 'As I understand it, Mr Quigley, you've been awarded some big contracts from the government, is that right?'

'That is correct.'

'Was Carol involved in these contracts in some way?'

'No.'

'Did your relationship with Carol predate the contracts?'

Quigley smiled. 'No,' he lied. 'I met her well after the contracts were signed.'

'Do you remember precisely when you met?'

'No.'

'But you remember it was after the contracts were signed.'

'Believe me,' Quigley said, 'I know that it was after the contracts were signed because it was what Carol found most attractive about me. I believe that she found money to be the most potent aphrodisiac of all.'

'Is there not one good thing you can say about her?' Vallance demanded, suddenly exasperated by Quigley's cynicism.

Quigley looked surprised. 'I'm not disparaging, Chief Inspector, far from it. I have nothing but admiration for Carol, though I believe that there are higher motives in life than financial gain. The only cause that she was ever believed in was her own. She never did understand the difference between ends and means.'

'What's that supposed to mean?'

Quigley brushed the question aside with a wave of his hand. 'Nothing of value to you, Chief Inspector. I just wish that her ferocious intelligence had been put to better use, that's all.'

'Like producing Nazi literature?' Vallance demanded angrily.

Quigley's solicitor was about to object but Quigley was there first. 'I would think very carefully before making unfounded allegations, Chief Inspector,' he warned.

'There's nothing unfounded about the allegations against you, Mr Quigley,' Vallance snapped back.

Quigley's smile was suddenly an angry sneer. 'Look at you,' he said. 'To think that you're responsible for upholding the values of decency and goodness. No wonder this country's going to the dogs.'

Vallance stood up. 'Decency and goodness? Two minutes ago you were raving on about giving Carol to someone else, and you were full of praise for her being so amoral. Don't try and lecture me, Mr Quigley, especially not when you're pedalling these things.' He threw down the terrorist manual.

'I would remind you, Chief Inspector,' Quigley's solicitor broke in calmly, 'that my client has not been charged with any offence. He is here voluntarily and if he wishes he may withdraw his co-operation at any moment.'

Vallance inhaled deeply and then sat down again. There was no point in losing his cool, no matter what the provocation. It rankled but he had no choice.

'What happened after Carol left your office?' he asked, taking up the thread once more.

Quigley paused for a second but then answered simply. 'I called Alison Maybury and told her that Grant Newman was going to come to work for me.'

'And you did that because you knew the news would be leaked back to Gavin Newman?'

'That is correct,' Quigley confirmed. 'I wanted the two brothers to split up; in that way there would be more chance of getting Grant to come to work for me. That was the last I saw of Carol, by the way. She returned to her office at around lunchtime.'

Sarah had been right. The argument with Gavin had been deliberately engineered by Quigley. It seemed as though Carol's manipulative personality was well matched by Quigley's.

'Tell me about Carol's interest in food and health,' Vallance suggested.

'Pardon?'

Vallance repeated the question. Quigley looked quizzically at his solicitor who nodded for him to continue. 'She was obsessed with nutrition and disease,' Quigley explained. 'She was a vegetarian, tried to eat organically produced fruit and vegetables and had a mania about toxins and disease. I can't say that I shared this mania, Chief Inspector, but she was convinced that unless she ate the right foods and vitamins she was going to get cancer or some other dread disease. I know that she sometimes pretended an interest in ecology or a wider concern with the world but I know that her primary concerns were entirely selfish.'

'You said vitamins,' Vallance pointed out. 'Tell me about that.'

Again the question seemed to throw Quigley. 'She took lots of them. It sometimes felt that she was doing nothing but swallowing pills and potions. Tell me, Chief Inspector, what is the relevance of all of this?'

'You don't have to worry about that,' Chiltern told him. 'Just answer the questions.'

'Did you have a key to Carol's office?' Vallance asked.

Quigley smiled, as though things were back on track again. 'No.'

'When was the last time you visited her office?'

'I can't tell you. Weeks, possibly months ago. There was simply no need for me to visit there; one call and Carol or Liz would come right over.'

Vallance suddenly felt exhausted. Quigley was being suspiciously helpful again, which meant that either he had nothing to hide or else he had everything beautifully worked out in advance. There was no doubt in his mind that Quigley was a dangerous man, and that he had been behind the bulletin board and the Nazi terror manual, but he was not convinced that he had killed Carol.

'Doesn't Carol's death make life a lot easier for you now?'

Quigley's solicitor blocked the question with a simple shake of the head. Vallance rephrased the question: 'Who benefits from Carol's death?'

Quigley smiled. 'Gavin Newman for one,' he said. 'And I imagine that Liz Farnham will sleep easier. As will Gerry Graham and Sarah Fairfax.'

'Why Sarah Fairfax?'

'Because now she has her martyr. It would be so easy to paint Carol as a saint who was killed by some dark demon. Where there was no story Sarah Fairfax can paint her paranoid fantasies and make something from nothing.'

It sounded like crap, as though Quigley wanted the police to take a swipe at Sarah on his behalf. 'Tell me about Gerry Graham and Carol,' he suggested instead.

'She pandered to his needs from time to time,' Quigley said. 'But in the end I think he was beginning to grow bored with her. You see, he was more interested in his career – which he sees as synonymous with the Science Park – than in her. Of course he was flattered that a pretty young woman like Carol would sleep with him, but later on I think he saw that he'd made a mistake. In his opinion Carol was threatening the stability of the Science Park, and that put the fear of God into him.'

'What was he doing at the Science Park tonight?'

'Perhaps he was there to help load those books,' Quigley replied with a grin. 'I really have no idea, Chief Inspector. I was there working late and I was as surprised to see him as I was to see you.'

'You didn't ask him what he was doing there?'

'I did, and he merely said that he was working late.'

'Did he talk to you about the men loading up the vans?'

'No.'

Vallance was incredulous. 'Isn't that odd? I mean he runs the place, wouldn't you expect him to wonder who these people are?'

'I would,' admitted Quigley.

'Did he ask about Carol?'

'Yes, he seemed very nervous about it, Chief Inspector.'

'Very nervous?'

Quigley grinned. 'Yes, he claimed that someone had poisoned her.'

That detail had been kept back. 'Poisoned? How did he know that?'

'Liz Farnham called him with the news, Chief Inspector. He seemed very nervous all the same.'

Gerry Graham was still in police custody, waiting to give a statement even though he was not considered a prime suspect. Sarah had vouched for him, and there had been every chance that he was going to be given an easy ride while Quigley took all the flak. That was going to change, but then, perhaps, Quigley was deliberately setting him up.

'Now,' Vallance continued, 'let's talk about these men loading the books into the van.'

Quigley looked bored again. 'Do we have to? We've been over this already.'

'Yes, we do have to. Do you know who the van belongs to?'

'No.'

'We have witnesses who saw you giving orders and directing these men,' Vallance said.

Quigley smiled coolly. 'Sarah Fairfax is lying, obviously.'

The plastic coffee cup was scalding hot and so thin that Sarah was afraid it would crack and cover her with the burning liquid that had poured out of the coffee machine. She carried it carefully back to her seat, one of a row outside the CID offices. The place was deserted; Vallance was still in one of the interview rooms with Quigley, who'd got himself an expensive solicitor by the look of things. She sat down, still balancing the coffee which she no longer wanted, and waited.

'Sarah, can we talk?'

She looked up at Dr Graham, looking exhausted, his beard unkempt and his suit terribly creased. 'Yes, of course,' she agreed, aware that something had changed about the way he regarded her.

'I know you're not who you pretended to be,' he said, taking the seat beside her. He spoke sadly, as though hurt by what he'd found out.

She looked him in the eye, unwilling to let him know that she felt guilty about deceiving him. 'Who told you?' she asked calmly.

'Brian. He says that you were at Epsley to make trouble, that you had no real interest in what we were doing there at all.'

How had Quigley found out? The question would have to wait for an answer later. 'Did you know that Quigley was running a Nazi computer system from his office?' she demanded.

'That's not true,' Dr Graham replied, but his heart wasn't in it.

'How long have you known?'

Dr Graham sat forward and held his head in his hands. 'It's

so hard to believe that things have turned out this way . . . You can't imagine how much time and effort I've put into that place. Do you know what it's like lecturing these days? It's a nightmare, Sarah, an absolute nightmare. We're squeezed on all sides, there's mountains of paperwork, hordes of students and no resources. They want miracles from us . . . They want us to prepare students for the future and yet they're constantly sniping at our budgets or sucking away at our time . . .'

Sarah sympathised but he was trying to justify himself. 'What's that got to do with what Brian Quigley was doing? You knew, didn't you?'

He shook his head. 'No, I didn't . . . You see, the Science Park was going to be the way out. I'd be freed for ever from the hapless and the hopeless, no more chasing after students too stupid to think for themselves, no more filling in endless bits of paper repeating the same information a dozen ways. I was sick of it, Sarah, sick to death of it.'

'Why didn't you put a stop to Quigley?' Sarah insisted. 'You could have stopped him, you could have pulled the plug on his computer network.'

He looked at her pleadingly. 'Don't you think I considered that? It's so easy for you to sit and make judgements from the sideline.'

'Then why didn't you do it?'

He looked away again. 'Once Carol was involved as well it was too late. I wished I'd never met either of them. Did you know that about Carol? Did you know that she shared Quigley's sick ideology?'

It was nonsense. Carol wasn't a Nazi — she couldn't be, could she? 'Then why didn't you put a stop to both of them?' she repeated.

He looked startled. There was something in his eyes that Sarah didn't catch and then he looked away. 'I couldn't put a stop to either of them,' he admitted. 'They had me over a barrel. Those books that were printed? They were produced on our equipment and Carol used our media budget to pay for them. By then it looked as if the Science Park was intricately involved in their activities. When I threatened to do something they laughed and threatened me with complete exposure.

233

Do you know that half the Venture Capital International board is Jewish?'

'And you mean to tell me that you put your career first?' Sarah was appalled. 'You preferred to let them use this as a base for their operations rather than taking a stand against it? My God, Gerry, is that really what you're like?'

He looked stung by her anger. 'You don't know what it's like,' he whined. 'And besides, look at what Carol was doing with you. Don't you think that you were part of her scheme too?'

'But I didn't know what was going on.'

'Who did? Come on, Sarah, if she hadn't taken the cyanide she'd still be at it. Wouldn't she?'

'And how long would you have turned a blind eye to it?' Sarah demanded. 'First it was books and a computer system. What next? Bombs? Guns? Where would you have drawn the line?'

He stood up, wearily. 'This is pointless,' he sighed. 'It's all over now anyway. You know the truth, and soon no doubt the name of Epsley Science Park is going to be dragged down into the mud. It didn't have to be this way. It still doesn't, does it? Don't you see? We're the real victims here, us.'

The idea sounded preposterous. 'What about Carol? Wasn't she a victim?'

'Of course she was,' he hastened to say. 'It was a tragic end to a life that had gone badly wrong a long time ago, Sarah. But look at us. Look at you, still here at this hour of the morning, still caught up in this whole complicated bloody mess. And look at me. Aren't we victims too? How do you think it feels for me? Brian called me up just before midnight and forced me to drive down to the Park. He was clearing his stuff out and he wanted me on hand in case he needed me. That's what I've been reduced to, acting as the bloody caretaker.'

'You could have called the police,' she pointed out.

'No I couldn't,' he insisted angrily. 'I was stuck, there was nothing else I could do but go along with their demands. Don't forget, I was the one taking all the flak from Liz for Carol's behaviour. And Carol used me, Sarah, she used me.

They all did and there wasn't a damned thing I could do about it. I know it's too late to bring Carol back; she's dead now, but at least those of us still here deserve a break. Don't let it end like this, Sarah, please, I'm begging you.'

She half expected him to get down on his knees and sob. She looked away from him, embarrassed by the pathetic demeanour and pitiful tone of voice. 'How can I help? It's not in my hands now, there's nothing I can do.'

It was as though he didn't hear her, or else he refused to believe what he was hearing. 'Please, Sarah,' he implored. 'Think of all those people working there. Think of Gavin and Grant. Think of Liz. Please, don't let things get to the stage where the Park is closed down. Please.'

'Are you suggesting that I help you cover things up?'

He sat down again, close to her, and took her hands in his. 'What I'm asking for, Sarah, is the chance to find a way through this mess. Let the police carry on their investigation, let them deal with Brian Quigley and all of his group.'

Sarah looked him in the eye and realised that she still felt something for him. He was, despite everything, an attractive man, and if he was reduced to pleading it was because he was in a desperate situation.

'Please?' he whispered.

It came to her suddenly, with an appalling clarity that almost made her sick. It was as though connections had been made and things had fallen naturally into place. She swallowed hard and looked away, unable to speak to him for a moment. How had he known that Carol had taken cyanide? Everything had been so confused. Had Liz known or not? Dr Graham was involved with an engineering faculty. He would have access to cyanide salts used in electro-plating, and Liz had dropped enough hints about his relationship with Carol . . . The last vestiges of attraction that she still felt disappeared in a spasm of horror.

'What are you going to do now?' he asked glumly, oblivious to her growing feeling of revulsion. 'Are you still planning on making your film about the Park?'

He was the murderer. Sarah knew it with absolute certainty and, if he was not so obsessed with his precious career, he would have realised that she knew. It was as though he could see no further than saving himself, he was blind to everything else. It explained why he was so stupid as to believe that he could get away with killing Carol, and why he had allowed himself to be manipulated and blackmailed so easily.

'I don't know what I'm going to do,' she told him, suddenly aware that they were alone in the empty corridor. She should have been afraid of him but he was so pathetic, so stupid, that she felt nothing but an icy contempt and a feeling of disappointment. After all the excitement and the intrigue it was ending as an anticlimax. Far from being the result of a grand conspiracy Carol's death was an inept and meaningless attempt at saving Dr Graham's career. Damn it! Why wasn't Quigley the murderer? It would have been better, much better . . .

'Things could have been so different,' he whispered to himself.

She stood up. 'I just need to go to the loo,' she said.

He looked up at her and nodded. 'Sure,' he said. 'Have you been in to give a statement yet?'

'No,' she lied.

'Please, Sarah,' he said quietly, 'can't we discuss this further? There's so much at stake here.'

She nodded. There was nothing of value at stake, nothing at all. 'I'll be back in a minute,' she promised him.

He attempted a smile but all that she could see was the desperation in his eyes. He wasn't even making an attempt to save himself. Not once had he tried to pin the blame elsewhere, to blame Quigley for example; it was as if he imagined that he was so totally above suspicion that he didn't need to make the effort.

She turned on her heel and marched off down the corridor, her footsteps echoing sadly through the silence. She rounded a corner and then walked briskly down to the front desk. The sergeant on duty was dealing with a drunken couple who could barely stand up. They would have to wait, she decided.

'Excuse me, Sergeant,' she said calmly, 'but I think you need to get Chief Inspector Vallance here immediately.'

EPILOGUE

The morning was hidden by a thick grey mist that pressed solidly against the window, obscuring everything but the dim lights from the buildings opposite and the opaque white lights from passing traffic. The sun was a pale white disc hanging in the mist, somewhere above where the horizon should be. Vallance regarded it for a moment, looking at the cold white circle of light that shed no heat and whose light was lost in the dense and immobile fog. He shivered and turned away, suddenly aware that the icy atmosphere was infiltrating his thoughts and feelings.

He felt tense and dissatisfied, unhappy at the way things had finally turned out. It hadn't taken long to get a confession out of Dr Graham. Sarah had been right: it had only taken a stupid slip of the tongue to point to his guilt. The lies he had tried spinning to cover his tracks had been hazy, ill-thought-out and finally had been abandoned. The forensic evidence to support the confession would be easily obtained. Gerry Graham seemed to be the only one surprised at having been caught out. It had certainly been no surprise to Brian Quigley, who clearly either knew the truth or had strong suspicions.

Case closed. Vallance slumped down heavily in his seat and let the exhaustion wash through him. He should have felt elation; after all, that was what he had wanted to do, it was what he was *supposed* to do. It was what justice was all about:

catching the criminal, punishing the guilty, serving society. And did he feel that justice had been done? No. And it pained him to think about it.

Where was the justice in watching Brian Quigley walk free? The hate-filled books and propaganda he had been producing were being passed to the Director of Public Prosecutions for comment. Vallance knew that there was little chance that anything would come of that. Besides which there was still little evidence that tied him directly to the production and dissemination of it. The most that could be hoped for would be a prosecution which might lead to a paltry fine. More likely the books would be pulped and that would be the end of it as far as the police were concerned. In the meantime there would be nothing to stop him or his associates starting another computer system or printing up new books and magazines.

The details of the alleged fraud were being passed to the Serious Fraud Office, but again there was a long road to travel from there to a successful prosecution. It did seem that Carol's allegations were true to some extent. The most likely explanation, in Vallance's opinion, was that Quigley had a group of supporters inside the Ministry of Defence. The provisions of the contracts were deliberately made loose so that Quigley could rake in the cash to fund his sick political activities. But that was still conjecture; the evidence to prove it might never be forthcoming.

Quigley should have been the murderer. It was the solution that Vallance had wished for more than anything else. Then there would have been no way that the bastard could walk out grinning, the way he had. The satisfaction of charging him with murder had been denied, and there was nothing but a grim feeling of duty in laying those charges at the door of someone as weak and as stupid as Dr Graham. The mocking, arrogant smile on Quigley's face had been the final insult, making Vallance feel sick with disgust and anger.

There were still questions unanswered though. Who had been in the car behind Sarah travelling down to Lyndhurst? Quigley insisted that he didn't know, and there was something in his denial that was convincing. In that case who had it been? It wasn't Grant: he had already been there at the hotel with Carol, though he had owned up to the threatening phone calls to Sarah, the death threat via email and more. In that case who else could it have been? It was a question that fed Sarah's paranoia.

As did the questions about Quigley's alleged police protection. It sounded unreal, but then it seemed so unlikely that Quigley could have gone on so long without coming to the attention of Special Branch or the Anti-Terrorist Squad. It made Vallance uncomfortable thinking about it, but Sarah had insisted on asking him precisely those questions.

Sarah. She felt less constrained than he did. She had no doubt as to what to do next. She was determined to hound Quigley. Already she was working on her notes, gathering together all the information that she could. As far as she was concerned she was going to expose him to the full glare of the media, despite the threats and the risk of retaliation that that entailed. The woman was bloody-minded but at least she was willing to follow things through.

His own troubles were far from over. Somewhere along the line he'd have to explain himself. He had been sexually involved with the murder victim and that meant he shouldn't have been on the case, and not even the fact that the case had been solved would save him. What he'd done was unjustifiable, and he knew that he'd made a big mistake in not handing over the case immediately. But what the hell, he felt at least some consolation in having seen it through to the end.

The knock at his office door startled him. He didn't want company. It was late and he wanted to get out, to go home and sleep away the feeling of depression that was beginning to overwhelm him.

'You got a good result, sir,' Cooper said, coming into the cramped and untidy little office.

'Thanks.' He didn't want congratulations, he didn't deserve it.

'Sarah Fairfax is still downstairs,' Cooper reported. 'She's waiting to see you before she goes home. She says she's willing to wait.'

Of course she was willing to wait. There was no stopping

her. 'I'll be down to see her in a minute,' Vallance said, realising that he'd have to help her nail Quigley no matter what the consequences.

'Before that though, I've got something you need to see,' Cooper said, beaming excitedly.

'You've done it,' Vallance guessed. The endless stream of security film at the shopping centre must have finally yielded something useful on Angela Wilding.

'That's right,' Cooper agreed happily. 'Marilyn was right after all. Angie did meet someone outside the shop. I've got the bastard on film, trying to pick her up by the look of it. You can see him trying it on, and she's not happy about it, I can tell you that. She storms off and he calls something after her. I'm amazed that no one else reported it but there was no one else about from what the film shows.'

'Who was it?' Vallance demanded, his pulse quickening.

'Who we want it to be,' Cooper reported.

Vallance's head spun with names and faces. 'Ted Coleman,' he said, summoning up the image of Jake Coleman's obnoxious father.

'That's right. The dirty bastard had banned his son from seeing Angie but he was more than willing to try it on himself. No wonder she was ballistic that day.'

Sleep would have to be postponed, Vallance realised. 'Let's pull the bastard in,' he said grimly. Not that it would do any good. Angie had killed and there was no way that could be changed. The most they could expect – and that was if they could prove conclusively that Coleman had tried it on – was some understanding for the poor kid. It would make no difference to her sentence, no difference at all, Vallance thought bitterly.

'It'll be a pleasure, sir.' Cooper couldn't see it. All he could think about was pulling Coleman in and giving him hell. Vallance stood up.

'I'd better see Sarah while you're getting him.'

'Yes, sir. Oh,' Cooper turned back at the door, 'and I think Mr Riley's waiting to see you too.'

Vallance nodded. It was time to face the music – again.

CRIME & PASSION

DEADLY AFFAIRS
by
Juliet Hastings

ISBN: 0 7535 0029 9
Publication date: 17 April 1997

Eddie Drax is a playboy businessman with a short fuse and a taste for blondes. A lot of people don't like him: ex-girlfriends, business rivals, even his colleagues. He's not an easy man to like. When Eddie is found asphyxiated at the wheel of his car, DCI John Anderson delves beneath the golf-clubbing, tree-lined respectability of suburban Surrey and uncovers the secret – and often complex – sex-lives of Drax's colleagues and associates.

He soon finds that Drax was murdered – and there are more killings to come. In the course of his investigations, Anderson becomes personally involved in Drax's circle of passionate women, jealous husbands and people who can't be trusted. He also has plenty of opportunities to find out more about his own sexual nature.

This is the first in the series of John Anderson mysteries.

CRIME & PASSION

A MOMENT OF MADNESS
by
Pan Pantziarka
ISBN: 0 7535 0024 8
Publication date: 17 April 1997

Tom Ryder is the charismatic head of the Ryder Forum – an organisation teaching slick management techniques to business people. Sarah Fairfax is investigating current management theories for a television programme called *Insight* and is attending a course at the Ryder Hall. All the women on the course think Ryder is dynamic, powerful and extremely attractive. Sarah agrees, but this doesn't mean that she's won over by his evangelical spiel; in fact, she's rather cynical about the whole thing.

When one of the course attendees – a high-ranking civil servant – is found dead in his room from a drugs overdose, Detective Chief Inspector Anthony Vallance is called in to investigate. Everyone has something to hide, except for Sarah Fairfax who is also keen to find out the truth about this suspicious death. As the mystery deepens and another death occurs, Fairfax and Vallance compete to unearth the truth. They discover dark, erotic secrets, lethal dangers and, to their mutual irritation, each other.

This is the first in a series of Fairfax and Vallance mysteries.

CRIME & PASSION

INTIMATE ENEMIES
by
Juliet Hastings

ISBN: 0 7535 0034 5
Publication date: 15 May 1997

Francesca Lyons is found dead in her art gallery. The cause of death isn't obvious but her bound hands suggest foul play. The previous evening she had an argument with her husband, she had sex with someone, and two men left messages on the gallery's answering machine. Detective Chief Inspector Anderson has plenty of suspects but can't find anyone with a motive.

When Stephanie Pinkney, an art researcher, is found dead in similar circumstances, Anderson's colleagues are sure the culprit is a serial killer. But Anderson is convinced that the murders are connected with something else entirely. Unravelling the threads leads him to Andrea Maguire, a vulnerable, sensuous art dealer with a quick-tempered husband and unsatisfied desires. Anderson can prove Andrea isn't the killer and finds himself strongly attracted to her. Is he making an untypical and dangerous mistake?

**Intimate Enemies is the second in the series
of John Anderson mysteries.**

CRIME & PASSION

A TANGLED WEB
by
Pan Pantziarka
ISBN: 0 7535 0155 4
Publication date: 19 June 1997

Michael Cunliffe was ordinary. He was an accountant for a small charity. He had a pretty wife and an executive home in a leafy estate. Now he's been found dead: shot in the back of the head at close range. The murder bears the hallmark of a gangland execution.

DCI Vallance soon discovers Cunliffe wasn't ordinary at all. The police investigation lifts the veneer of suburban respectability to reveal blackmail, extortion, embezzlement, and a network of sexual intrigue. One of Cunliffe's businesses has been the subject of an investigation by the television programme, *Insight*, which means that Vallance has an excuse to get in touch again with Sarah Fairfax. Soon they're getting on each other's nerves and in each other's way, but they cannot help working well together.

A Tangled Web is the second in the series of Fairfax and Vallance mysteries.

CRIME & PASSION

A WAITING GAME
by
Juliet Hastings
ISBN: 0 7535 0109 0
Publication date: 21 August 1997

A child is abducted and held to ransom. As the boy's mother is a prospective MP and his father is a friend of the Chief Constable, Detective Chief Inspector Anderson is required to wrap up the case cleanly and efficiently.

But the kidnappers, although cunning and well-organised, make up a triangle of lust and jealousy. Somehow Anderson's tactics are being betrayed to the kidnappers and, after a series of mishaps and errors, and a violent death, Anderson's latest sexual conquest and his ex-wife become involved in the conspiracy. Anderson's legendary patience and willpower are stretched to the limit as he risks his own life trying to save others.

This is the third in the series of John Anderson mysteries.

CRIME & PASSION

TO DIE FOR
by
Peter Birch
ISBN: 0 7535 0034 5
Publication date: 18 September 1997

The cool and efficient Detective Chief Inspector is keen to re-establish his reputation as a skilled investigator. The body of Charles Draper has been found in the mud flats of a Devon estuary. The murdered man was a law-abiding citizen and there appears to be no motive for the killing. There are also very few clues.

When Anderson is sent to assist the Devon and Cornwall constabulary, he's led towards dubious evidence and suspects whose alibis are watertight. The investigation also brings him in contact with forensics assistant Anna Ferreira whose intellect and physical attractiveness make her irresistible.

The only suspect is then found murdered. Local antiques dealer Nathan Cutts fits the murderer's profile but Anderson feels he's not the man they're looking for. Against the backdrop of windswept Dartmoor, the chase to catch a killer is on.

This is the fourth in the series of John Anderson mysteries.

CRIME & PASSION

TIME TO KILL
by
Margaret Bingley
ISBN: 0 7535 0164 3
Publication date: 16 October 1997

Lisa Allan's body is found in the corner of her kitchen by her husband, Ralph. Everyone knows Lisa was ill, suffering from a complicated heart condition, but no one expected her to die – least of all her doctor. DCI Anderson met Lisa socially only two days before her death. He found her desirable but disliked her husband on sight.

Two autopsy reports pose more questions than answers and as Anderson struggles to untangle the relationships of the dysfunctional Allan family, he becomes involved with Pippa Wright, Ralph's attractive PA and ex-mistress. When a second murder occurs, Anderson realises that getting to know Pippa was not one of his better ideas. Against a background of sexual intrigue and hidden secrets, he needs to harness all his skills and intuition if he is to ensure that justice is done.

This is the fifth in the series of John Anderson mysteries.

CRIME & PASSION

DAMAGED GOODS
by
Georgina Franks
ISBN: 0 7535 0124 4
Publication date: 20 November 1997

A high-performance car has spun out of control on a test drive. The driver has suffered multiple injuries and is suing Landor Motors for negligence. He says the airbag inflated for no reason, causing him to lose control of the car.

This is the third and most serious claim Landor Motors have had to make this year. The insurance company aren't happy, and they bring in Victoria Donovan to assist in their investigations.

Landor Motors is a high-profile car showroom situated in the stockbroker belt. But the Landor family have a history of untimely deaths and brooding resentments. Soon, Vic is up to her neck in a complex web of drug-dealing, sexual jealousy and deception involving Derek Landor's wayward and very attractive son. When Derek Landor is kidnapped, only Vic knows what's going on. Will anyone take her seriously before time runs out for Derek Landor?

This is the first Victoria Donovan mystery.

CRIME & PASSION

GAMES OF DECEIT
by
Pan Pantziarka
ISBN: 0 7535 0119 8
Publication date: 4 December 1997

Detective Chief Inspector Anthony Vallance and television
journalist Sarah Fairfax team up once more when an old
friend of Sarah's is caught up in the strange goings-on at the
science park where she's working. Carol Davis says someone
there is trying to kill her but the squeaky clean credentials of
her colleagues don't tally with the dangerous and violent
nature of the attacks.

When Vallance becomes sexually involved with Carol Davis,
he begins to realise that she has a dark side to her nature:
she's manipulative, kinky and possibly unstable. As Fairfax and
Vallance peel away the layers of respectability to reveal a
background of corporate coercion, deceit and neo–Nazism,
they discover that Carol has not been telling the truth about
the people she's working for. But who is going to reveal
what's really going on when Carol winds up dead?

This is the third in the series of Fairfax and Vallance novels.

CRIME & PASSION

ANGEL OF DEATH
by
Richard Shaw
ISBN: 0 7535 0255 0
Publication date: 15 January 1998

Victoria Donovan is called in to investigate the theft of valuable marble statues from Blythwood Cemetery. This should be a straightforward piece of detection. However, it soon transpires that the lives of the cemetery staff are as tangled as the undergrowth which surrounds them. Vic's plan is to nail the thieves and stay out of harm's way but a lot of surveillance takes place at night – a time when the cemetery becomes dangerous. One of the management team is having perverse liaisons by moonlight with a Blythwood security guard; a recently released mentally ill patient is on the loose, looking for the 'daughter of darkness', and the rest of the ground staff are lining their pockets.

When a body is found which shouldn't yet be in the ground, accusations start flying and Vic suddenly finds herself involved in a murder investigation. Unfortunately, the police are less than co-operative and when one of the grave-diggers is arrested and charged with murder, Vic strongly suspects they've got the wrong man. To add to all this, her current lover is getting friendly with the manipulative Chloe, the cemetery's assistant manageress, and her family is giving her problems. How can she find the time to see that justice is done?

**This is the second in the series of
Victoria Donovan mysteries.**

GAMES OF DECEIT

The lights flashed suddenly, blinding Sarah completely. She stopped, shielded her eyes, caught in the harsh white glare. Carol was beside her, also covering her eyes and trying to make out the car in front of them. The engine was gunned loudly, and roared with an angry, suppressed power. The tyres screamed against the tarmac and Carol cried out at the same time.

Sarah could feel the car racing towards her, the raw power of the engine pushing the vehicle to its limits. The light was so powerful . . . She stood still, unable to move, trapped by the twin beams as the car accelerated towards her. Time stopped. It felt as if her heart was bursting inside her; her hands were shaking so much that the papers fluttered from her fingers.

It was almost upon her.

A MOMENT OF MADNESS
A TANGLED WEB
GAMES OF DECEIT
Fairfax and Vallance mysteries

DEADLY AFFAIRS
INTIMATE ENEMIES
A WAITING GAME
TO DIE FOR
TIME TO KILL
John Anderson mysteries

DAMAGED GOODS
A Victoria Donovan mystery